IN FOX'S FOREST

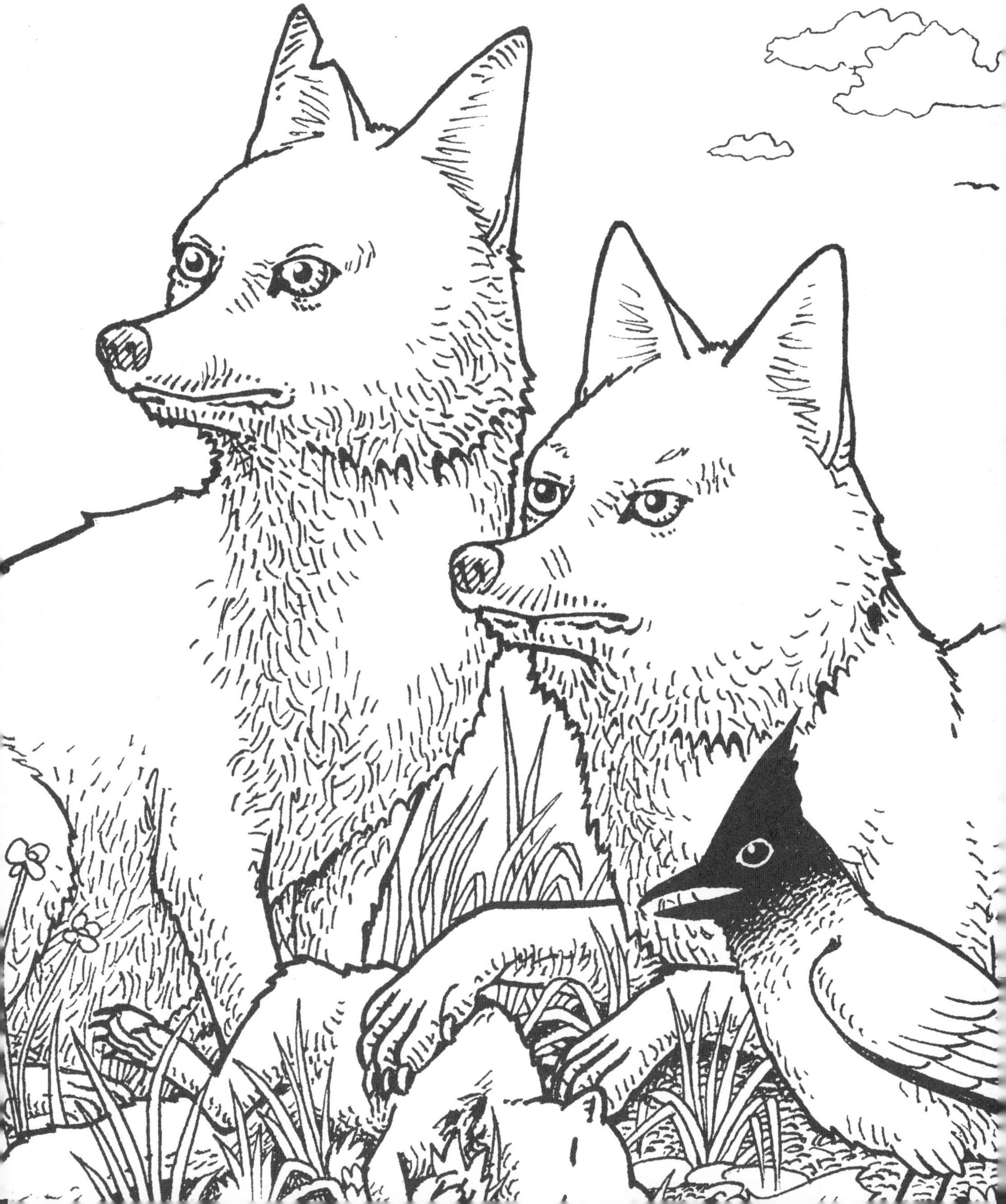

Edited by Gary Groth
Designed by Guy Colwell and Keeli McCarthy
Production by Paul Baresh
Associate Publisher: Eric Reynolds
Publisher: Gary Groth

Fantagraphics Books, Inc.
7563 Lake City Way NE
Seattle, WA 98115

First Printing: September 2016

ISBN 978-1-60699-956-1
Library of Congress Control Number: 2016940736

Printed in China

IN FOX'S FOREST

GUY COLWELL

FANTAGRAPHICS BOOKS

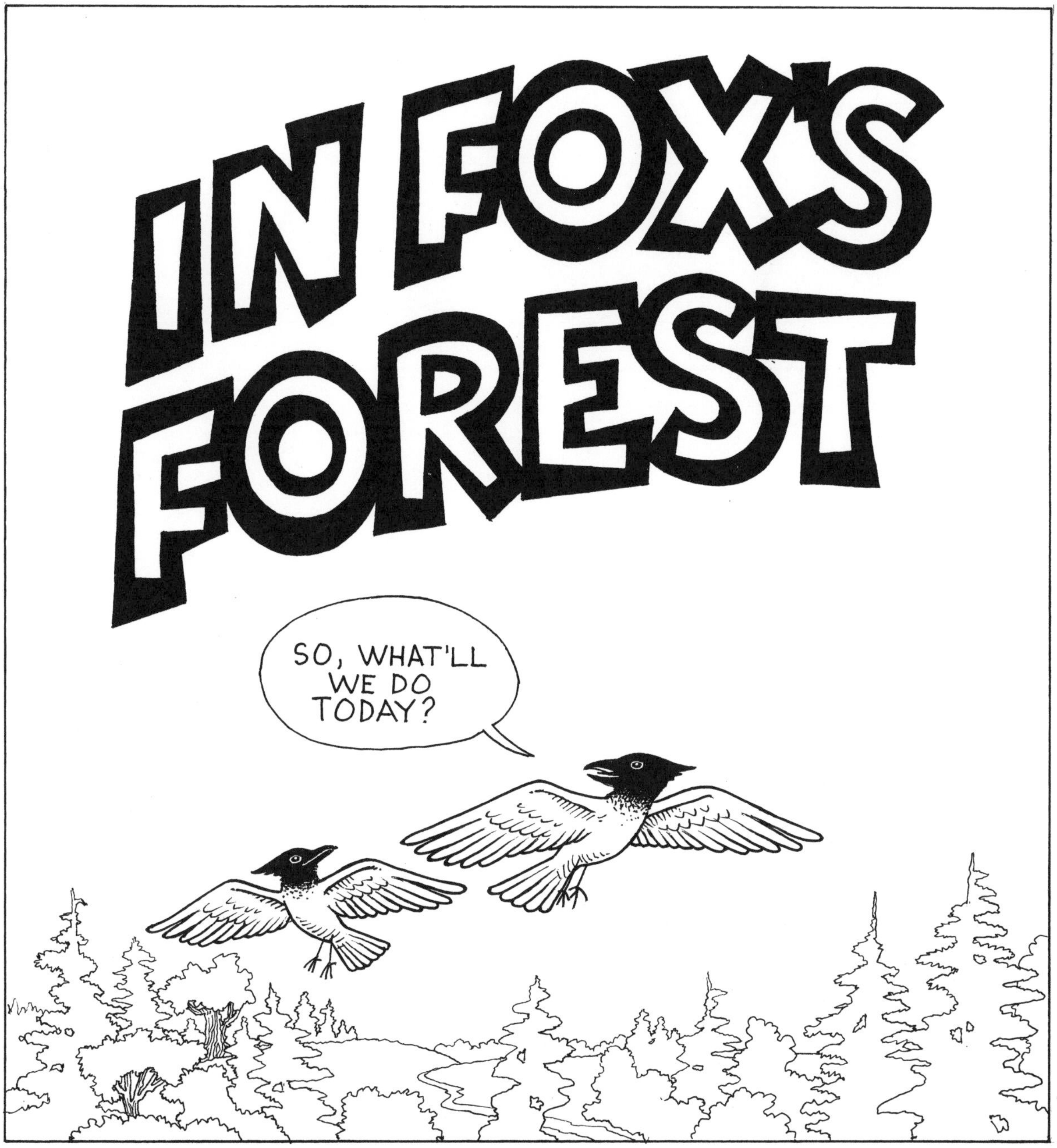
IN FOX'S FOREST
SO, WHAT'LL WE DO TODAY?

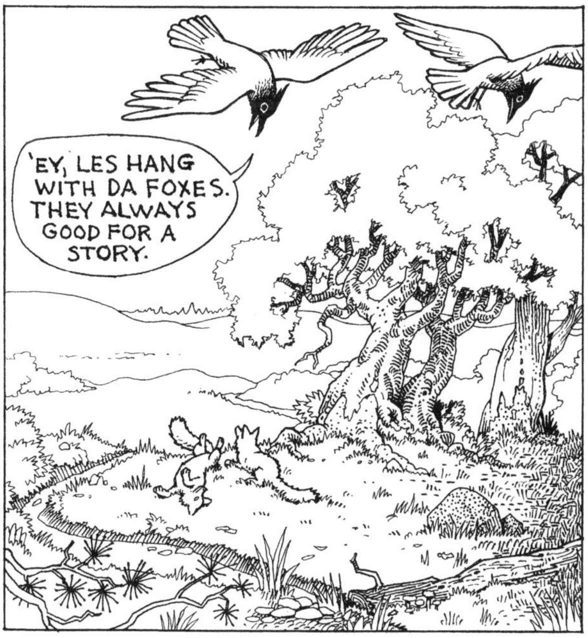
'EY, LES HANG WITH DA FOXES. THEY ALWAYS GOOD FOR A STORY.

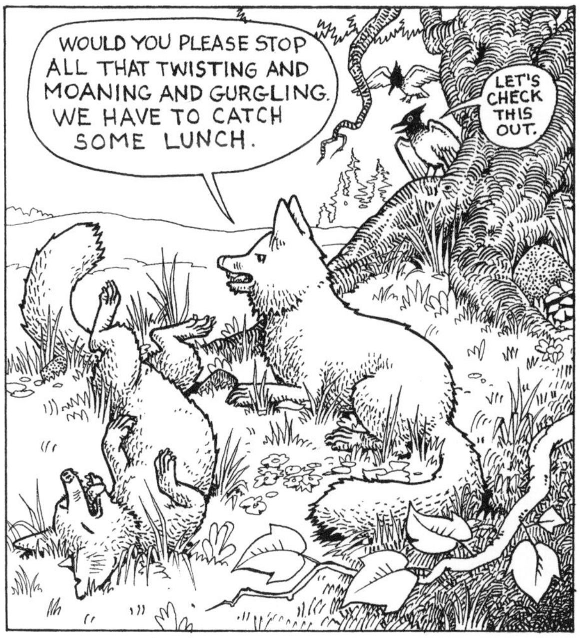
WOULD YOU PLEASE STOP ALL THAT TWISTING AND MOANING AND GURGLING. WE HAVE TO CATCH SOME LUNCH.
LET'S CHECK THIS OUT.

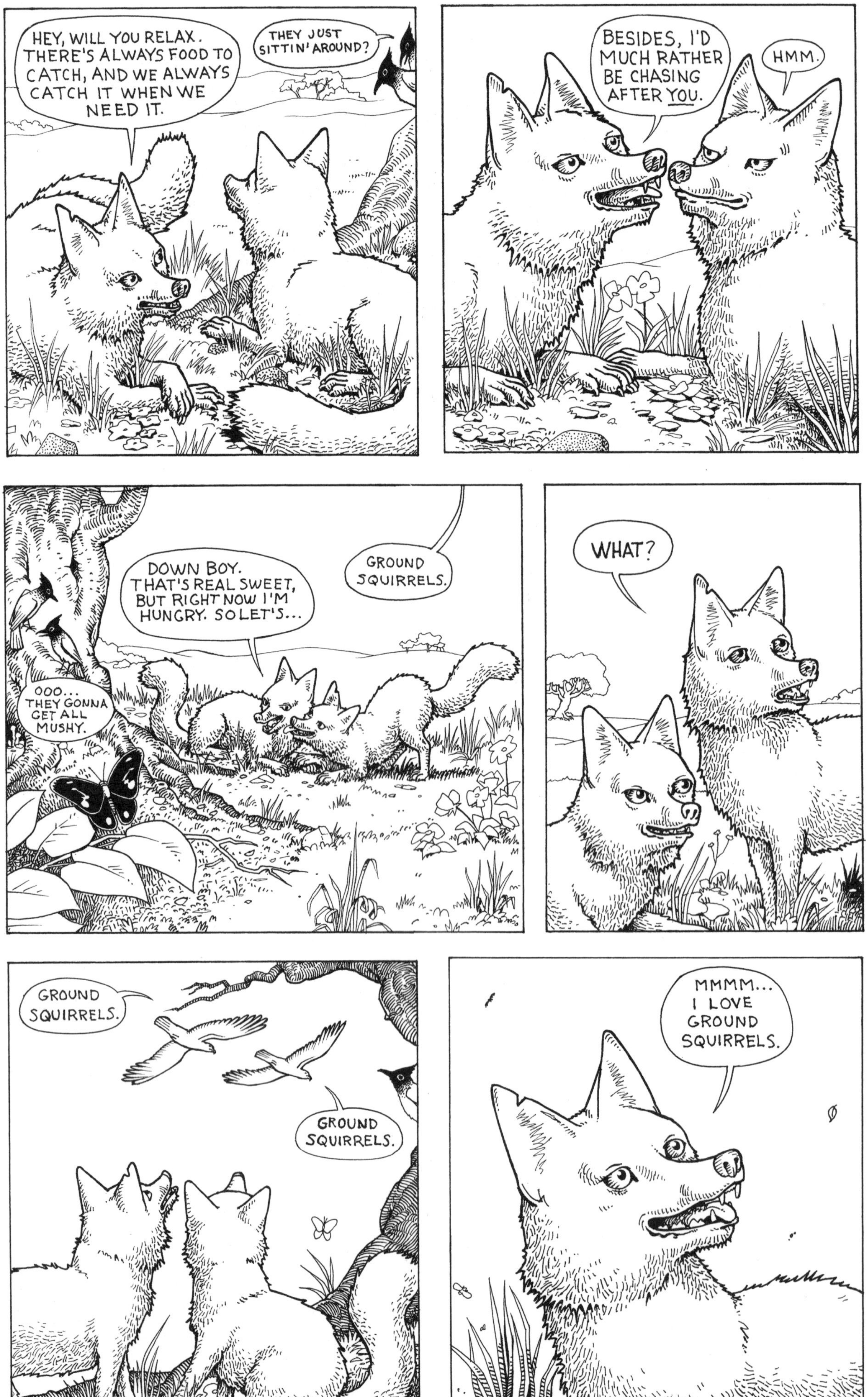
HEY, WILL YOU RELAX. THERE'S ALWAYS FOOD TO CATCH, AND WE ALWAYS CATCH IT WHEN WE NEED IT.
THEY JUST SITTIN' AROUND?
BESIDES, I'D MUCH RATHER BE CHASING AFTER YOU.
HMM.
DOWN BOY. THAT'S REAL SWEET, BUT RIGHT NOW I'M HUNGRY. SO LET'S...
GROUND SQUIRRELS.
OOO... THEY GONNA GET ALL MUSHY.
WHAT?
GROUND SQUIRRELS.
GROUND SQUIRRELS.
MMMM... I LOVE GROUND SQUIRRELS.

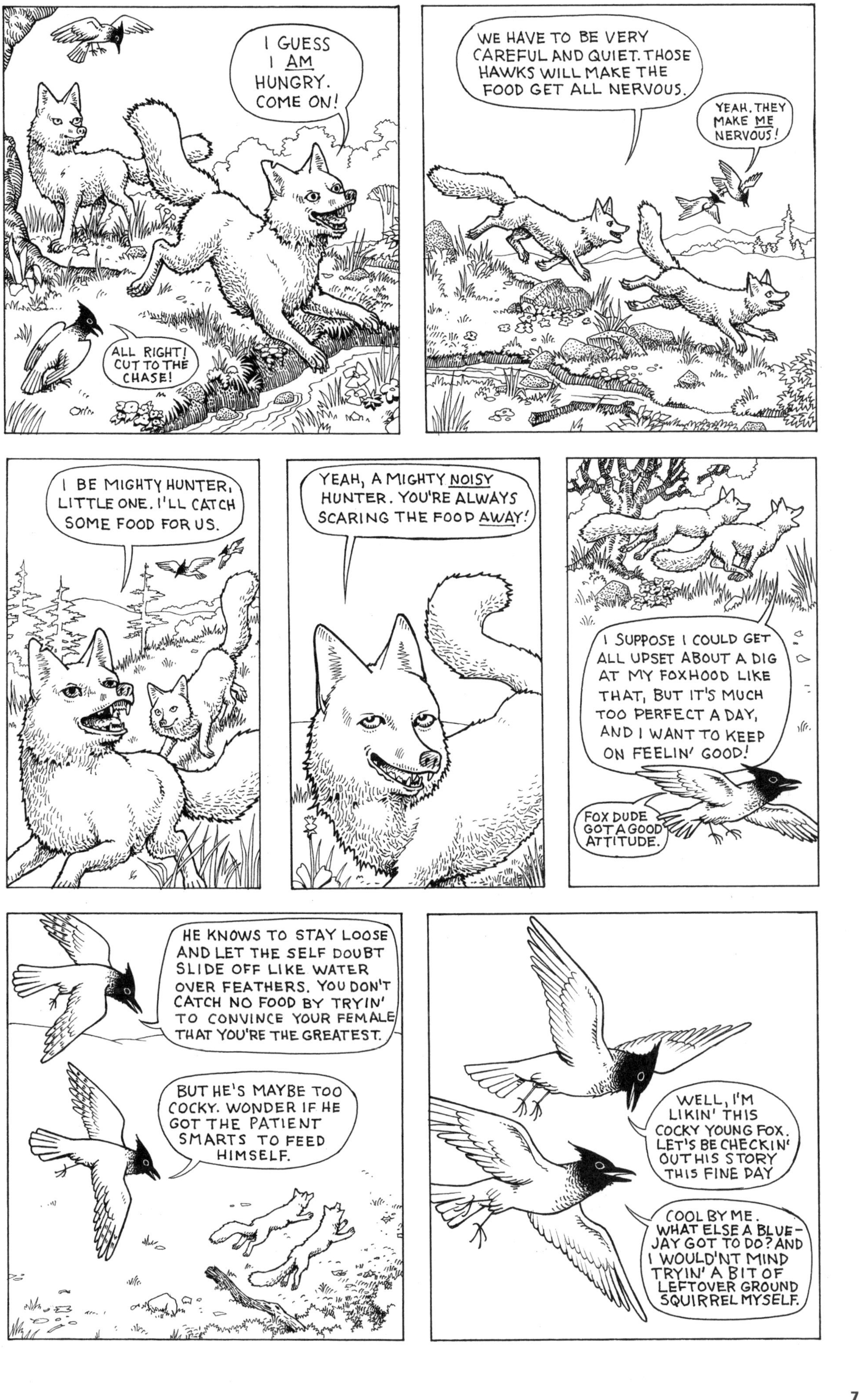
I GUESS I AM HUNGRY. COME ON!
ALL RIGHT! CUT TO THE CHASE!
WE HAVE TO BE VERY CAREFUL AND QUIET. THOSE HAWKS WILL MAKE THE FOOD GET ALL NERVOUS.
YEAH. THEY MAKE ME NERVOUS!
I BE MIGHTY HUNTER, LITTLE ONE. I'LL CATCH SOME FOOD FOR US.
YEAH, A MIGHTY NOISY HUNTER. YOU'RE ALWAYS SCARING THE FOOD AWAY!
I SUPPOSE I COULD GET ALL UPSET ABOUT A DIG AT MY FOXHOOD LIKE THAT, BUT IT'S MUCH TOO PERFECT A DAY, AND I WANT TO KEEP ON FEELIN' GOOD!
FOX DUDE GOT A GOOD ATTITUDE.
HE KNOWS TO STAY LOOSE AND LET THE SELF DOUBT SLIDE OFF LIKE WATER OVER FEATHERS. YOU DON'T CATCH NO FOOD BY TRYIN' TO CONVINCE YOUR FEMALE THAT YOU'RE THE GREATEST.
BUT HE'S MAYBE TOO COCKY. WONDER IF HE GOT THE PATIENT SMARTS TO FEED HIMSELF.
WELL, I'M LIKIN' THIS COCKY YOUNG FOX. LET'S BE CHECKIN' OUT HIS STORY THIS FINE DAY
COOL BY ME. WHAT ELSE A BLUE-JAY GOT TO DO? AND I WOULD'NT MIND TRYIN' A BIT OF LEFTOVER GROUND SQUIRREL MYSELF.

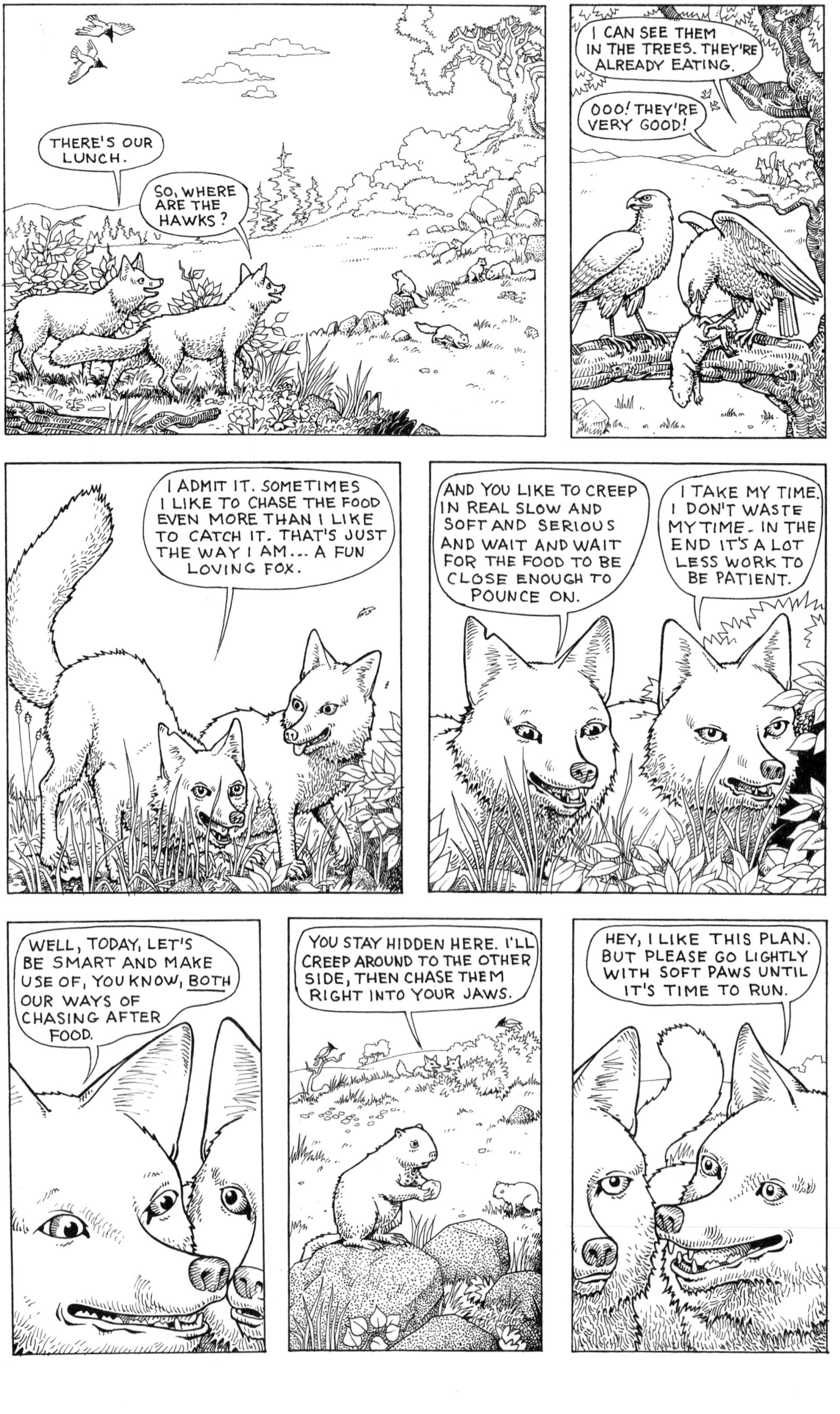
THERE'S OUR LUNCH.
SO, WHERE ARE THE HAWKS?
I CAN SEE THEM IN THE TREES. THEY'RE ALREADY EATING.
OOO! THEY'RE VERY GOOD!
I ADMIT IT. SOMETIMES I LIKE TO CHASE THE FOOD EVEN MORE THAN I LIKE TO CATCH IT. THAT'S JUST THE WAY I AM... A FUN LOVING FOX.
AND YOU LIKE TO CREEP IN REAL SLOW AND SOFT AND SERIOUS AND WAIT AND WAIT FOR THE FOOD TO BE CLOSE ENOUGH TO POUNCE ON.
I TAKE MY TIME. I DON'T WASTE MY TIME. IN THE END IT'S A LOT LESS WORK TO BE PATIENT.
WELL, TODAY, LET'S BE SMART AND MAKE USE OF, YOU KNOW, BOTH OUR WAYS OF CHASING AFTER FOOD.
YOU STAY HIDDEN HERE. I'LL CREEP AROUND TO THE OTHER SIDE, THEN CHASE THEM RIGHT INTO YOUR JAWS.
HEY, I LIKE THIS PLAN. BUT PLEASE GO LIGHTLY WITH SOFT PAWS UNTIL IT'S TIME TO RUN.

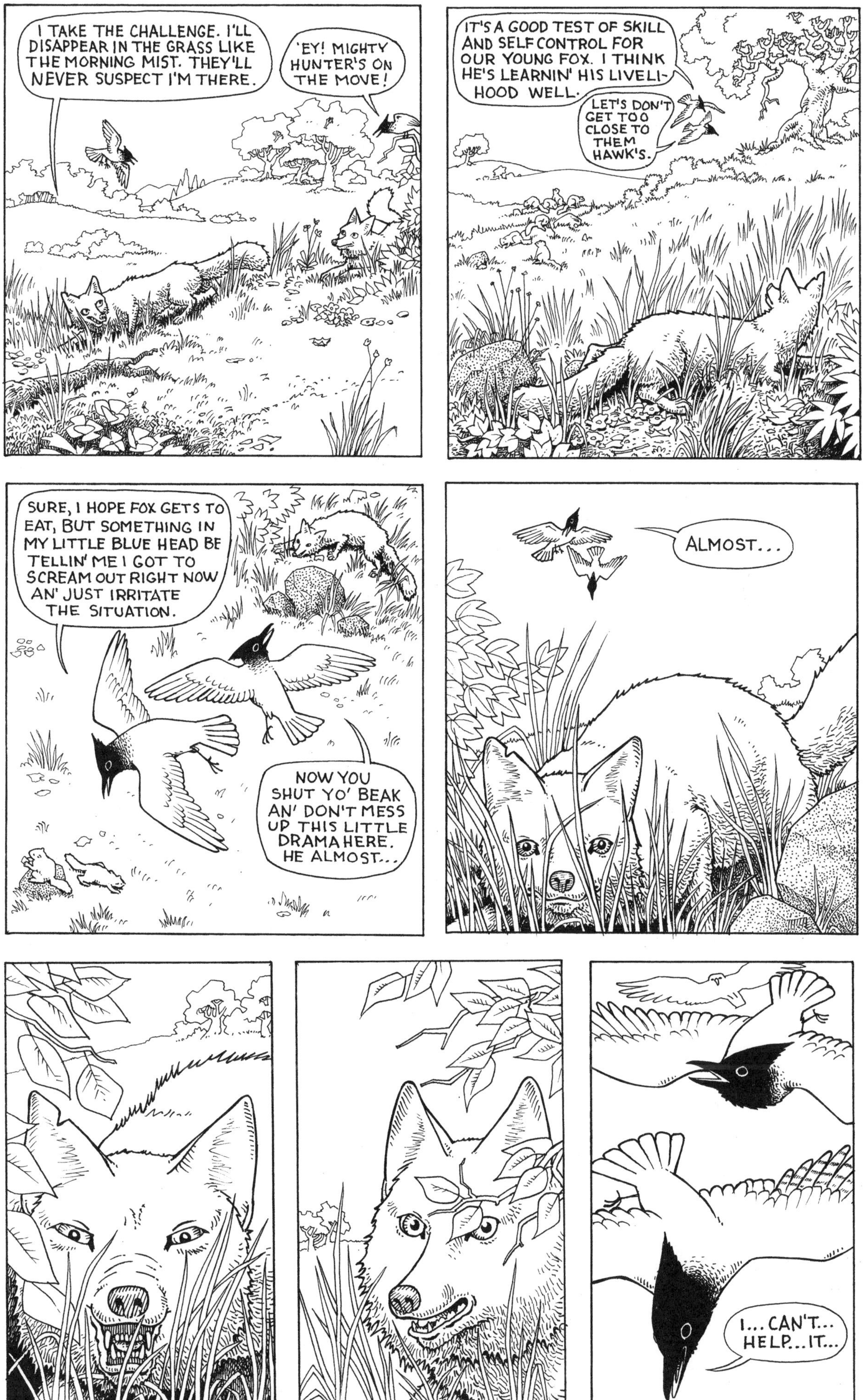
I TAKE THE CHALLENGE. I'LL DISAPPEAR IN THE GRASS LIKE THE MORNING MIST. THEY'LL NEVER SUSPECT I'M THERE.
'EY! MIGHTY HUNTER'S ON THE MOVE!
IT'S A GOOD TEST OF SKILL AND SELF CONTROL FOR OUR YOUNG FOX. I THINK HE'S LEARNIN' HIS LIVELIHOOD WELL.
LET'S DON'T GET TOO CLOSE TO THEM HAWK'S.
SURE, I HOPE FOX GETS TO EAT, BUT SOMETHING IN MY LITTLE BLUE HEAD BE TELLIN' ME I GOT TO SCREAM OUT RIGHT NOW AN' JUST IRRITATE THE SITUATION.
NOW YOU SHUT YO' BEAK AN' DON'T MESS UP THIS LITTLE DRAMA HERE. HE ALMOST...
ALMOST...
I... CAN'T... HELP... IT...

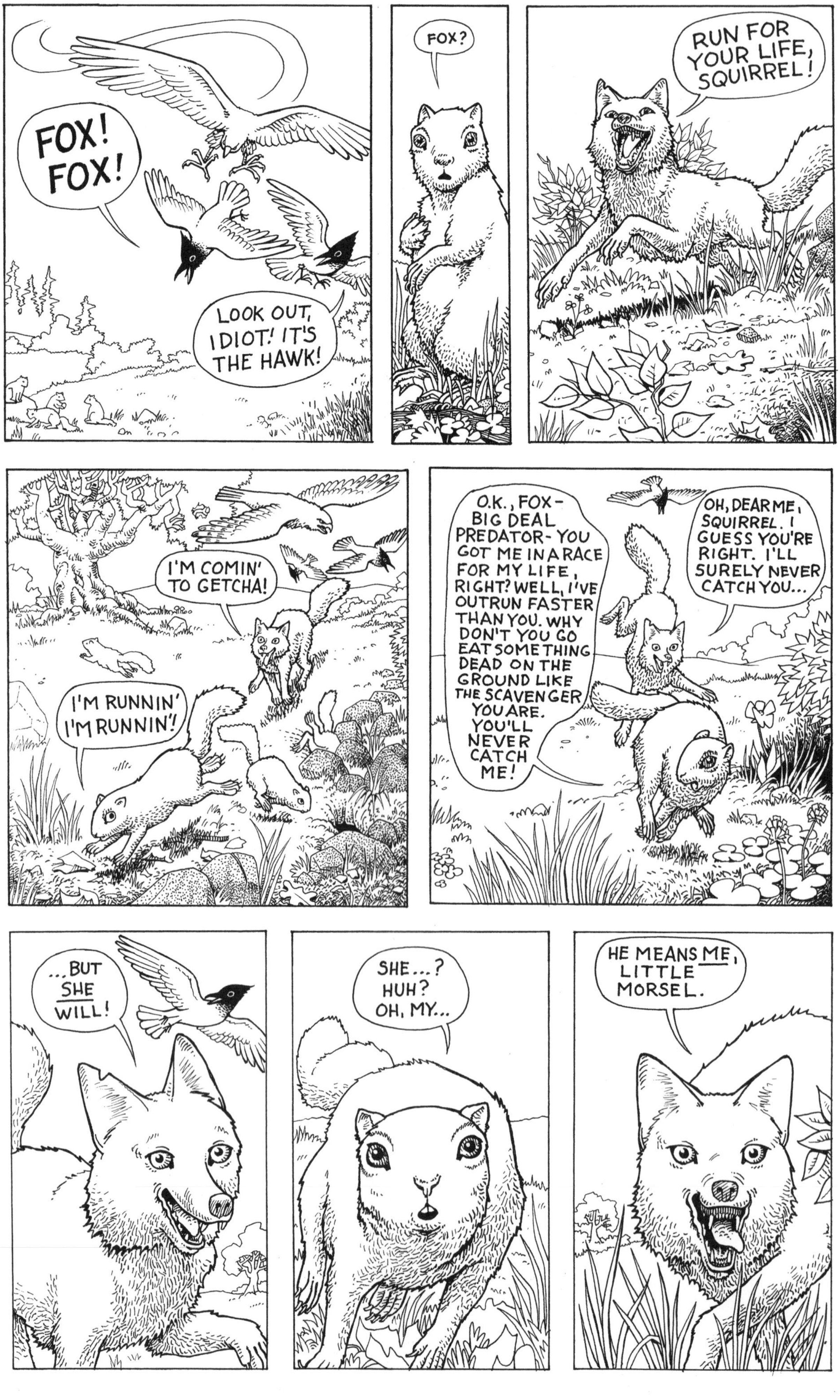
FOX! FOX!
LOOK OUT, IDIOT! IT'S THE HAWK!
FOX?
RUN FOR YOUR LIFE, SQUIRREL!
I'M COMIN' TO GETCHA!
I'M RUNNIN' I'M RUNNIN'!
O.K., FOX- BIG DEAL PREDATOR- YOU GOT ME IN A RACE FOR MY LIFE, RIGHT? WELL, I'VE OUTRUN FASTER THAN YOU. WHY DON'T YOU GO EAT SOMETHING DEAD ON THE GROUND LIKE THE SCAVENGER YOU ARE. YOU'LL NEVER CATCH ME!
OH, DEAR ME, SQUIRREL. I GUESS YOU'RE RIGHT. I'LL SURELY NEVER CATCH YOU...
...BUT SHE WILL!
SHE...? HUH? OH, MY...
HE MEANS ME, LITTLE MORSEL.

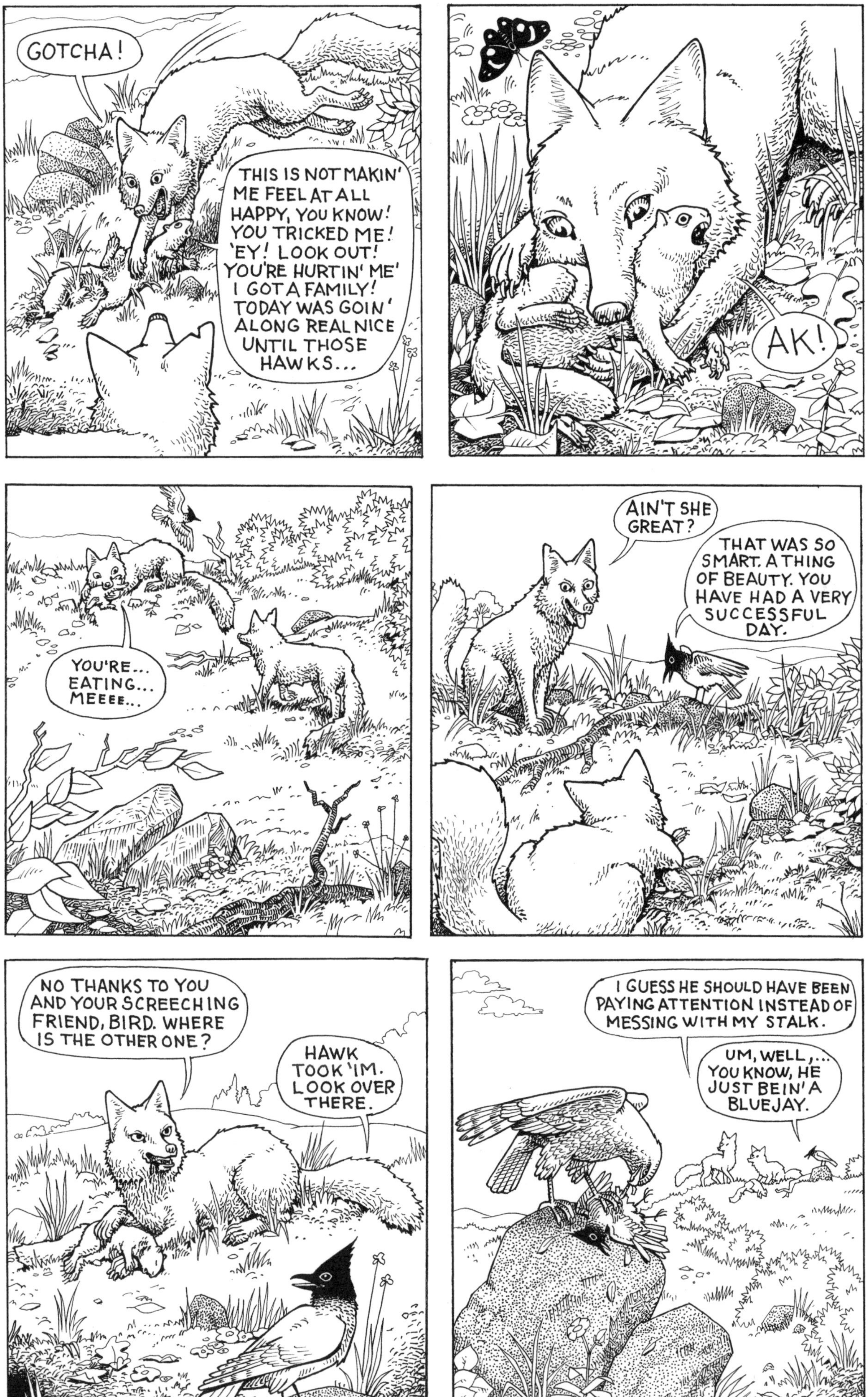
GOTCHA!
THIS IS NOT MAKIN' ME FEEL AT ALL HAPPY, YOU KNOW! YOU TRICKED ME! 'EY! LOOK OUT! YOU'RE HURTIN' ME' I GOT A FAMILY! TODAY WAS GOIN' ALONG REAL NICE UNTIL THOSE HAWKS...
AK!
YOU'RE... EATING... MEEEE...
AIN'T SHE GREAT?
THAT WAS SO SMART. A THING OF BEAUTY. YOU HAVE HAD A VERY SUCCESSFUL DAY.
NO THANKS TO YOU AND YOUR SCREECHING FRIEND, BIRD. WHERE IS THE OTHER ONE?
HAWK TOOK 'IM. LOOK OVER THERE.
I GUESS HE SHOULD HAVE BEEN PAYING ATTENTION INSTEAD OF MESSING WITH MY STALK.
UM, WELL,... YOU KNOW, HE JUST BEIN' A BLUEJAY.

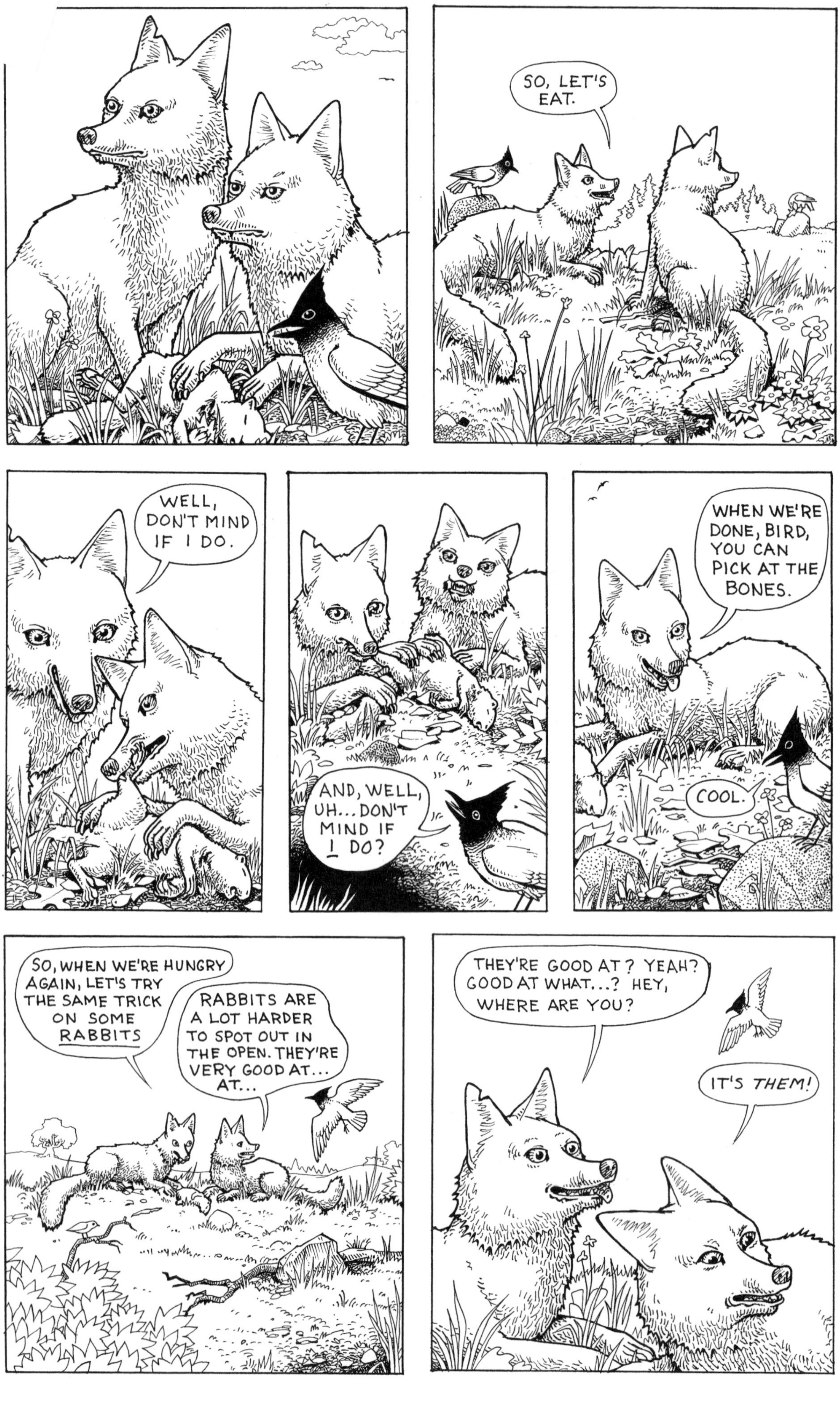
SO, LET'S EAT.
WELL, DON'T MIND IF I DO.
AND, WELL, UH... DON'T MIND IF I DO?
WHEN WE'RE DONE, BIRD, YOU CAN PICK AT THE BONES.
COOL.
SO, WHEN WE'RE HUNGRY AGAIN, LET'S TRY THE SAME TRICK ON SOME RABBITS
RABBITS ARE A LOT HARDER TO SPOT OUT IN THE OPEN. THEY'RE VERY GOOD AT... AT...
THEY'RE GOOD AT? YEAH? GOOD AT WHAT...? HEY, WHERE ARE YOU?
IT'S *THEM*!

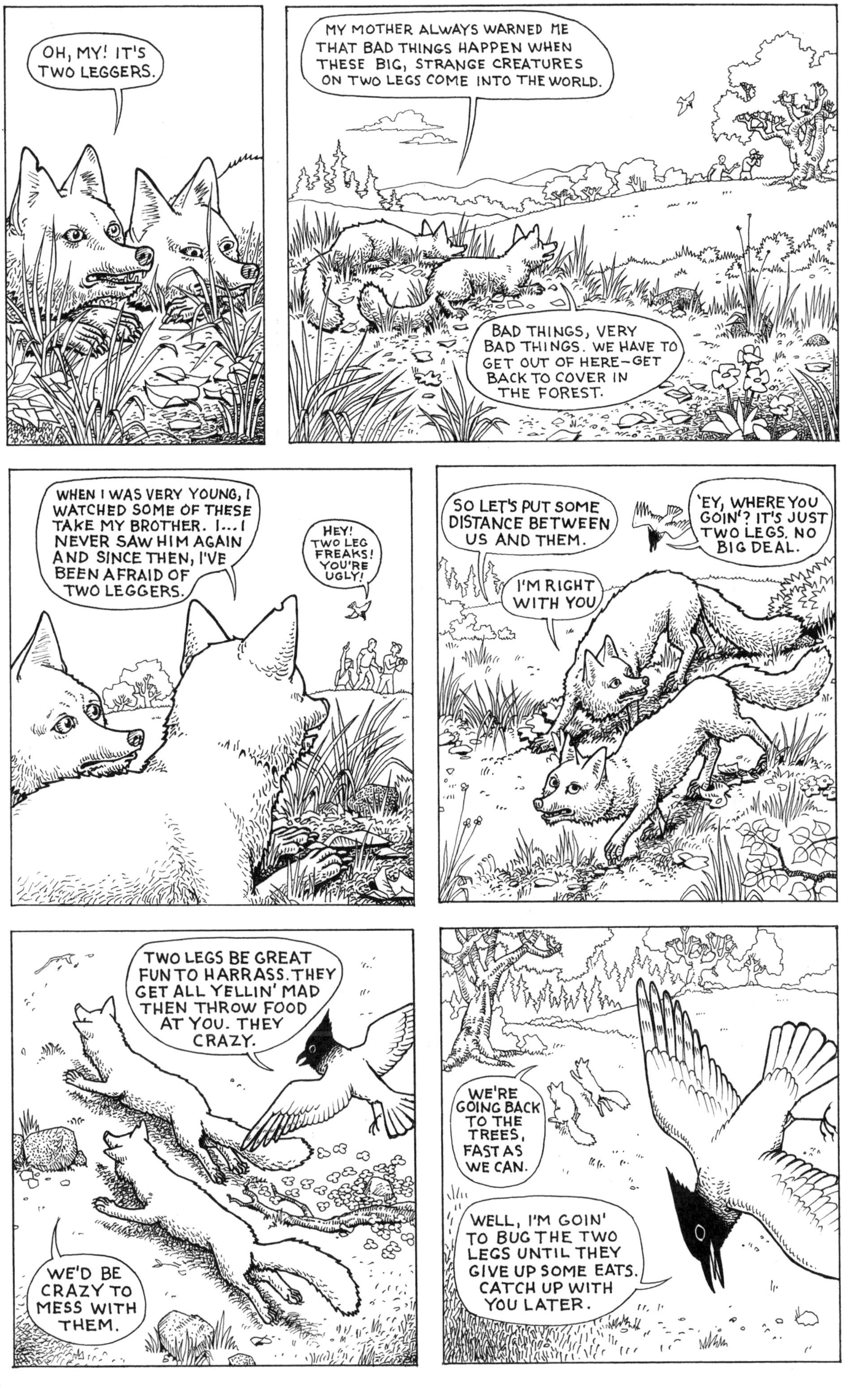
OH, MY! IT'S TWO LEGGERS.
MY MOTHER ALWAYS WARNED ME THAT BAD THINGS HAPPEN WHEN THESE BIG, STRANGE CREATURES ON TWO LEGS COME INTO THE WORLD.
BAD THINGS, VERY BAD THINGS. WE HAVE TO GET OUT OF HERE—GET BACK TO COVER IN THE FOREST.
WHEN I WAS VERY YOUNG, I WATCHED SOME OF THESE TAKE MY BROTHER. I...I NEVER SAW HIM AGAIN AND SINCE THEN, I'VE BEEN AFRAID OF TWO LEGGERS.
HEY! TWO LEG FREAKS! YOU'RE UGLY!
SO LET'S PUT SOME DISTANCE BETWEEN US AND THEM.
'EY, WHERE YOU GOIN'? IT'S JUST TWO LEGS. NO BIG DEAL.
I'M RIGHT WITH YOU
TWO LEGS BE GREAT FUN TO HARRASS. THEY GET ALL YELLIN' MAD THEN THROW FOOD AT YOU. THEY CRAZY.
WE'D BE CRAZY TO MESS WITH THEM.
WE'RE GOING BACK TO THE TREES, FAST AS WE CAN.
WELL, I'M GOIN' TO BUG THE TWO LEGS UNTIL THEY GIVE UP SOME EATS. CATCH UP WITH YOU LATER.

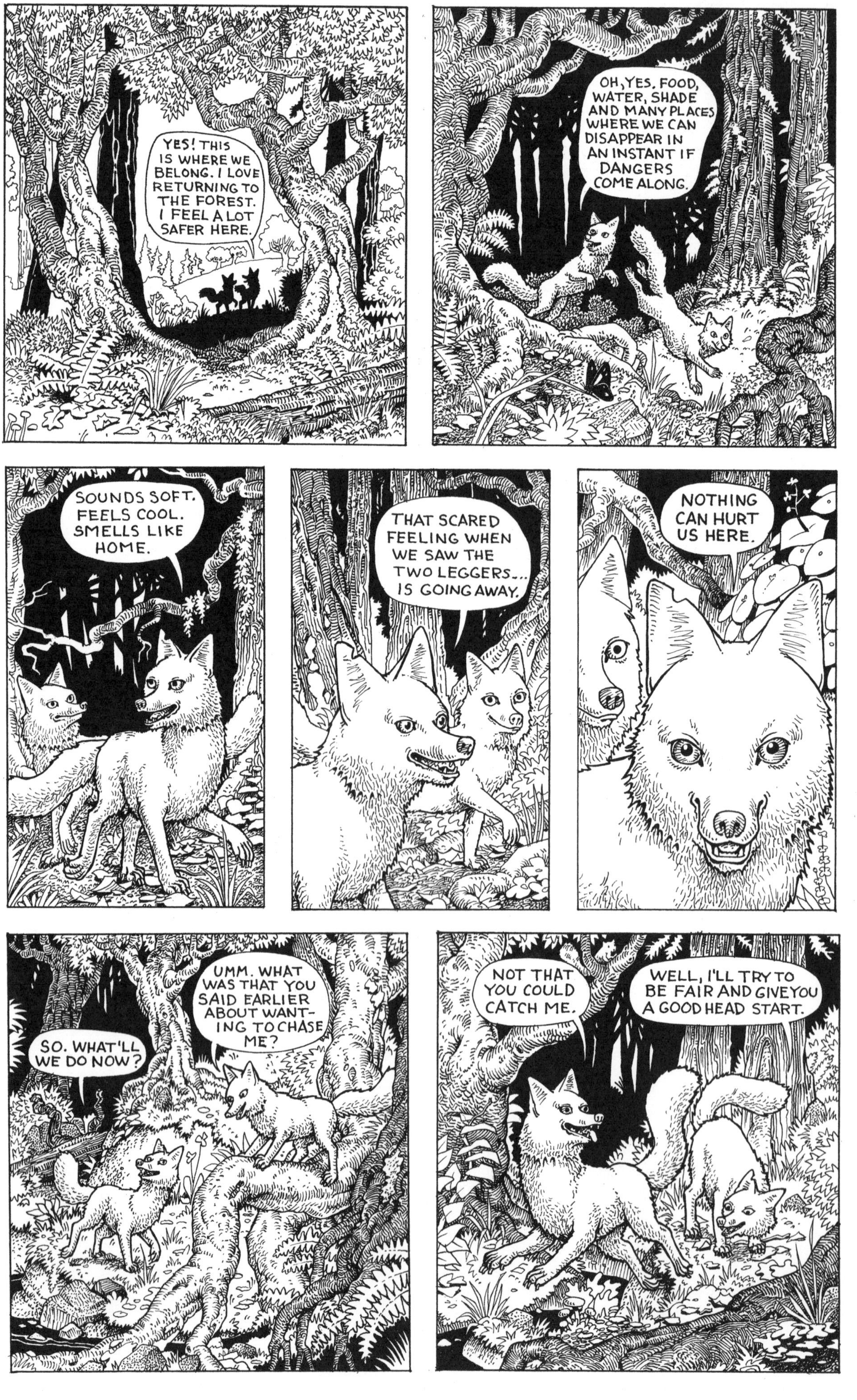
YES! THIS IS WHERE WE BELONG. I LOVE RETURNING TO THE FOREST. I FEEL A LOT SAFER HERE.
OH, YES. FOOD, WATER, SHADE AND MANY PLACES WHERE WE CAN DISAPPEAR IN AN INSTANT IF DANGERS COME ALONG.
SOUNDS SOFT. FEELS COOL. SMELLS LIKE HOME.
THAT SCARED FEELING WHEN WE SAW THE TWO LEGGERS... IS GOING AWAY.
NOTHING CAN HURT US HERE.
SO. WHAT'LL WE DO NOW?
UMM. WHAT WAS THAT YOU SAID EARLIER ABOUT WANTING TO CHASE ME?
NOT THAT YOU COULD CATCH ME.
WELL, I'LL TRY TO BE FAIR AND GIVE YOU A GOOD HEAD START.

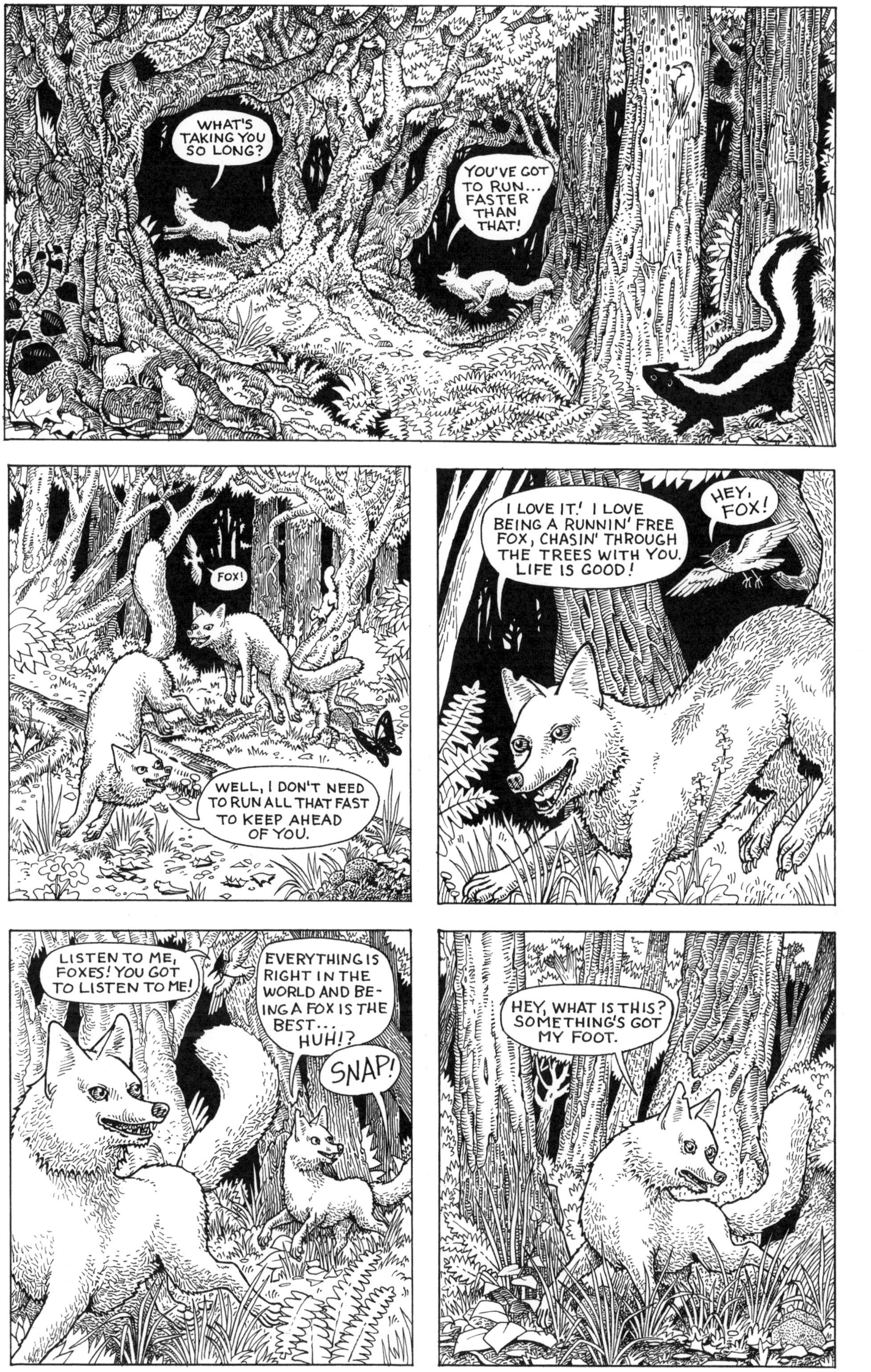
WHAT'S TAKING YOU SO LONG?
YOU'VE GOT TO RUN... FASTER THAN THAT!
FOX!
WELL, I DON'T NEED TO RUN ALL THAT FAST TO KEEP AHEAD OF YOU.
I LOVE IT! I LOVE BEING A RUNNIN' FREE FOX, CHASIN' THROUGH THE TREES WITH YOU. LIFE IS GOOD!
HEY, FOX!
LISTEN TO ME, FOXES! YOU GOT TO LISTEN TO ME!
EVERYTHING IS RIGHT IN THE WORLD AND BEING A FOX IS THE BEST... HUH!?
SNAP!
HEY, WHAT IS THIS? SOMETHING'S GOT MY FOOT.

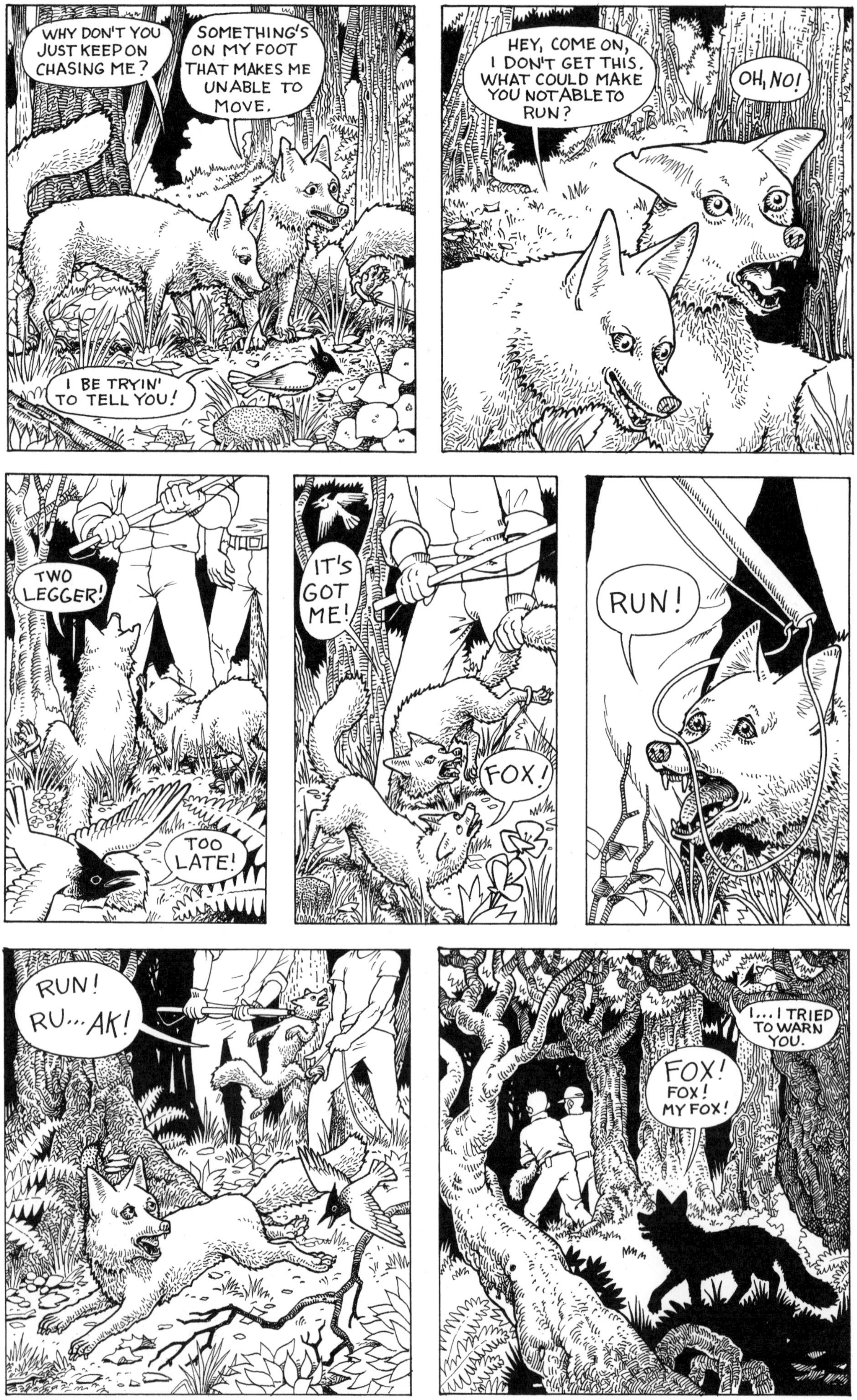
WHY DON'T YOU JUST KEEP ON CHASING ME?
SOMETHING'S ON MY FOOT THAT MAKES ME UNABLE TO MOVE.
I BE TRYIN' TO TELL YOU!
HEY, COME ON, I DON'T GET THIS. WHAT COULD MAKE YOU NOT ABLE TO RUN?
OH, NO!
TWO LEGGER!
TOO LATE!
IT'S GOT ME!
FOX!
RUN!
RUN! RU...AK!
I...I TRIED TO WARN YOU.
FOX! FOX! MY FOX!

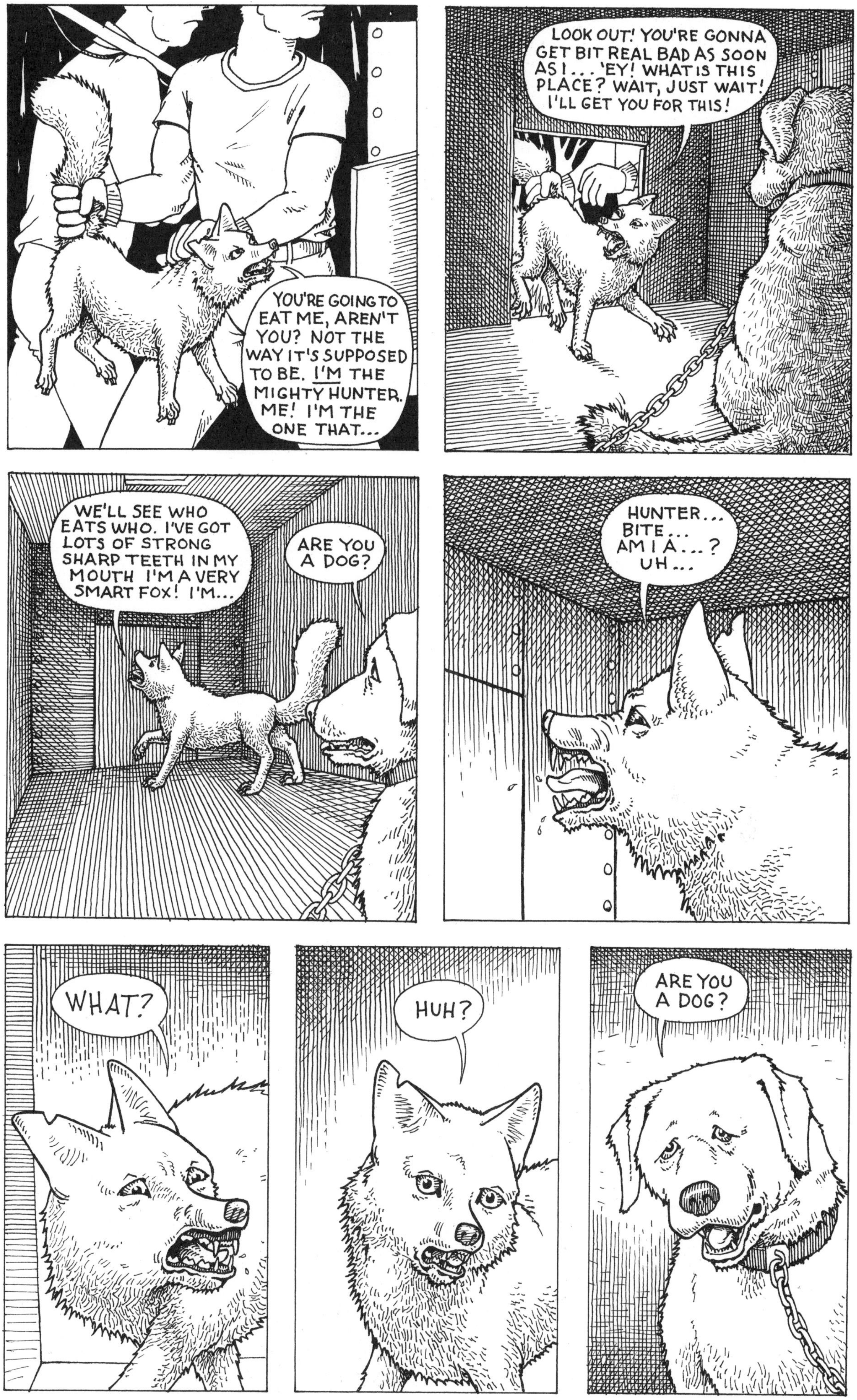
YOU'RE GOING TO EAT ME, AREN'T YOU? NOT THE WAY IT'S SUPPOSED TO BE. I'M THE MIGHTY HUNTER. ME! I'M THE ONE THAT...
LOOK OUT! YOU'RE GONNA GET BIT REAL BAD AS SOON AS I... 'EY! WHAT IS THIS PLACE? WAIT, JUST WAIT! I'LL GET YOU FOR THIS!
WE'LL SEE WHO EATS WHO. I'VE GOT LOTS OF STRONG SHARP TEETH IN MY MOUTH I'M A VERY SMART FOX! I'M...
ARE YOU A DOG?
HUNTER... BITE... AM I A...? UH...
WHAT?
HUH?
ARE YOU A DOG?

?
BETTER NOT GET TOO CLOSE TO ME. I MIGHT HAVE TO SNARL AT YOU OR EVEN BITE YOU.
ME? WHY BITE ME?
WELL, BECAUSE I'M A DOG. THAT'S WHAT I DO.
YOU ARE A DOG, AREN'T YOU?
WUH... OF COURSE NOT. I'M A FOX.
HUMMPH! WELL, YOU SURE LOOK A LOT LIKE A DOG.
WHAT'S THAT?
IT'S OUR TWO LEG MASTERS MAKING THE ROOM MOVE TO A NEW PLACE.

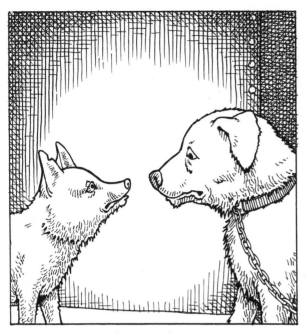

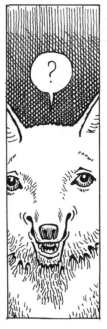

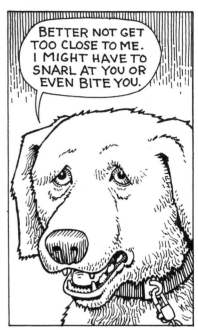

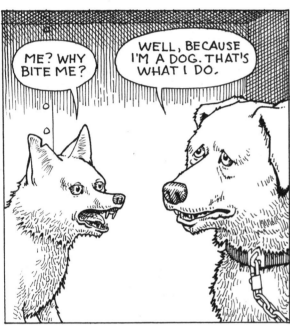

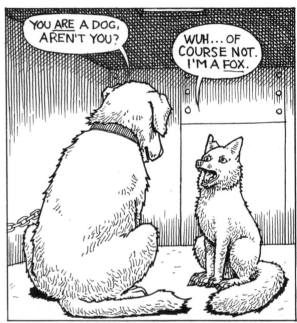

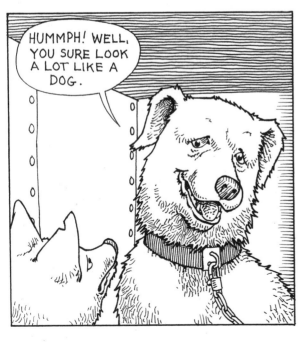

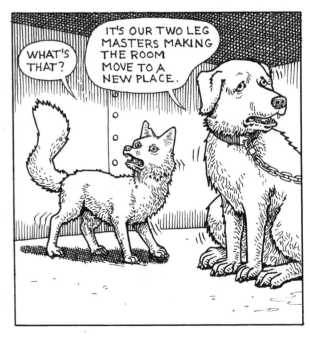

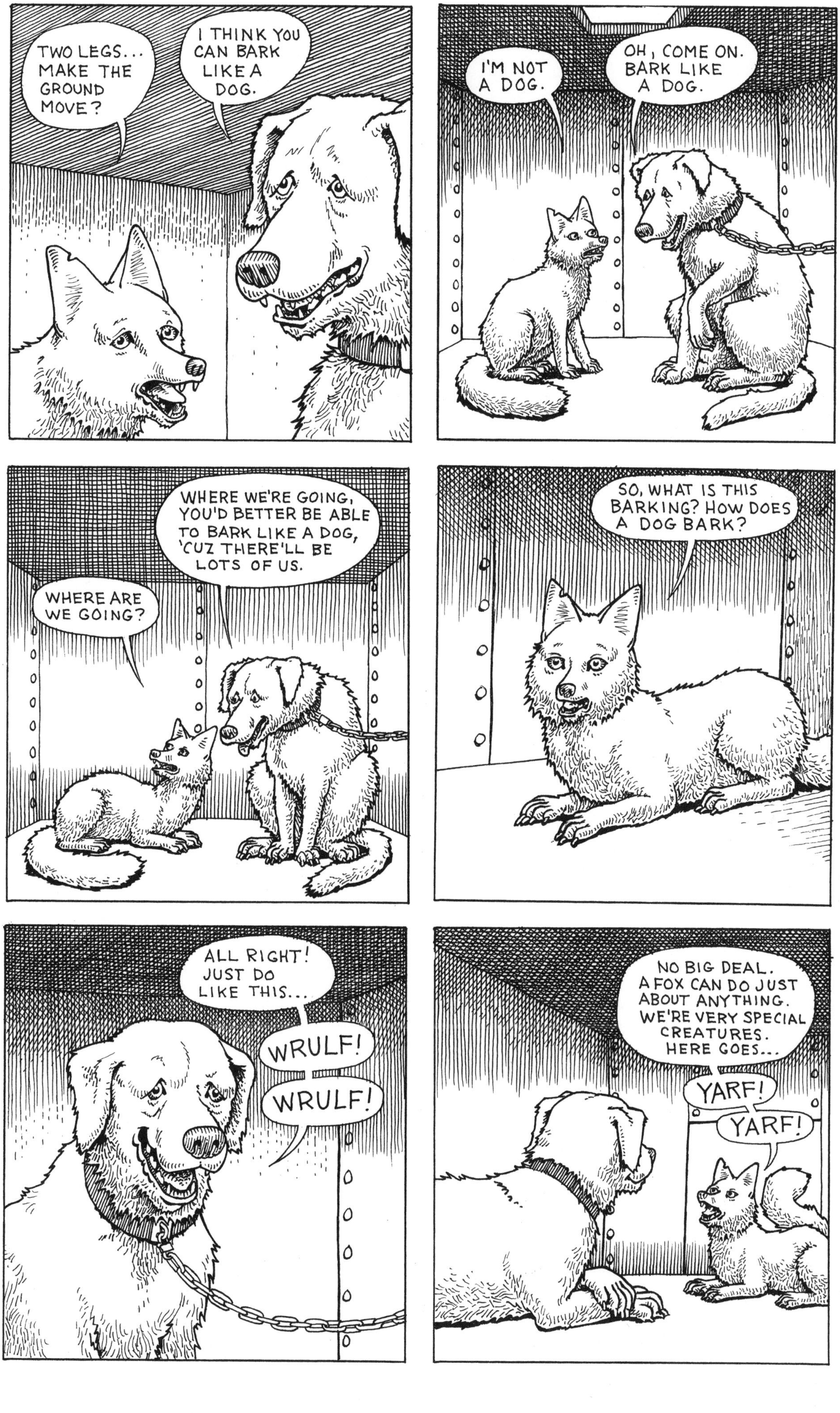
TWO LEGS... MAKE THE GROUND MOVE?
I THINK YOU CAN BARK LIKE A DOG.
I'M NOT A DOG.
OH, COME ON. BARK LIKE A DOG.
WHERE WE'RE GOING, YOU'D BETTER BE ABLE TO BARK LIKE A DOG, 'CUZ THERE'LL BE LOTS OF US.
WHERE ARE WE GOING?
SO, WHAT IS THIS BARKING? HOW DOES A DOG BARK?
ALL RIGHT! JUST DO LIKE THIS...
WRULF!
WRULF!
NO BIG DEAL. A FOX CAN DO JUST ABOUT ANYTHING. WE'RE VERY SPECIAL CREATURES. HERE GOES...
YARF!
YARF!

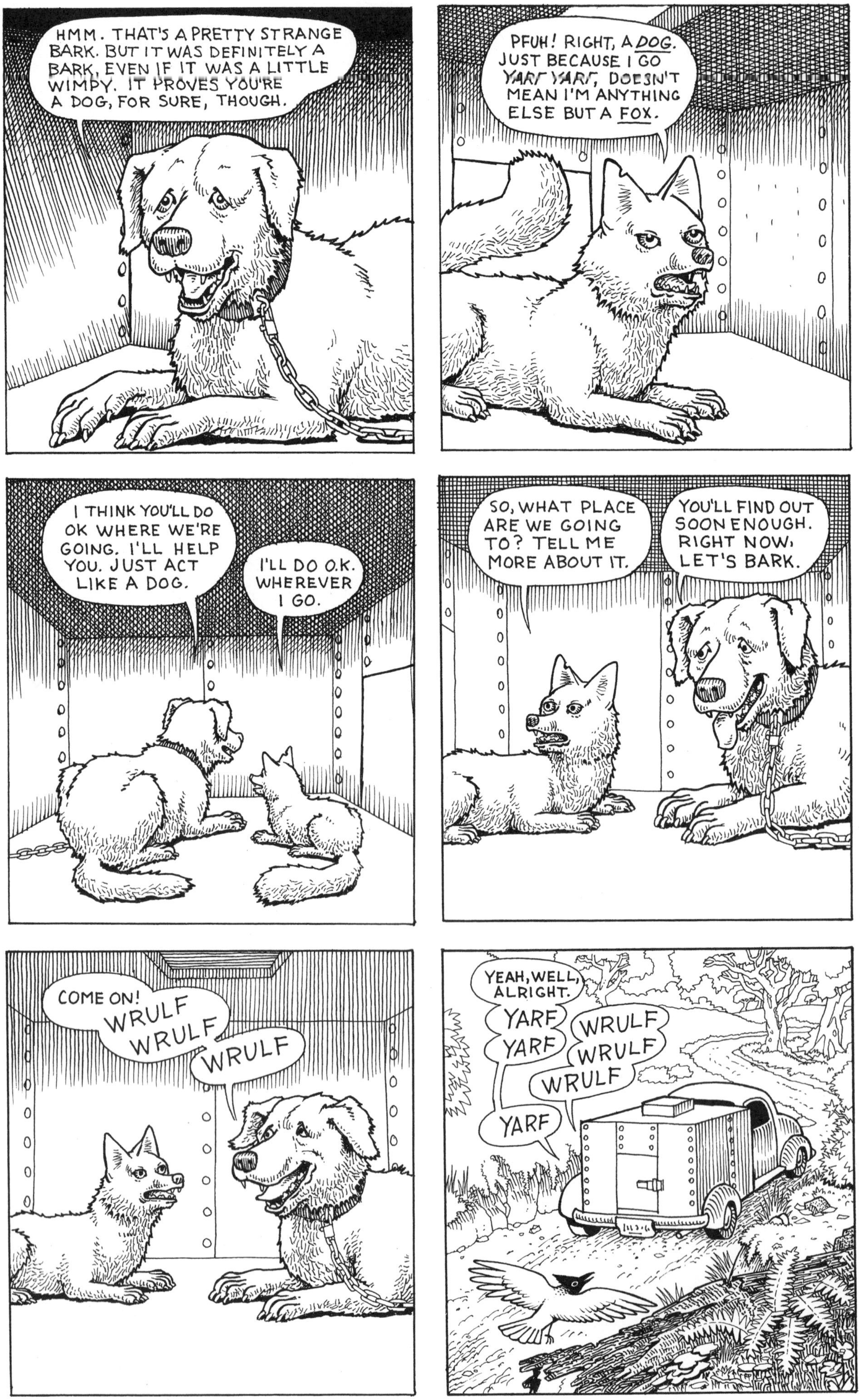
HMM. THAT'S A PRETTY STRANGE BARK. BUT IT WAS DEFINITELY A BARK, EVEN IF IT WAS A LITTLE WIMPY. IT PROVES YOU'RE A DOG, FOR SURE, THOUGH.
PFUH! RIGHT, A DOG. JUST BECAUSE I GO YARF YARF, DOESN'T MEAN I'M ANYTHING ELSE BUT A FOX.
I THINK YOU'LL DO OK WHERE WE'RE GOING. I'LL HELP YOU. JUST ACT LIKE A DOG.
I'LL DO O.K. WHEREVER I GO.
SO, WHAT PLACE ARE WE GOING TO? TELL ME MORE ABOUT IT.
YOU'LL FIND OUT SOON ENOUGH. RIGHT NOW, LET'S BARK.
COME ON! WRULF WRULF
WRULF
YEAH, WELL, ALRIGHT.
YARF YARF
WRULF WRULF WRULF
YARF

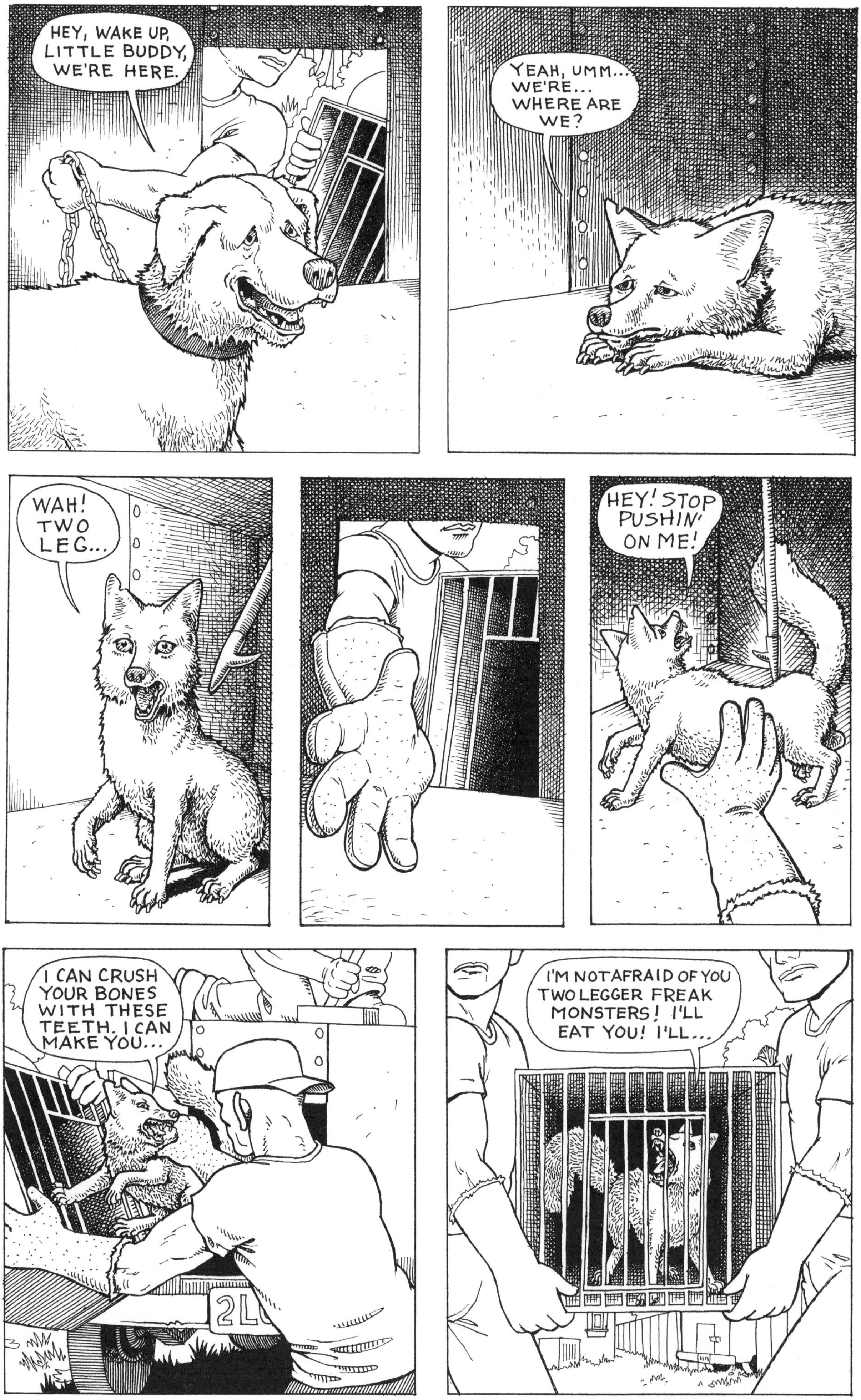
HEY, WAKE UP, LITTLE BUDDY, WE'RE HERE.
YEAH, UMM... WE'RE... WHERE ARE WE?
WAH! TWO LEG...
HEY! STOP PUSHIN' ON ME!
I CAN CRUSH YOUR BONES WITH THESE TEETH. I CAN MAKE YOU...
I'M NOT AFRAID OF YOU TWOLEGGER FREAK MONSTERS! I'LL EAT YOU! I'LL...

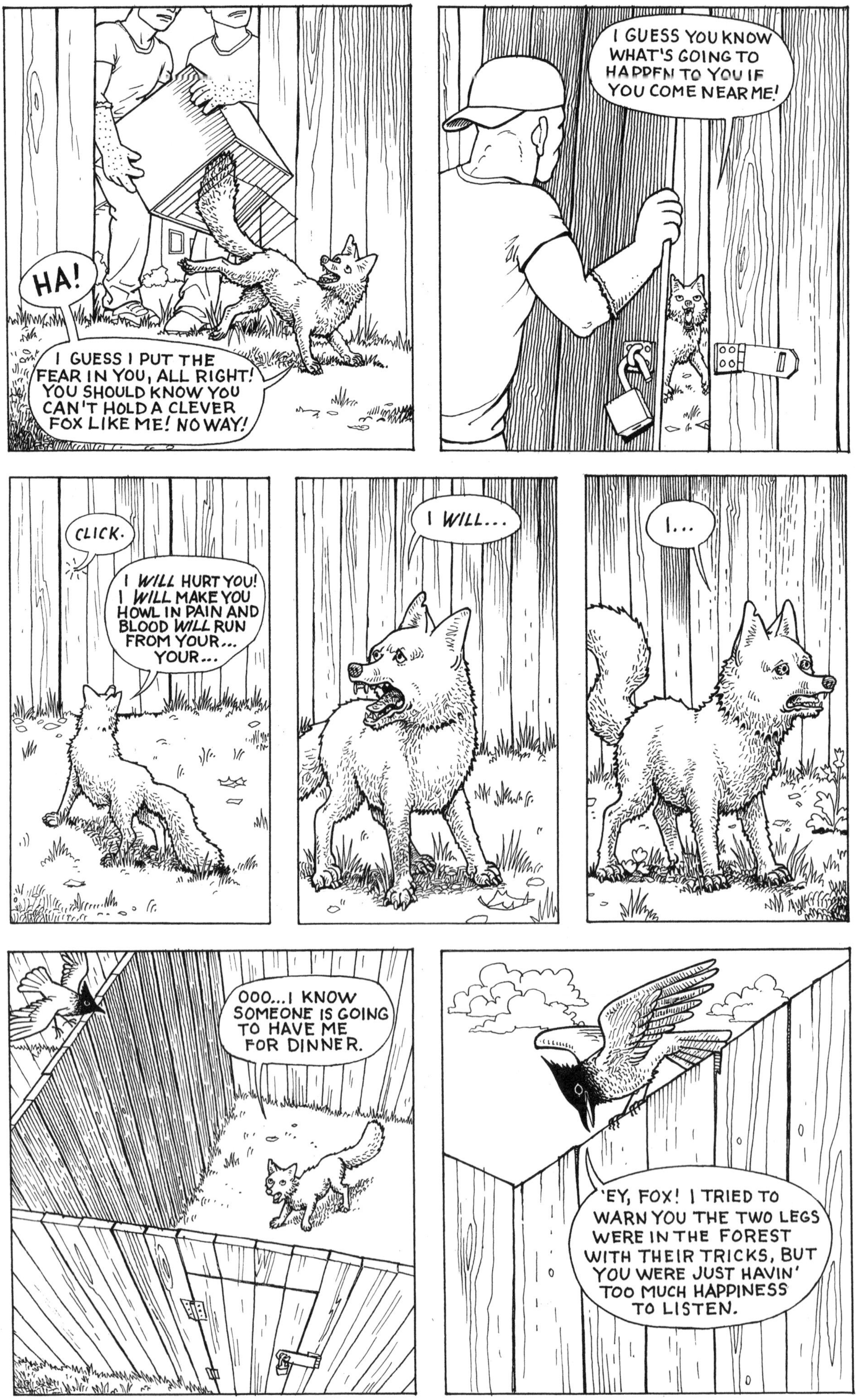
HA!
I GUESS I PUT THE FEAR IN YOU, ALL RIGHT! YOU SHOULD KNOW YOU CAN'T HOLD A CLEVER FOX LIKE ME! NO WAY!
I GUESS YOU KNOW WHAT'S GOING TO HAPPEN TO YOU IF YOU COME NEAR ME!
CLICK.
I *WILL* HURT YOU! I *WILL* MAKE YOU HOWL IN PAIN AND BLOOD *WILL* RUN FROM YOUR... YOUR...
I *WILL*...
I...
OOO...I KNOW SOMEONE IS GOING TO HAVE ME FOR DINNER.
'EY, FOX! I TRIED TO WARN YOU THE TWO LEGS WERE IN THE FOREST WITH THEIR TRICKS, BUT YOU WERE JUST HAVIN' TOO MUCH HAPPINESS TO LISTEN.

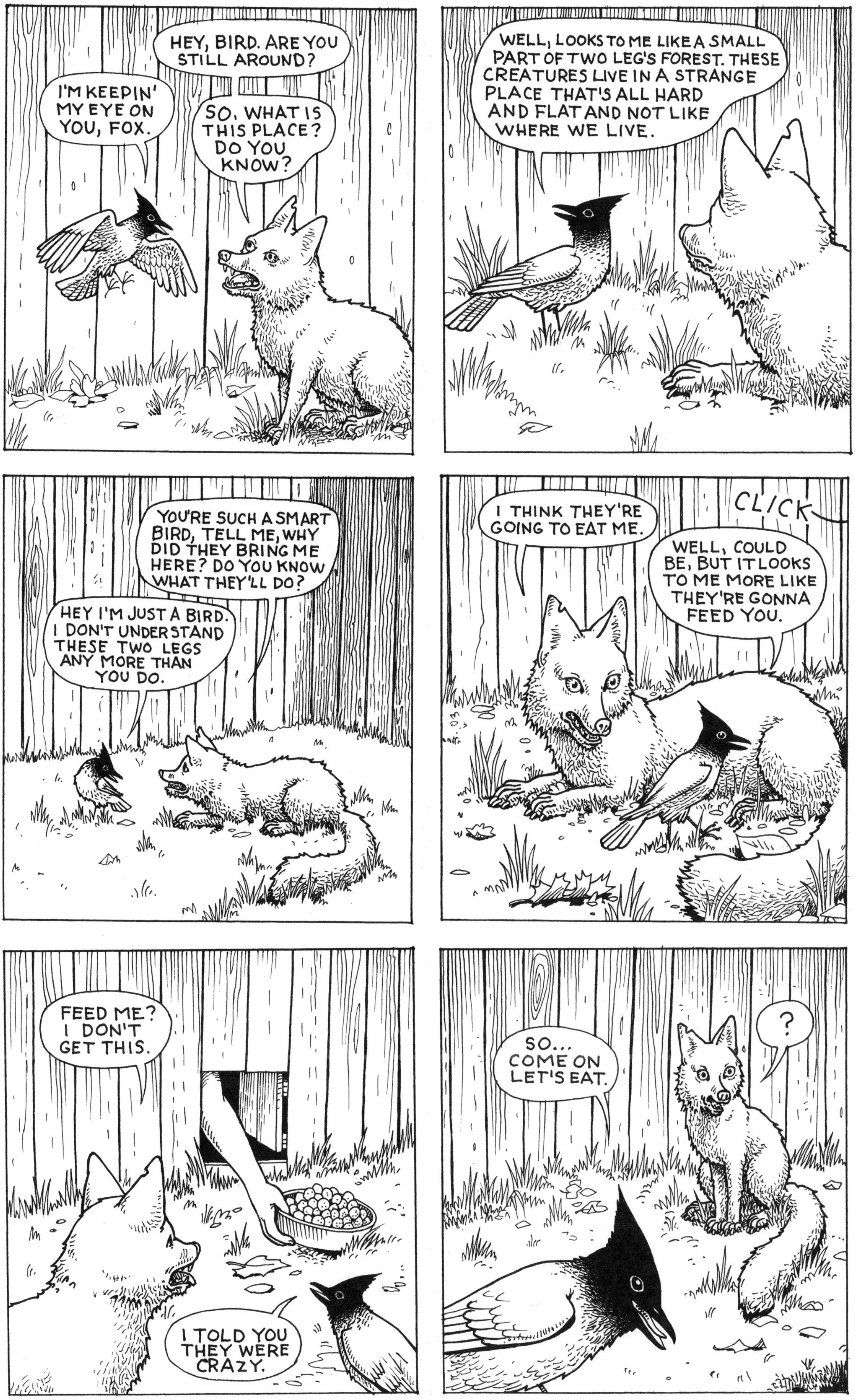
HEY, BIRD. ARE YOU STILL AROUND?
I'M KEEPIN' MY EYE ON YOU, FOX.
SO, WHAT IS THIS PLACE? DO YOU KNOW?
WELL, LOOKS TO ME LIKE A SMALL PART OF TWO LEG'S FOREST. THESE CREATURES LIVE IN A STRANGE PLACE THAT'S ALL HARD AND FLAT AND NOT LIKE WHERE WE LIVE.
YOU'RE SUCH A SMART BIRD, TELL ME, WHY DID THEY BRING ME HERE? DO YOU KNOW WHAT THEY'LL DO?
HEY I'M JUST A BIRD. I DON'T UNDERSTAND THESE TWO LEGS ANY MORE THAN YOU DO.
I THINK THEY'RE GOING TO EAT ME.
CLICK
WELL, COULD BE, BUT IT LOOKS TO ME MORE LIKE THEY'RE GONNA FEED YOU.
FEED ME? I DON'T GET THIS.
I TOLD YOU THEY WERE CRAZY.
SO... COME ON LET'S EAT.
?

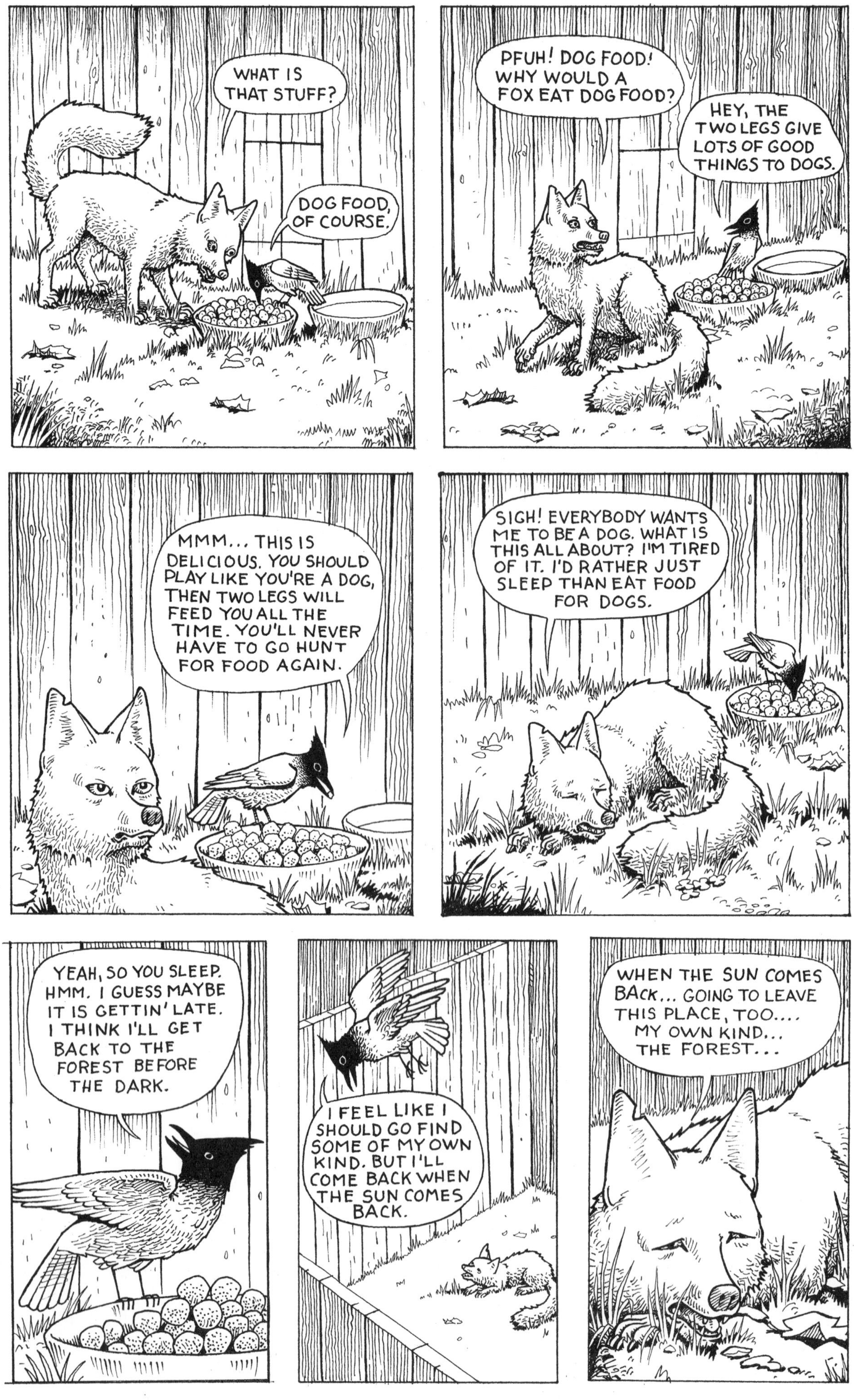
WHAT IS THAT STUFF?
DOG FOOD, OF COURSE.
PFUH! DOG FOOD! WHY WOULD A FOX EAT DOG FOOD?
HEY, THE TWO LEGS GIVE LOTS OF GOOD THINGS TO DOGS.
MMM... THIS IS DELICIOUS. YOU SHOULD PLAY LIKE YOU'RE A DOG, THEN TWO LEGS WILL FEED YOU ALL THE TIME. YOU'LL NEVER HAVE TO GO HUNT FOR FOOD AGAIN.
SIGH! EVERYBODY WANTS ME TO BE A DOG. WHAT IS THIS ALL ABOUT? I'M TIRED OF IT. I'D RATHER JUST SLEEP THAN EAT FOOD FOR DOGS.
YEAH, SO YOU SLEEP. HMM. I GUESS MAYBE IT IS GETTIN' LATE. I THINK I'LL GET BACK TO THE FOREST BEFORE THE DARK.
I FEEL LIKE I SHOULD GO FIND SOME OF MY OWN KIND. BUT I'LL COME BACK WHEN THE SUN COMES BACK.
WHEN THE SUN COMES BACK... GOING TO LEAVE THIS PLACE, TOO.... MY OWN KIND... THE FOREST...

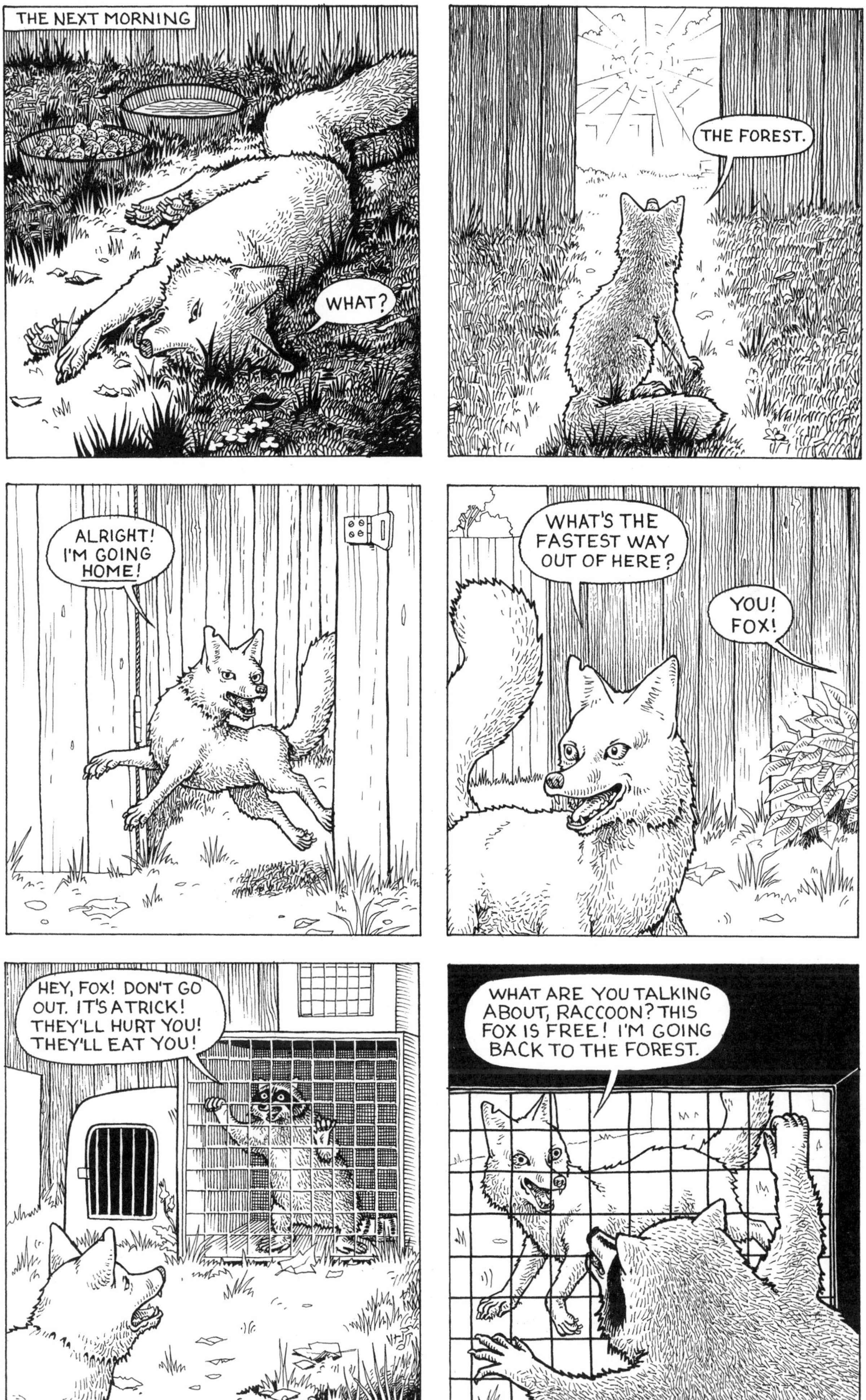
THE NEXT MORNING
WHAT?
THE FOREST.
ALRIGHT! I'M GOING HOME!
WHAT'S THE FASTEST WAY OUT OF HERE?
YOU! FOX!
HEY, FOX! DON'T GO OUT. IT'S A TRICK! THEY'LL HURT YOU! THEY'LL EAT YOU!
WHAT ARE YOU TALKING ABOUT, RACCOON? THIS FOX IS FREE! I'M GOING BACK TO THE FOREST.

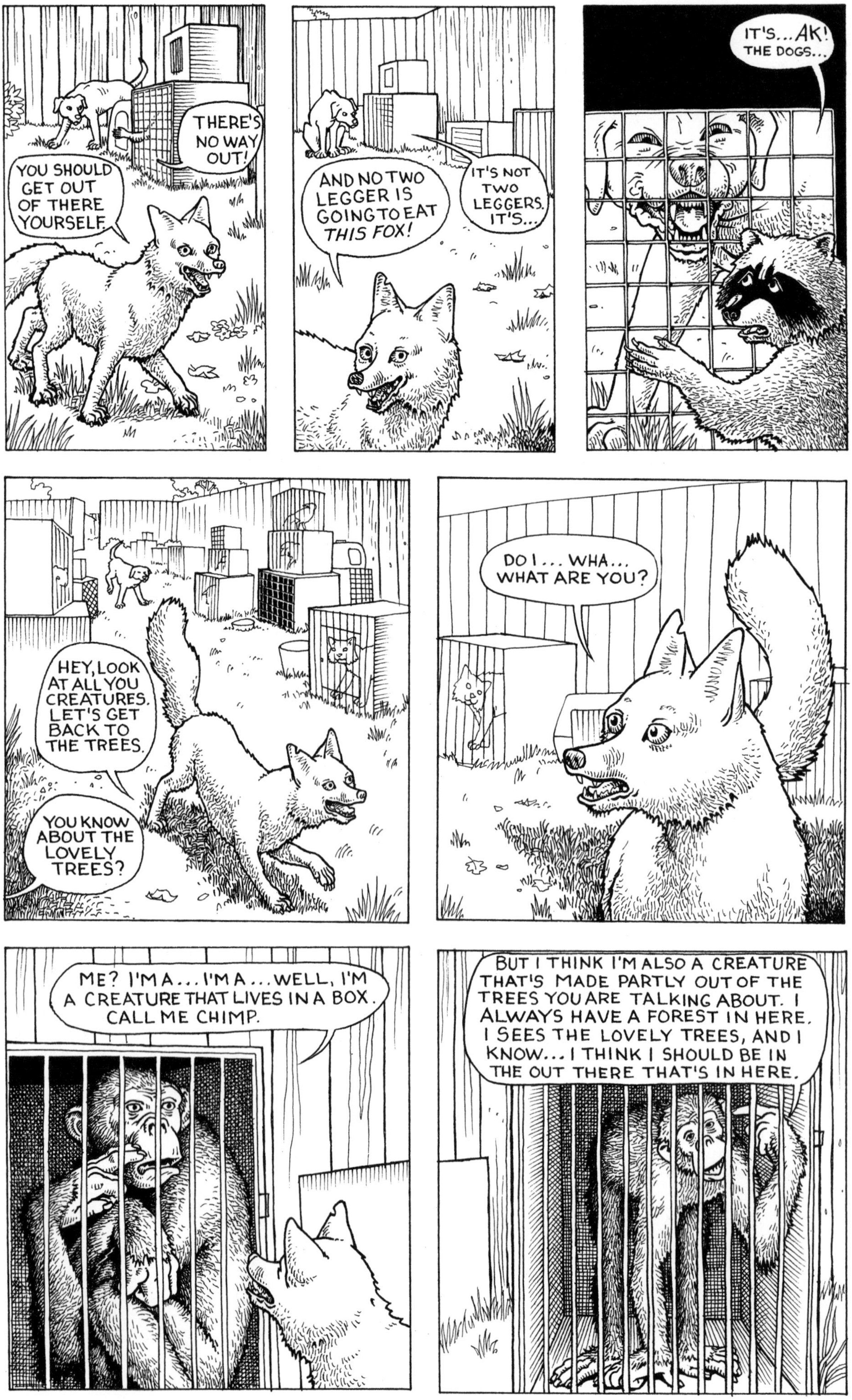
THERE'S NO WAY OUT!
YOU SHOULD GET OUT OF THERE YOURSELF.
AND NO TWO LEGGER IS GOING TO EAT *THIS FOX!*
IT'S NOT TWO LEGGERS. IT'S...
IT'S...AK! THE DOGS...
HEY, LOOK AT ALL YOU CREATURES. LET'S GET BACK TO THE TREES.
YOU KNOW ABOUT THE LOVELY TREES?
DO I... WHA... WHAT ARE YOU?
ME? I'M A... I'M A... WELL, I'M A CREATURE THAT LIVES IN A BOX. CALL ME CHIMP.
BUT I THINK I'M ALSO A CREATURE THAT'S MADE PARTLY OUT OF THE TREES YOU ARE TALKING ABOUT. I ALWAYS HAVE A FOREST IN HERE. I SEES THE LOVELY TREES, AND I KNOW... I THINK I SHOULD BE IN THE OUT THERE THAT'S IN HERE.

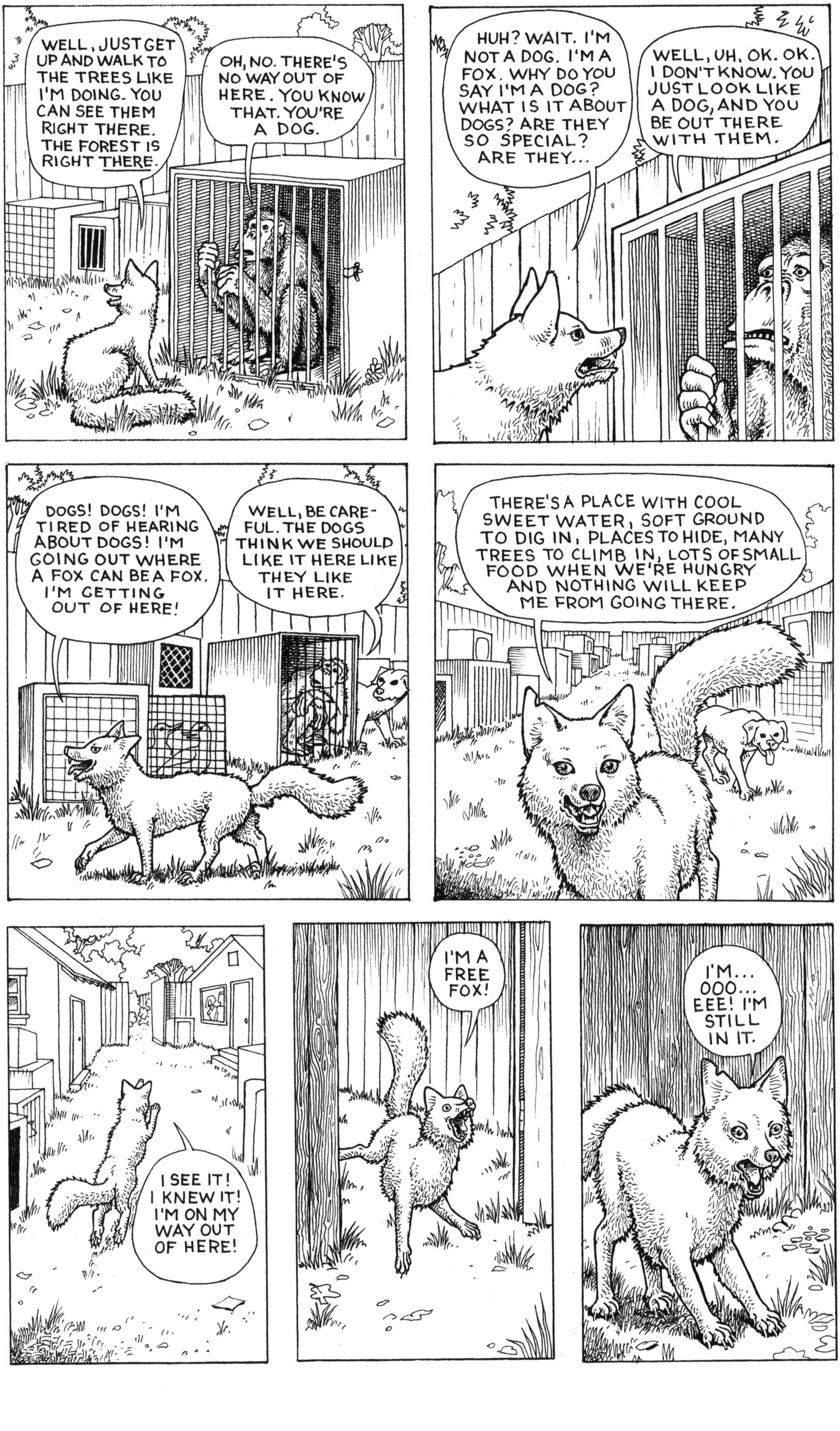
WELL, JUST GET UP AND WALK TO THE TREES LIKE I'M DOING. YOU CAN SEE THEM RIGHT THERE. THE FOREST IS RIGHT THERE.
OH, NO. THERE'S NO WAY OUT OF HERE. YOU KNOW THAT. YOU'RE A DOG.
HUH? WAIT. I'M NOT A DOG. I'M A FOX. WHY DO YOU SAY I'M A DOG? WHAT IS IT ABOUT DOGS? ARE THEY SO SPECIAL? ARE THEY...
WELL, UH, OK. OK. I DON'T KNOW. YOU JUST LOOK LIKE A DOG, AND YOU BE OUT THERE WITH THEM.
DOGS! DOGS! I'M TIRED OF HEARING ABOUT DOGS! I'M GOING OUT WHERE A FOX CAN BE A FOX. I'M GETTING OUT OF HERE!
WELL, BE CARE-FUL. THE DOGS THINK WE SHOULD LIKE IT HERE LIKE THEY LIKE IT HERE.
THERE'S A PLACE WITH COOL SWEET WATER, SOFT GROUND TO DIG IN, PLACES TO HIDE, MANY TREES TO CLIMB IN, LOTS OF SMALL FOOD WHEN WE'RE HUNGRY AND NOTHING WILL KEEP ME FROM GOING THERE.
I SEE IT! I KNEW IT! I'M ON MY WAY OUT OF HERE!
I'M A FREE FOX!
I'M... OOO... EEE! I'M STILL IN IT.

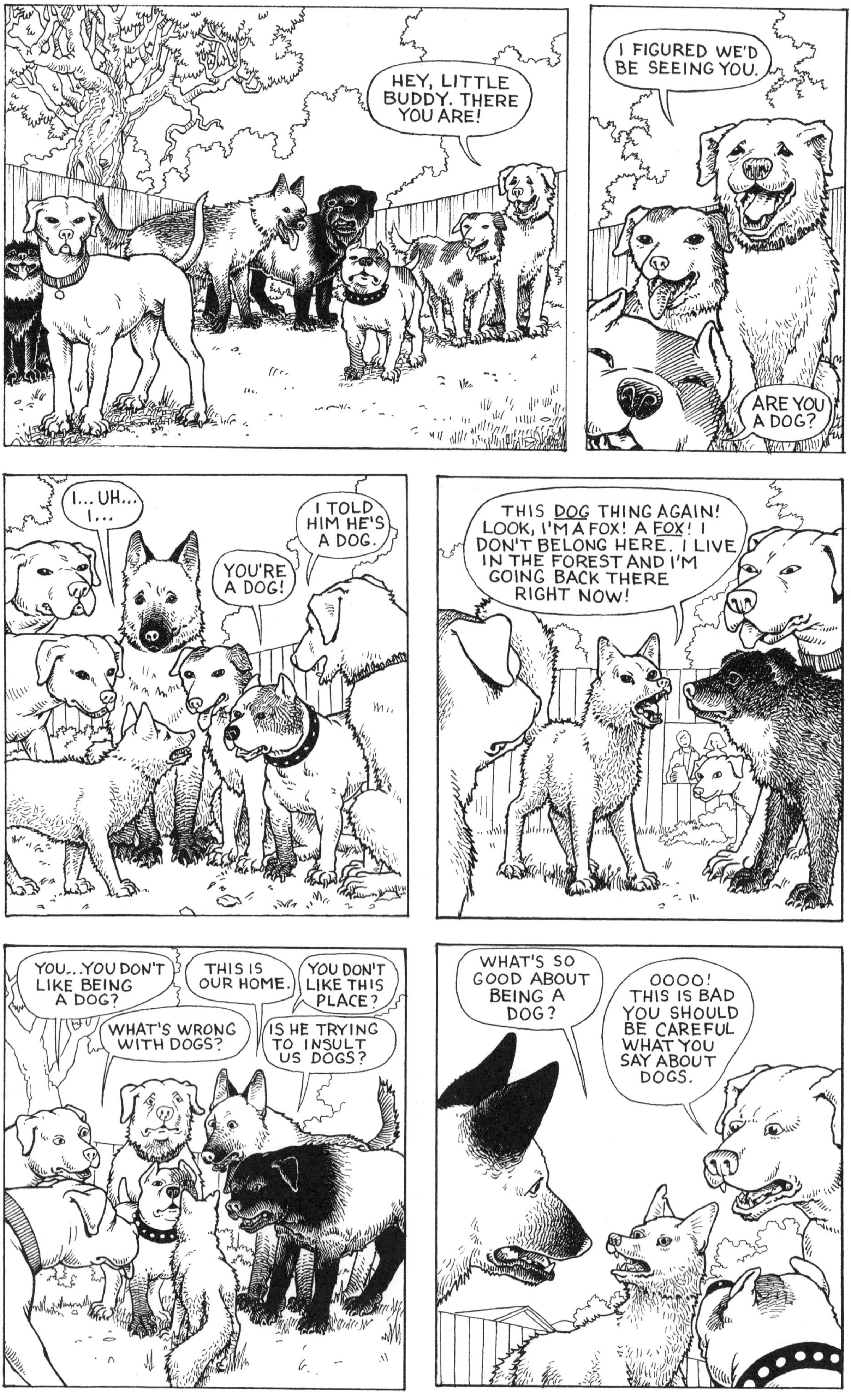
HEY, LITTLE BUDDY. THERE YOU ARE!
I FIGURED WE'D BE SEEING YOU.
ARE YOU A DOG?
I... UH... I...
I TOLD HIM HE'S A DOG.
YOU'RE A DOG!
THIS DOG THING AGAIN! LOOK, I'M A FOX! A FOX! I DON'T BELONG HERE. I LIVE IN THE FOREST AND I'M GOING BACK THERE RIGHT NOW!
YOU... YOU DON'T LIKE BEING A DOG?
THIS IS OUR HOME.
YOU DON'T LIKE THIS PLACE?
WHAT'S WRONG WITH DOGS?
IS HE TRYING TO INSULT US DOGS?
WHAT'S SO GOOD ABOUT BEING A DOG?
OOOO! THIS IS BAD YOU SHOULD BE CAREFUL WHAT YOU SAY ABOUT DOGS.

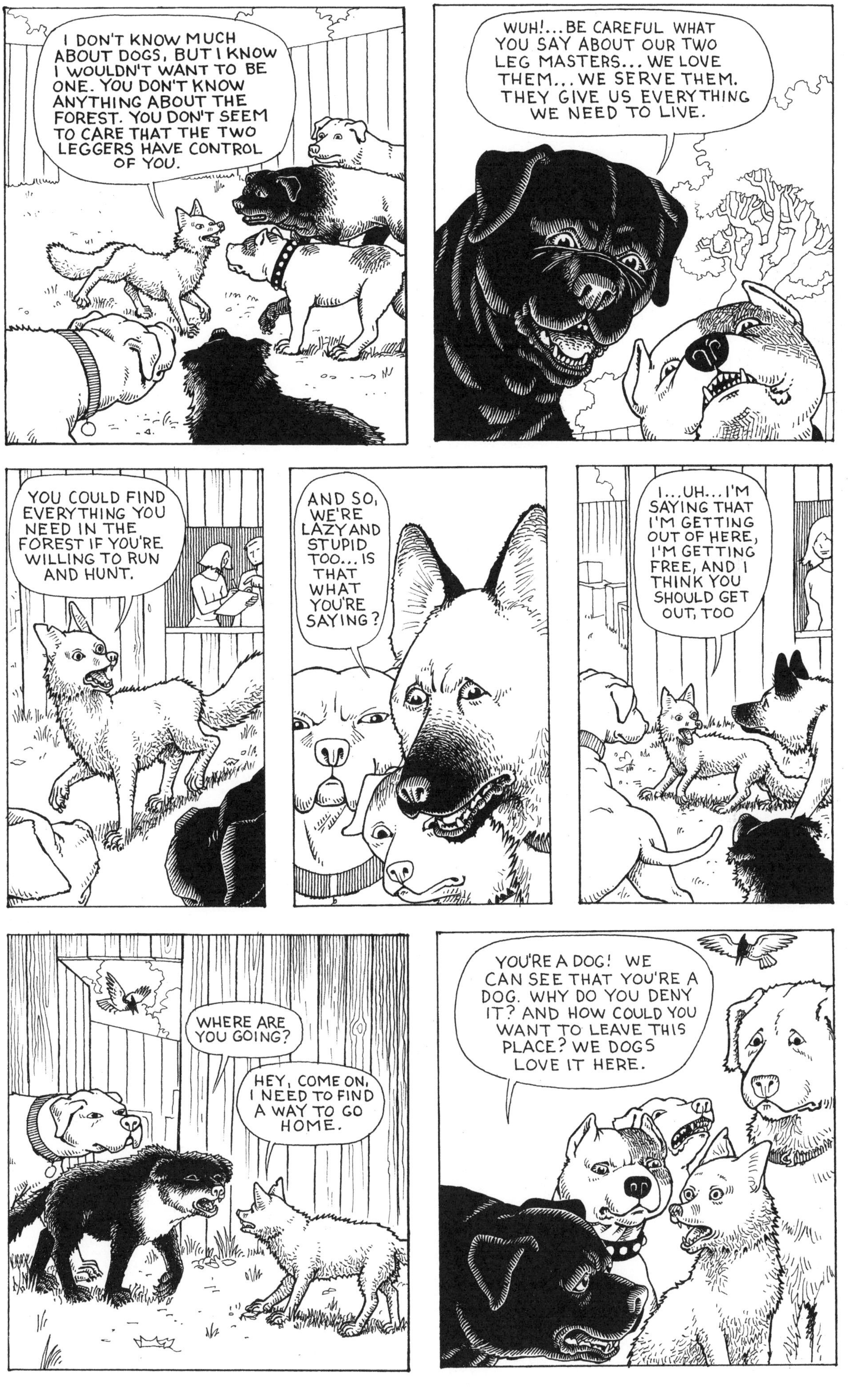
I DON'T KNOW MUCH ABOUT DOGS, BUT I KNOW I WOULDN'T WANT TO BE ONE. YOU DON'T KNOW ANYTHING ABOUT THE FOREST. YOU DON'T SEEM TO CARE THAT THE TWO LEGGERS HAVE CONTROL OF YOU.
WUH!...BE CAREFUL WHAT YOU SAY ABOUT OUR TWO LEG MASTERS... WE LOVE THEM... WE SERVE THEM. THEY GIVE US EVERYTHING WE NEED TO LIVE.
YOU COULD FIND EVERYTHING YOU NEED IN THE FOREST IF YOU'RE WILLING TO RUN AND HUNT.
AND SO, WE'RE LAZY AND STUPID TOO... IS THAT WHAT YOU'RE SAYING?
I...UH...I'M SAYING THAT I'M GETTING OUT OF HERE, I'M GETTING FREE, AND I THINK YOU SHOULD GET OUT, TOO
WHERE ARE YOU GOING?
HEY, COME ON, I NEED TO FIND A WAY TO GO HOME.
YOU'RE A DOG! WE CAN SEE THAT YOU'RE A DOG. WHY DO YOU DENY IT? AND HOW COULD YOU WANT TO LEAVE THIS PLACE? WE DOGS LOVE IT HERE.

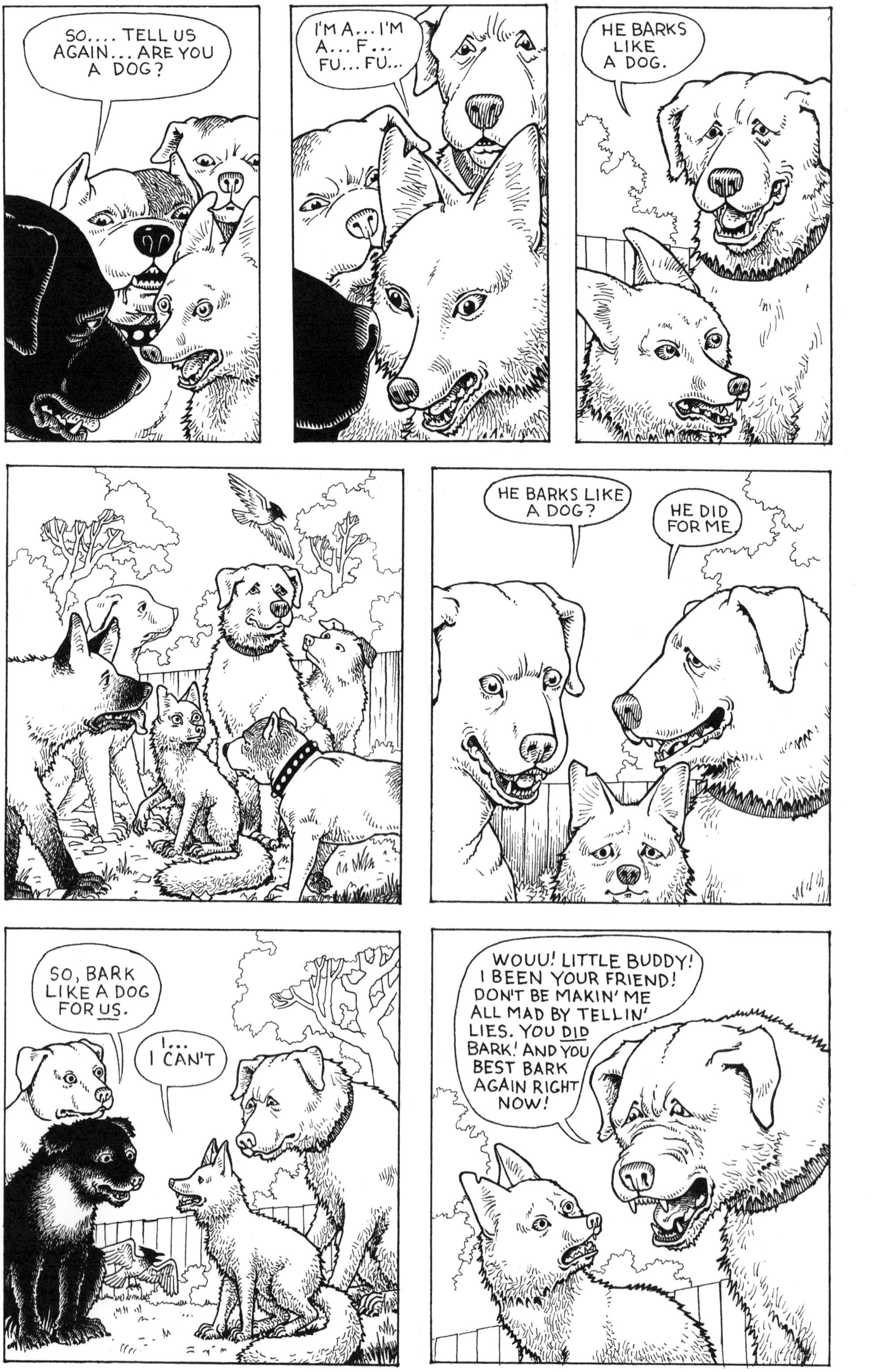
SO.... TELL US AGAIN... ARE YOU A DOG?
I'M A... I'M A... F... FU... FU...
HE BARKS LIKE A DOG.
HE BARKS LIKE A DOG?
HE DID FOR ME
SO, BARK LIKE A DOG FOR US.
I... I CAN'T
WOUU! LITTLE BUDDY! I BEEN YOUR FRIEND! DON'T BE MAKIN' ME ALL MAD BY TELLIN' LIES. YOU DID BARK! AND YOU BEST BARK AGAIN RIGHT NOW!

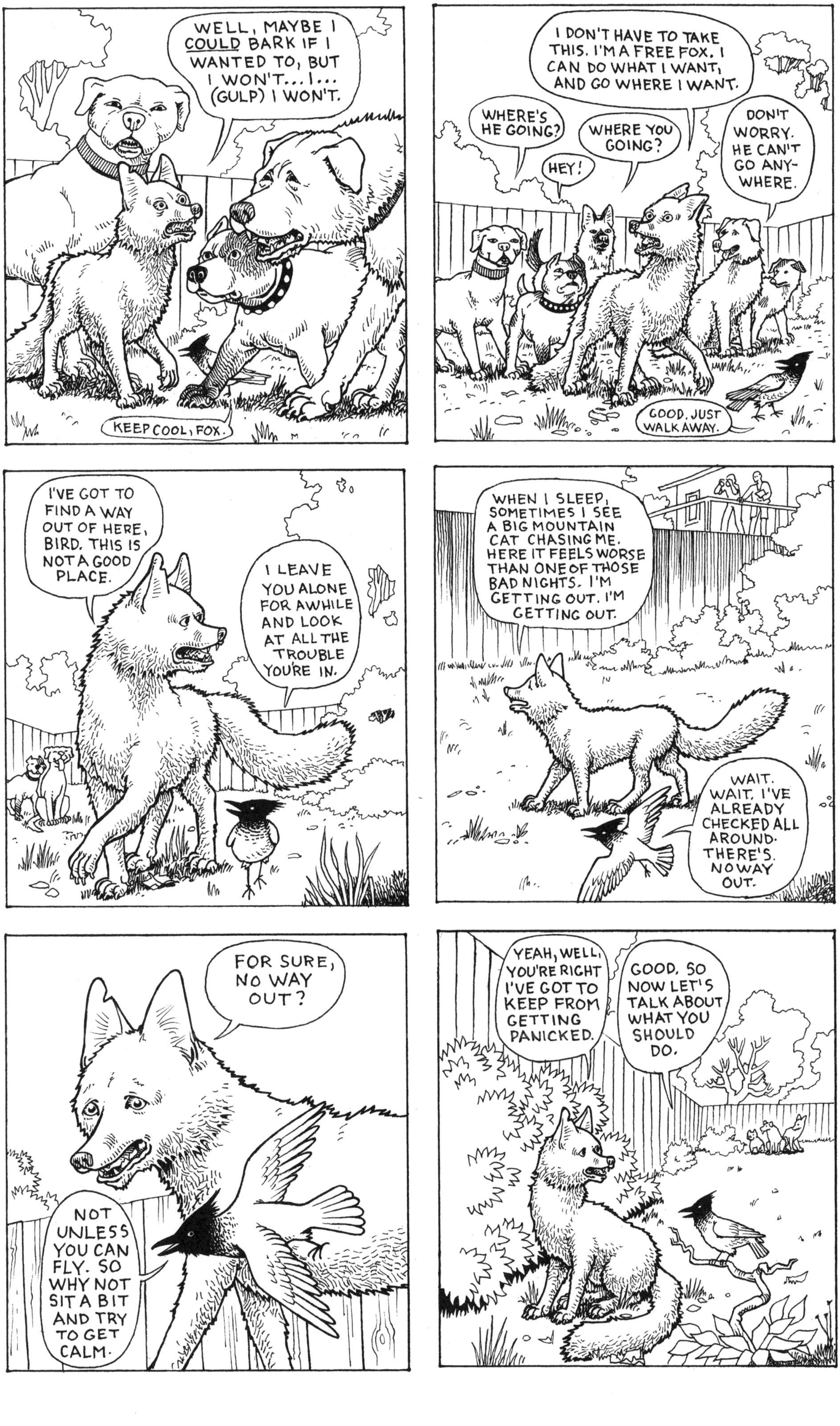
WELL, MAYBE I COULD BARK IF I WANTED TO, BUT I WON'T... I... (GULP) I WON'T.
KEEP COOL, FOX.
I DON'T HAVE TO TAKE THIS. I'M A FREE FOX. I CAN DO WHAT I WANT, AND GO WHERE I WANT.
WHERE'S HE GOING?
HEY!
WHERE YOU GOING?
DON'T WORRY. HE CAN'T GO ANYWHERE.
GOOD. JUST WALK AWAY.
I'VE GOT TO FIND A WAY OUT OF HERE, BIRD. THIS IS NOT A GOOD PLACE.
I LEAVE YOU ALONE FOR AWHILE AND LOOK AT ALL THE TROUBLE YOU'RE IN.
WHEN I SLEEP, SOMETIMES I SEE A BIG MOUNTAIN CAT CHASING ME. HERE IT FEELS WORSE THAN ONE OF THOSE BAD NIGHTS. I'M GETTING OUT. I'M GETTING OUT.
WAIT. WAIT. I'VE ALREADY CHECKED ALL AROUND. THERE'S NO WAY OUT.
FOR SURE, NO WAY OUT?
NOT UNLESS YOU CAN FLY. SO WHY NOT SIT A BIT AND TRY TO GET CALM.
YEAH, WELL, YOU'RE RIGHT I'VE GOT TO KEEP FROM GETTING PANICKED.
GOOD. SO NOW LET'S TALK ABOUT WHAT YOU SHOULD DO.

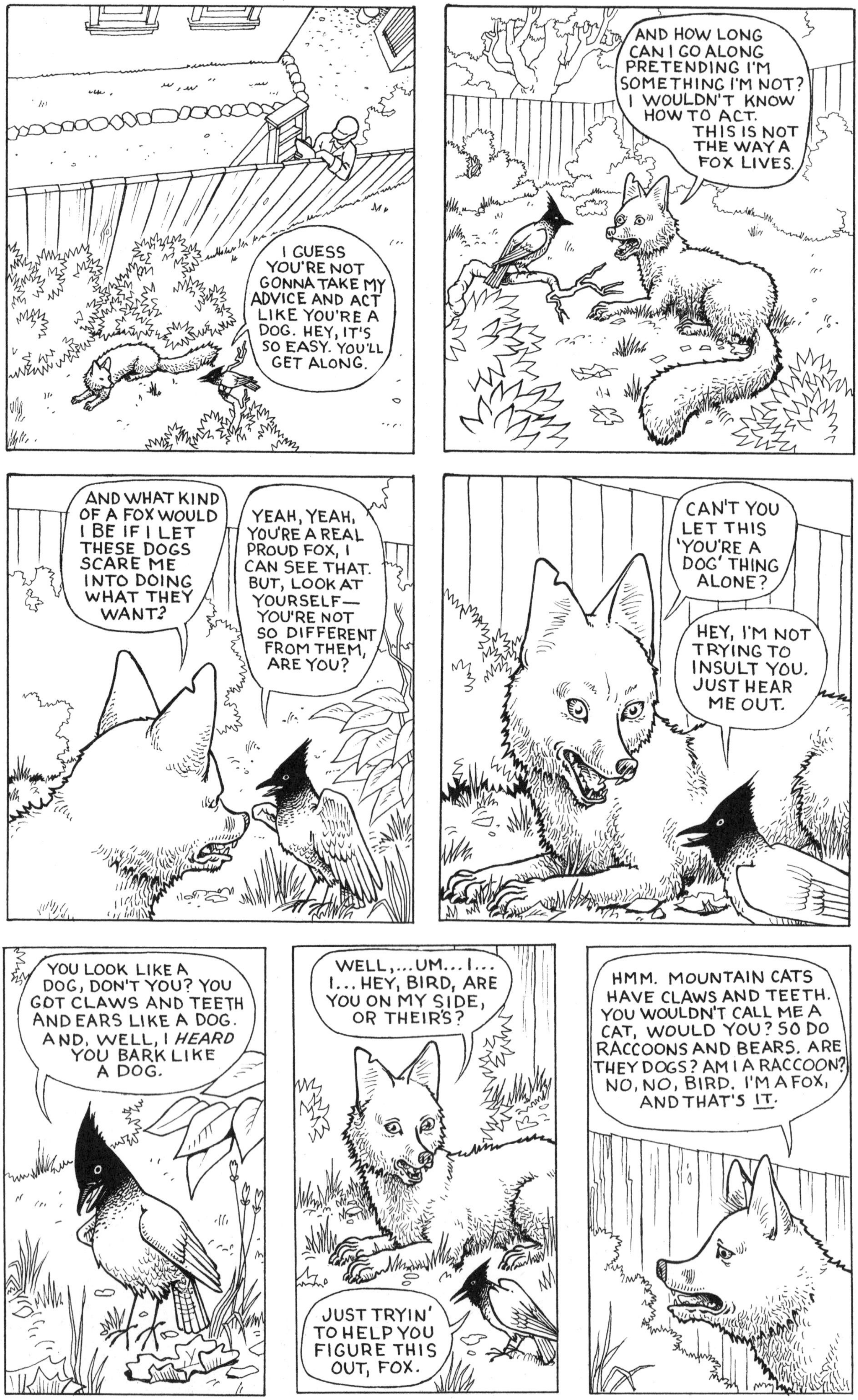
I GUESS YOU'RE NOT GONNA TAKE MY ADVICE AND ACT LIKE YOU'RE A DOG. HEY, IT'S SO EASY. YOU'LL GET ALONG.
AND HOW LONG CAN I GO ALONG PRETENDING I'M SOMETHING I'M NOT? I WOULDN'T KNOW HOW TO ACT.
THIS IS NOT THE WAY A FOX LIVES.
AND WHAT KIND OF A FOX WOULD I BE IF I LET THESE DOGS SCARE ME INTO DOING WHAT THEY WANT?
YEAH, YEAH, YOU'RE A REAL PROUD FOX, I CAN SEE THAT. BUT, LOOK AT YOURSELF— YOU'RE NOT SO DIFFERENT FROM THEM, ARE YOU?
CAN'T YOU LET THIS 'YOU'RE A DOG' THING ALONE?
HEY, I'M NOT TRYING TO INSULT YOU. JUST HEAR ME OUT.
YOU LOOK LIKE A DOG, DON'T YOU? YOU GOT CLAWS AND TEETH AND EARS LIKE A DOG. AND, WELL, I *HEARD* YOU BARK LIKE A DOG.
WELL,...UM...I... I... HEY, BIRD, ARE YOU ON MY SIDE, OR THEIR'S?
JUST TRYIN' TO HELP YOU FIGURE THIS OUT, FOX.
HMM. MOUNTAIN CATS HAVE CLAWS AND TEETH. YOU WOULDN'T CALL ME A CAT, WOULD YOU? SO DO RACCOONS AND BEARS. ARE THEY DOGS? AM I A RACCOON? NO, NO, BIRD. I'M A FOX, AND THAT'S IT.

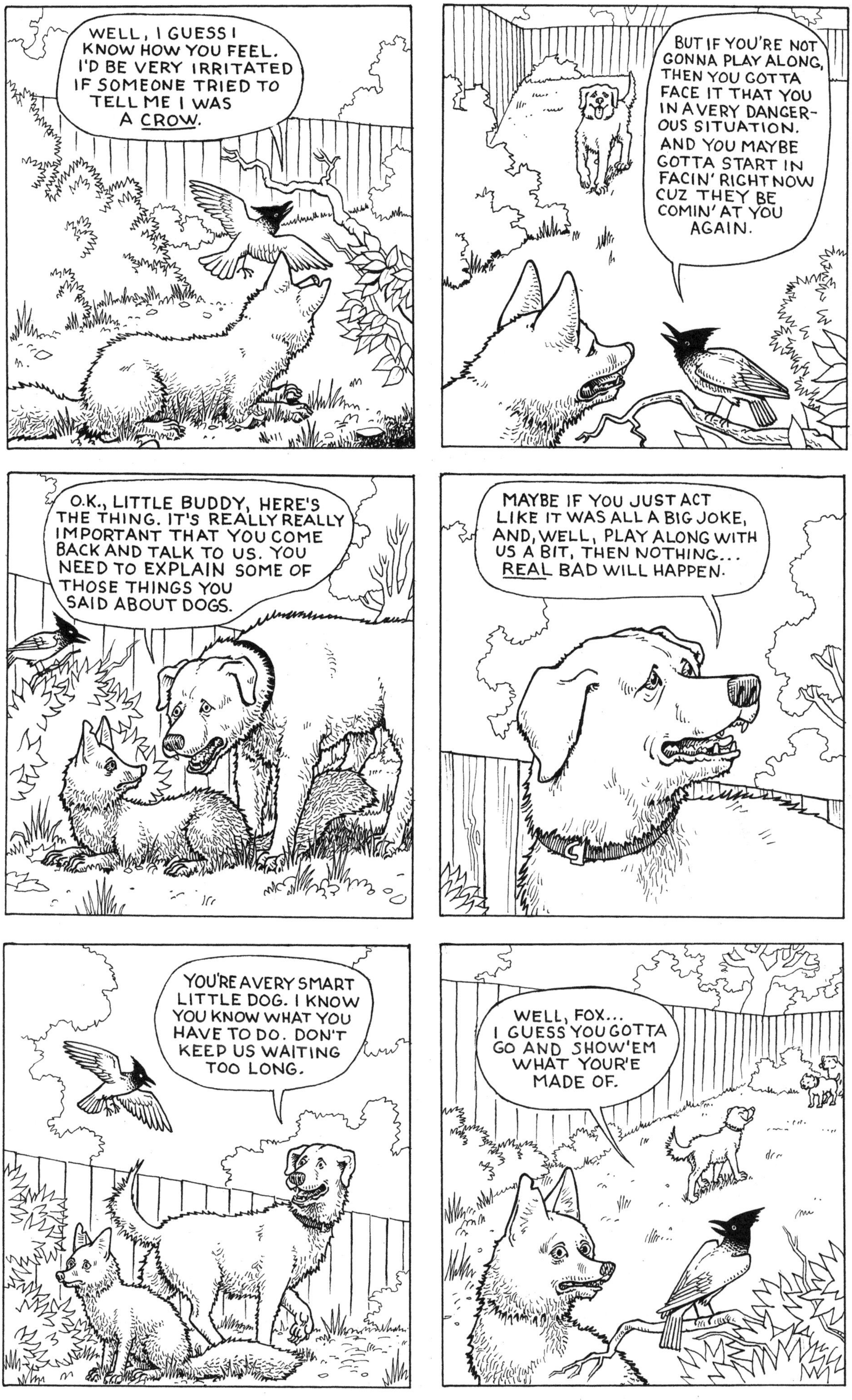
WELL, I GUESS I KNOW HOW YOU FEEL. I'D BE VERY IRRITATED IF SOMEONE TRIED TO TELL ME I WAS A CROW.
BUT IF YOU'RE NOT GONNA PLAY ALONG, THEN YOU GOTTA FACE IT THAT YOU IN A VERY DANGER-OUS SITUATION. AND YOU MAYBE GOTTA START IN FACIN' RIGHT NOW CUZ THEY BE COMIN' AT YOU AGAIN.
O.K., LITTLE BUDDY, HERE'S THE THING. IT'S REALLY REALLY IMPORTANT THAT YOU COME BACK AND TALK TO US. YOU NEED TO EXPLAIN SOME OF THOSE THINGS YOU SAID ABOUT DOGS.
MAYBE IF YOU JUST ACT LIKE IT WAS ALL A BIG JOKE, AND, WELL, PLAY ALONG WITH US A BIT, THEN NOTHING... REAL BAD WILL HAPPEN.
YOU'RE A VERY SMART LITTLE DOG. I KNOW YOU KNOW WHAT YOU HAVE TO DO. DON'T KEEP US WAITING TOO LONG.
WELL, FOX... I GUESS YOU GOTTA GO AND SHOW'EM WHAT YOUR'E MADE OF.

SIGH! WELL, O.K., HERE GOES. I'VE GOT TO DEAL WITH THIS STRAIGHT ON, NOSE TO NOSE. I KNOW YOU'RE RIGHT.
SO, DOGS... DO YOU WANT TO KNOW HOW A FOX LIVES IN THE FOREST AND NEVER TAKES A THING FROM TWO LEGS?
FORGET YOUR FOREST! WE DON'T WANT TO HEAR ANY MORE ABOUT YOUR FOREST!
WE JUST WANT TO HEAR YOU SAY THAT YOU'RE A DOG AND BEING A DOG IS A GOOD THING.
WE MOSTLY WANT TO HEAR YOU BARK LIKE A DOG.
BARK LIKE A DOG!
BARK!
COME ON! BARK LIKE A DOG!
YOU WILL BARK LIKE A DOG!
I DON'T THINK SO.

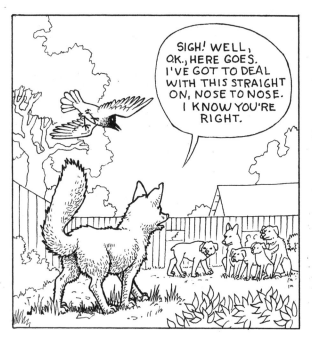

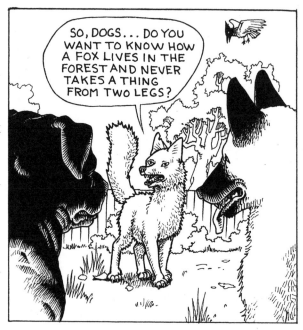

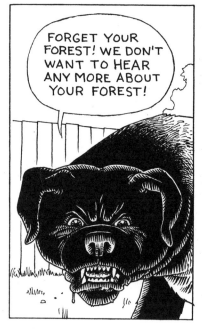

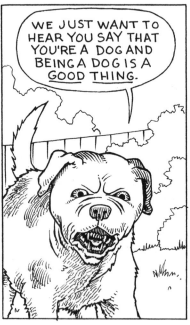

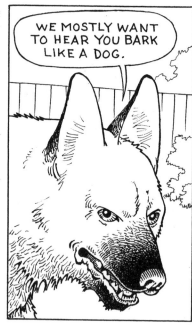

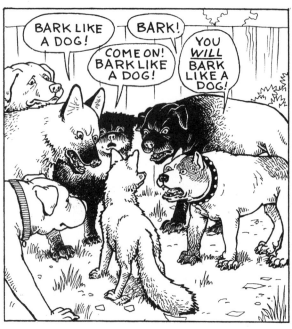

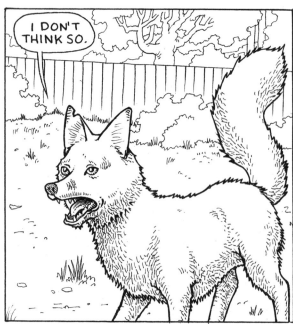

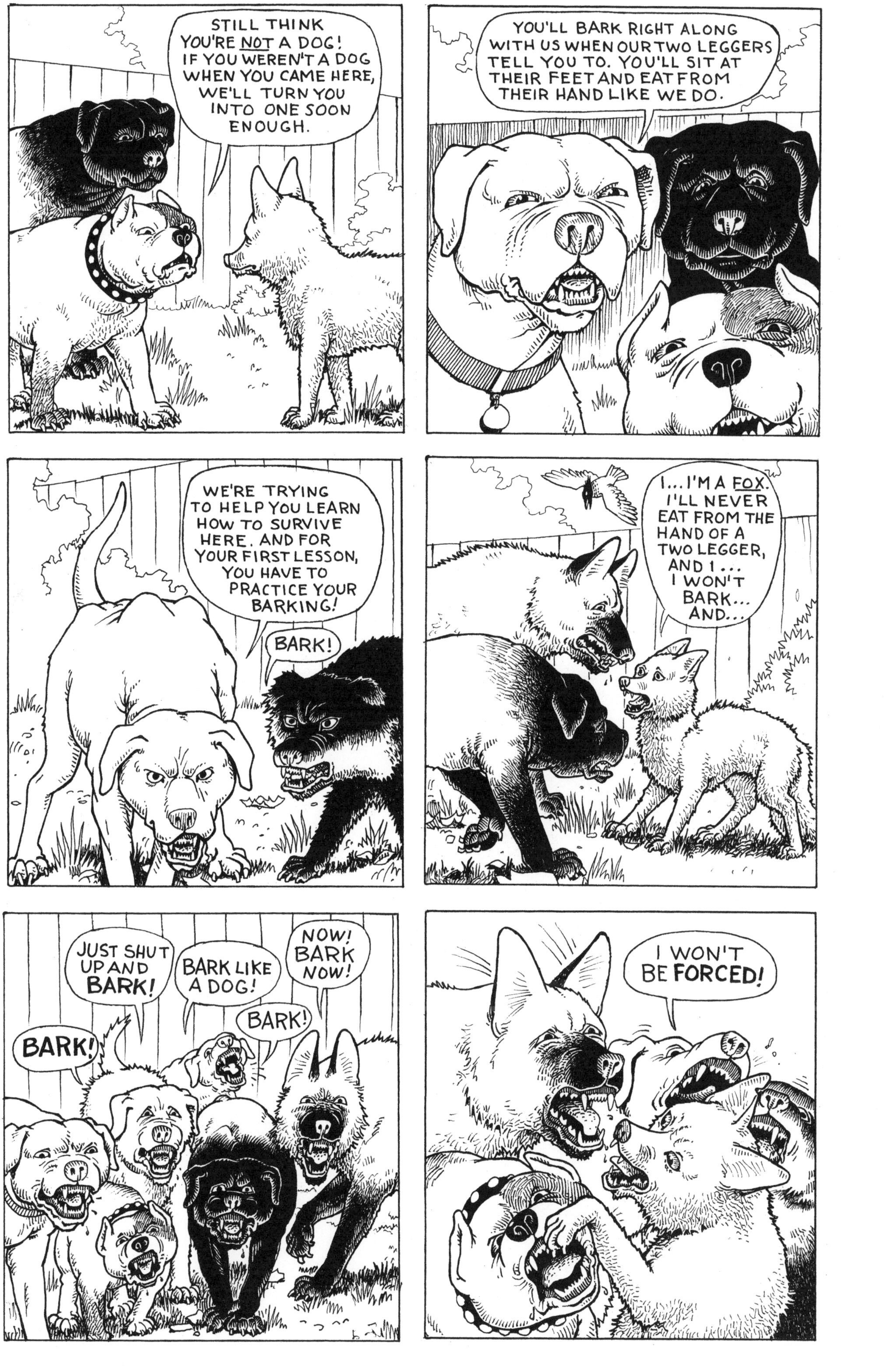
STILL THINK YOU'RE NOT A DOG! IF YOU WEREN'T A DOG WHEN YOU CAME HERE, WE'LL TURN YOU INTO ONE SOON ENOUGH.
YOU'LL BARK RIGHT ALONG WITH US WHEN OUR TWO LEGGERS TELL YOU TO. YOU'LL SIT AT THEIR FEET AND EAT FROM THEIR HAND LIKE WE DO.
WE'RE TRYING TO HELP YOU LEARN HOW TO SURVIVE HERE. AND FOR YOUR FIRST LESSON, YOU HAVE TO PRACTICE YOUR BARKING!
BARK!
I... I'M A FOX. I'LL NEVER EAT FROM THE HAND OF A TWO LEGGER, AND I... I WON'T BARK... AND...
JUST SHUT UP AND BARK!
BARK LIKE A DOG!
NOW! BARK NOW!
BARK!
BARK!
I WON'T BE FORCED!

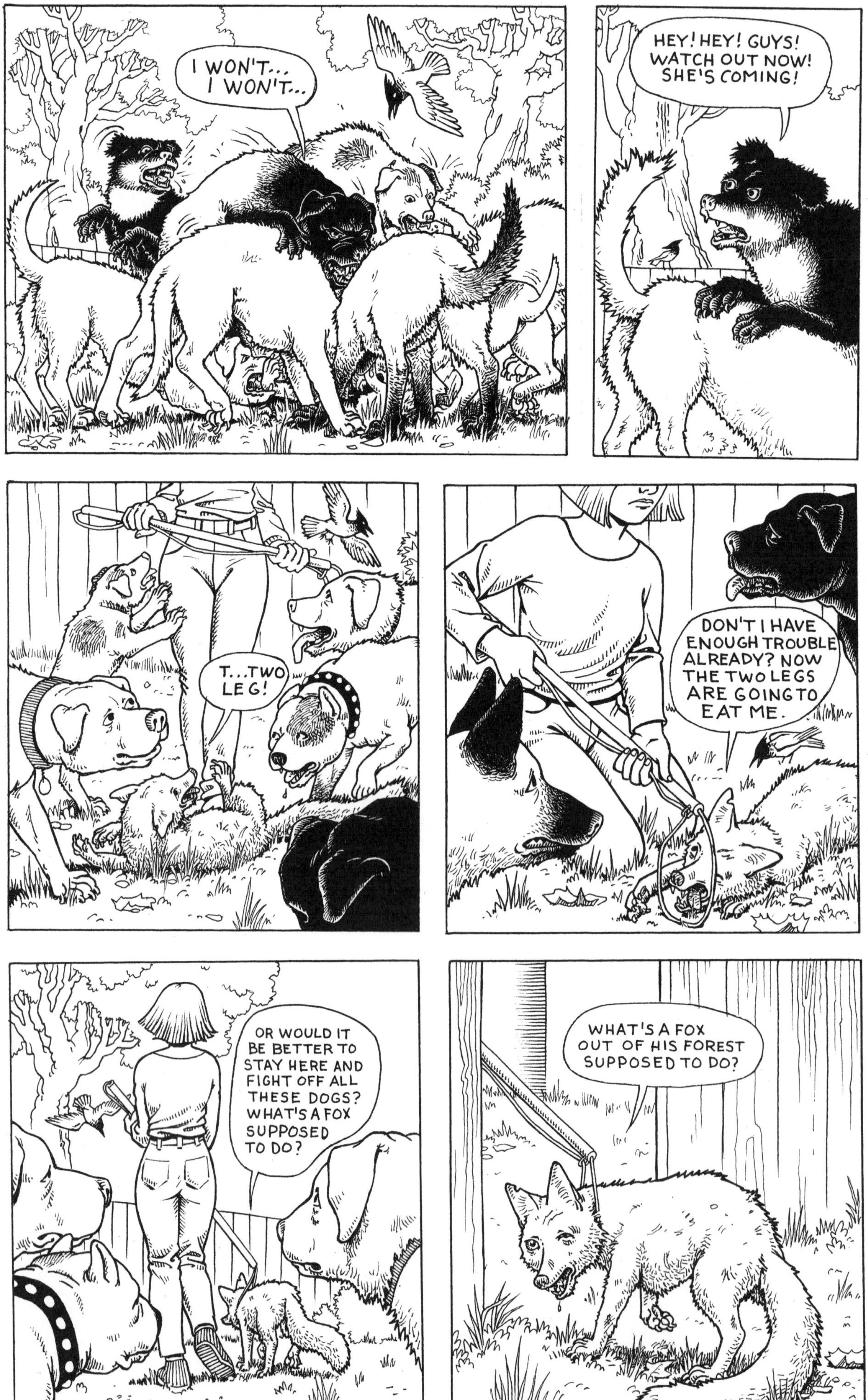
I WON'T... I WON'T...
HEY! HEY! GUYS! WATCH OUT NOW! SHE'S COMING!
T...TWO LEG!
DON'T I HAVE ENOUGH TROUBLE ALREADY? NOW THE TWO LEGS ARE GOING TO EAT ME.
OR WOULD IT BE BETTER TO STAY HERE AND FIGHT OFF ALL THESE DOGS? WHAT'S A FOX SUPPOSED TO DO?
WHAT'S A FOX OUT OF HIS FOREST SUPPOSED TO DO?

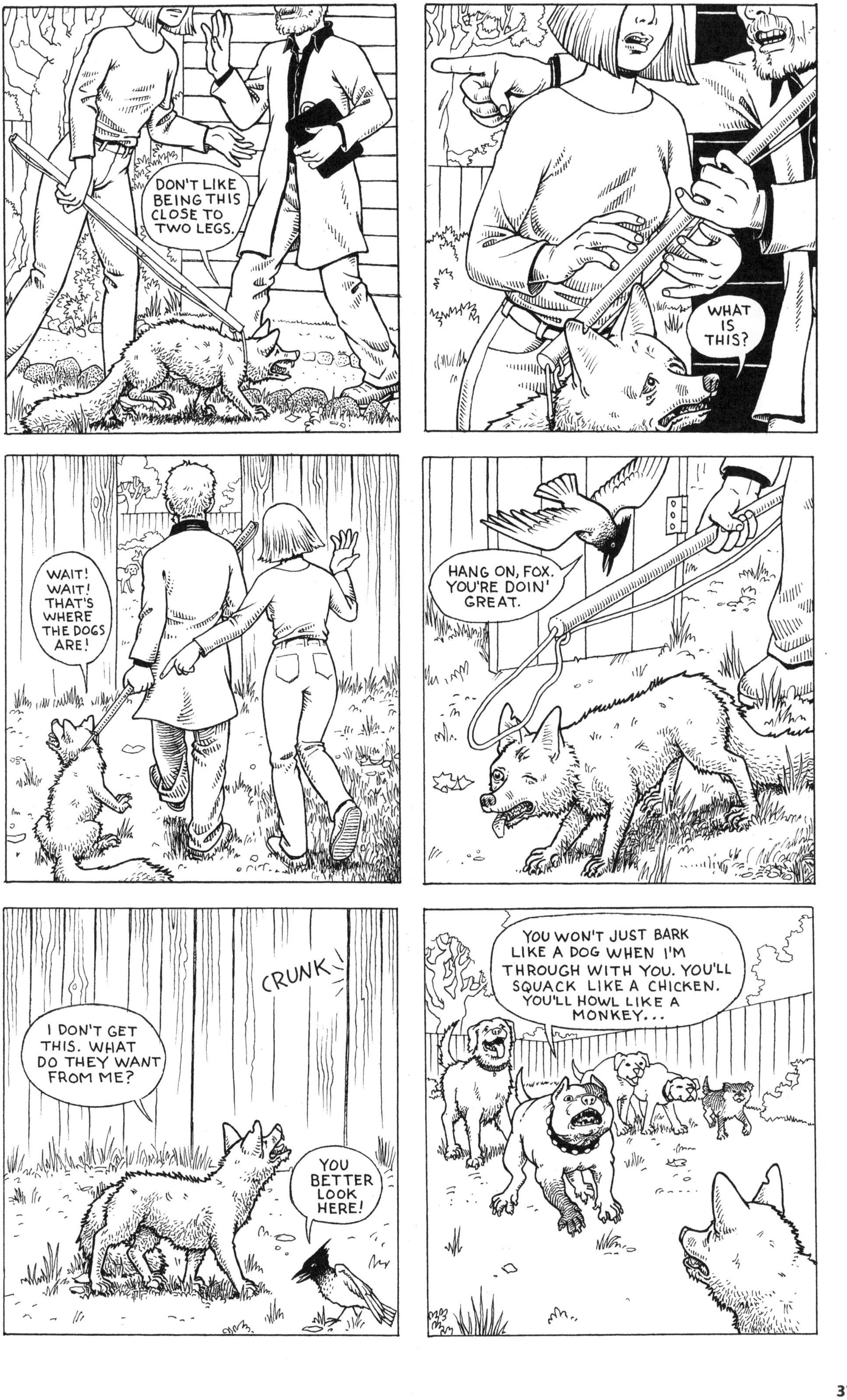
DON'T LIKE BEING THIS CLOSE TO TWO LEGS.
WHAT IS THIS?
WAIT! WAIT! THAT'S WHERE THE DOGS ARE!
HANG ON, FOX. YOU'RE DOIN' GREAT.
CRUNK!
I DON'T GET THIS. WHAT DO THEY WANT FROM ME?
YOU BETTER LOOK HERE!
YOU WON'T JUST BARK LIKE A DOG WHEN I'M THROUGH WITH YOU. YOU'LL SQUACK LIKE A CHICKEN. YOU'LL HOWL LIKE A MONKEY...

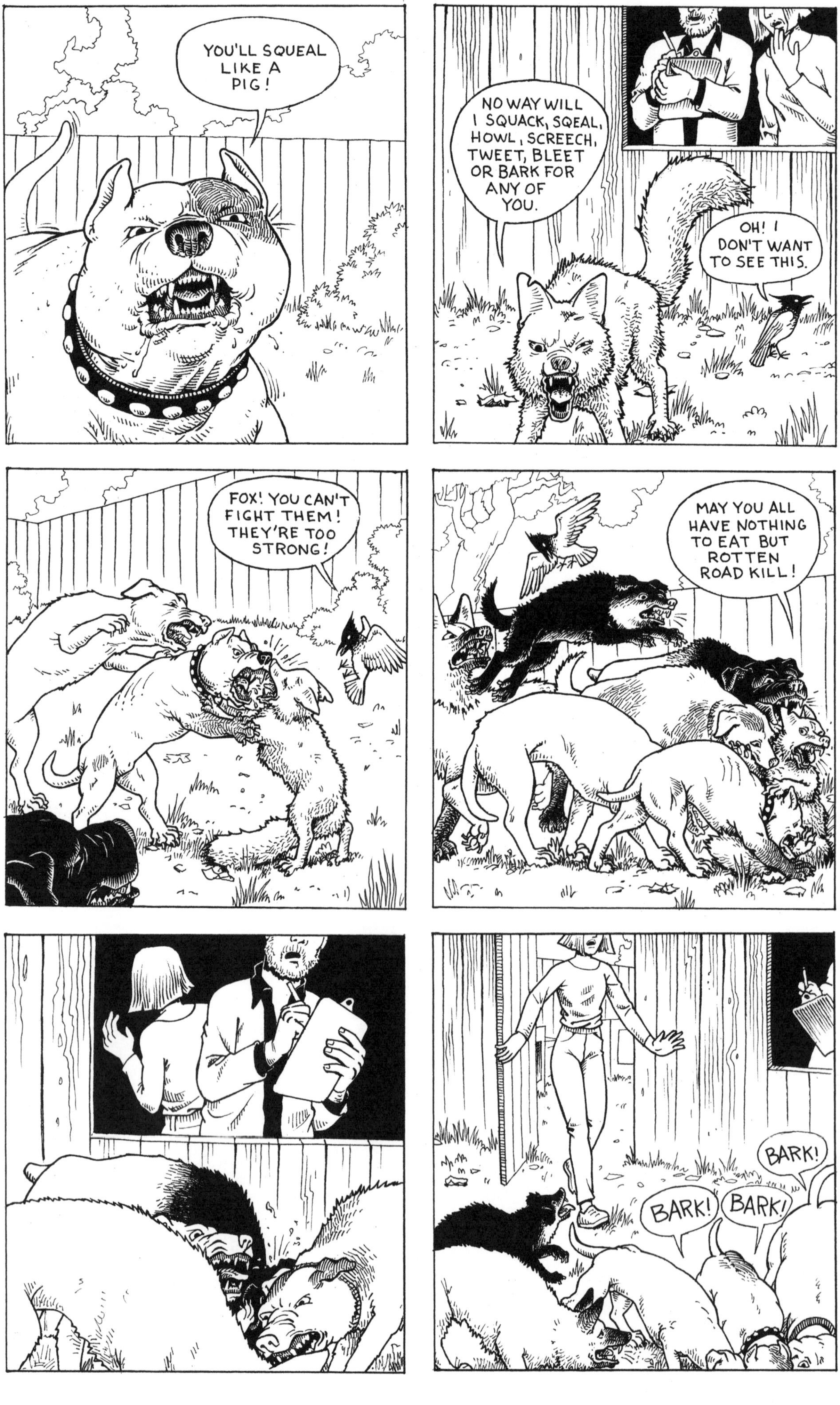
YOU'LL SQUEAL LIKE A PIG!
NO WAY WILL I SQUACK, SQEAL, HOWL, SCREECH, TWEET, BLEET OR BARK FOR ANY OF YOU.
OH! I DON'T WANT TO SEE THIS.
FOX! YOU CAN'T FIGHT THEM! THEY'RE TOO STRONG!
MAY YOU ALL HAVE NOTHING TO EAT BUT ROTTEN ROAD KILL!
BARK!
BARK!
BARK!

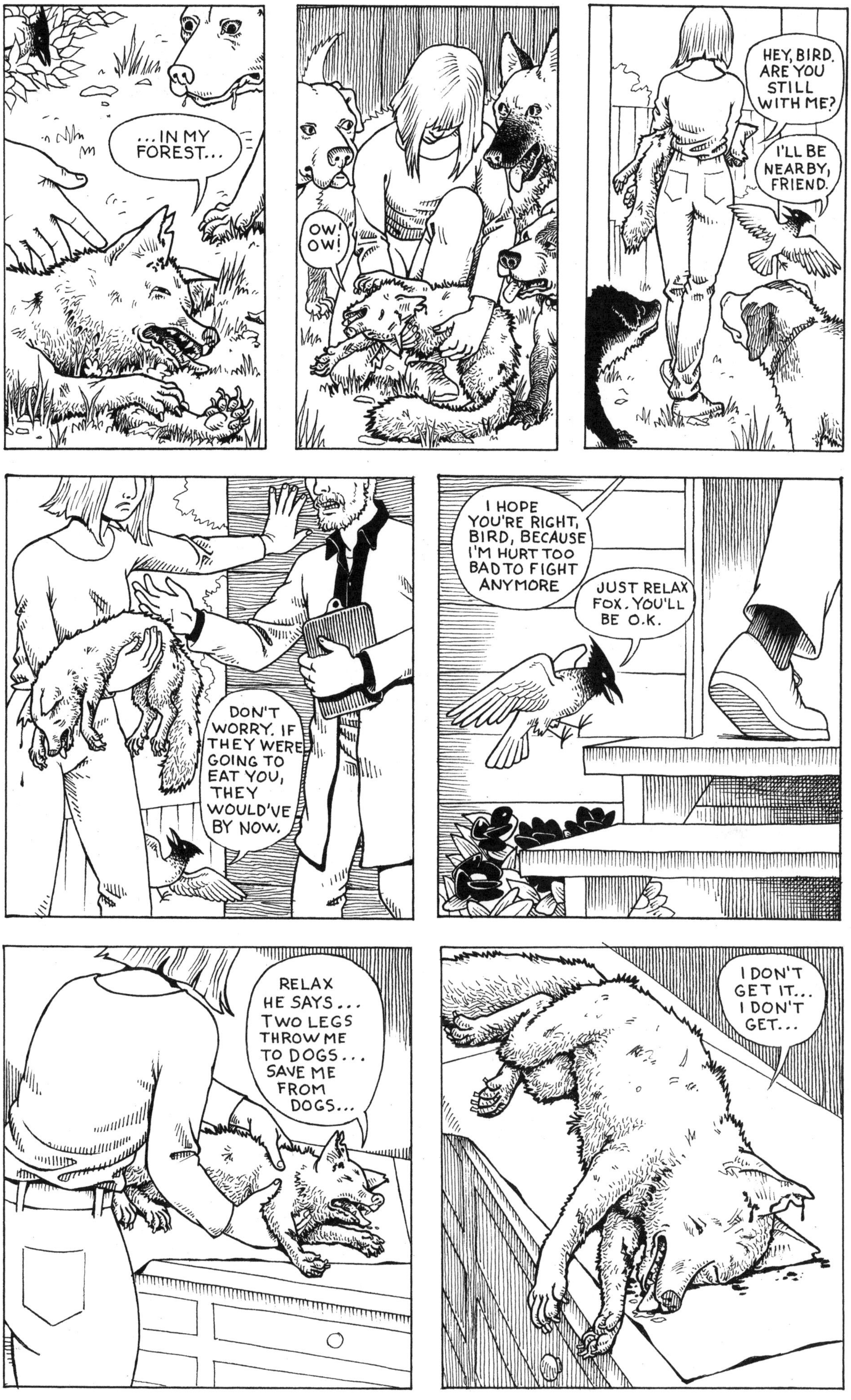
...IN MY FOREST...
OW! OW!
HEY, BIRD. ARE YOU STILL WITH ME?
I'LL BE NEARBY, FRIEND.
DON'T WORRY. IF THEY WERE GOING TO EAT YOU, THEY WOULD'VE BY NOW.
I HOPE YOU'RE RIGHT, BIRD, BECAUSE I'M HURT TOO BAD TO FIGHT ANYMORE
JUST RELAX FOX. YOU'LL BE O.K.
RELAX HE SAYS... TWO LEGS THROW ME TO DOGS... SAVE ME FROM DOGS...
I DON'T GET IT... I DON'T GET...

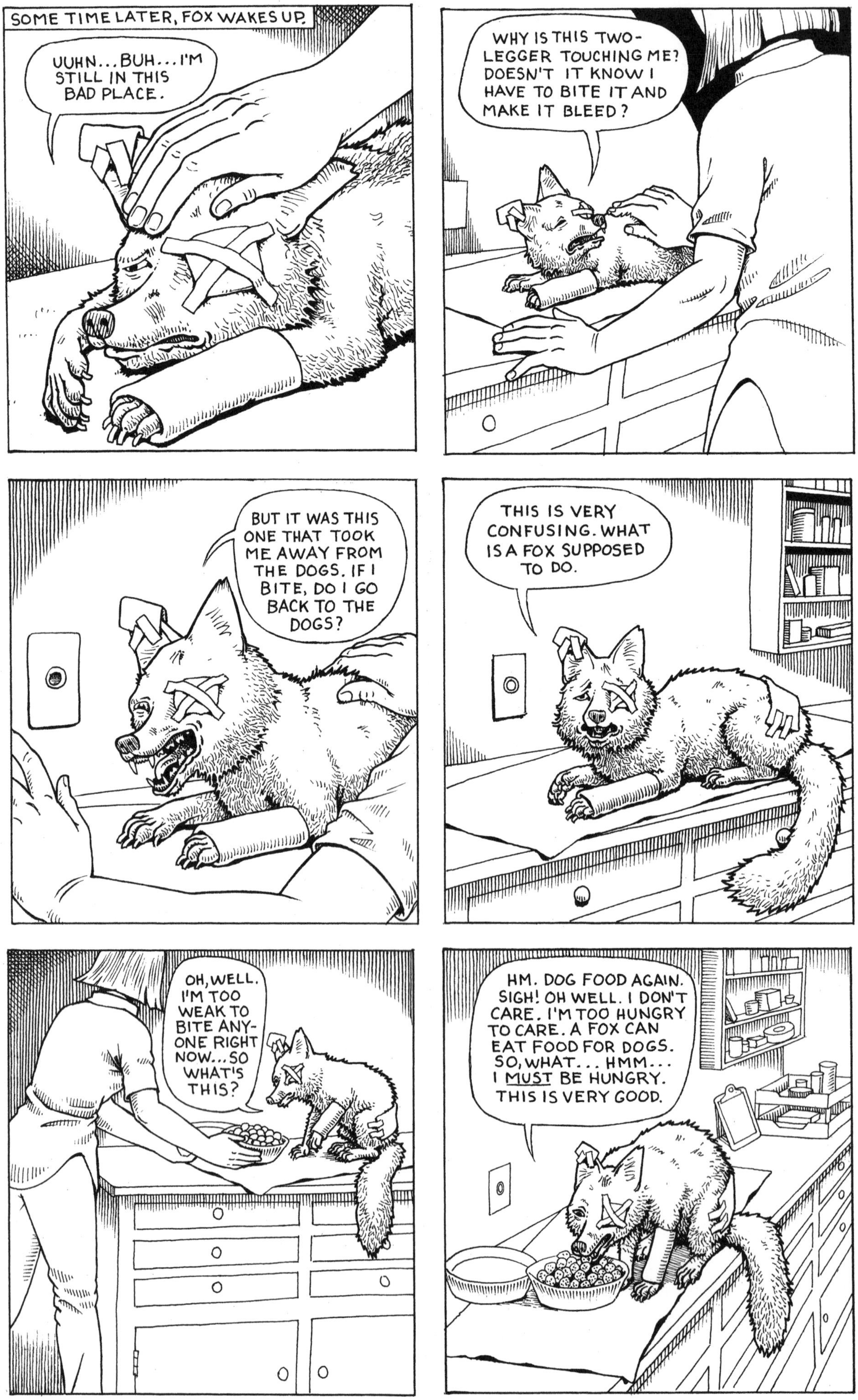
SOME TIME LATER, FOX WAKES UP.
UUHN... BUH... I'M STILL IN THIS BAD PLACE.
WHY IS THIS TWO-LEGGER TOUCHING ME? DOESN'T IT KNOW I HAVE TO BITE IT AND MAKE IT BLEED?
BUT IT WAS THIS ONE THAT TOOK ME AWAY FROM THE DOGS. IF I BITE, DO I GO BACK TO THE DOGS?
THIS IS VERY CONFUSING. WHAT IS A FOX SUPPOSED TO DO.
OH, WELL. I'M TOO WEAK TO BITE ANY-ONE RIGHT NOW... SO WHAT'S THIS?
HM. DOG FOOD AGAIN. SIGH! OH WELL. I DON'T CARE. I'M TOO HUNGRY TO CARE. A FOX CAN EAT FOOD FOR DOGS. SO, WHAT... HMM... I MUST BE HUNGRY. THIS IS VERY GOOD.

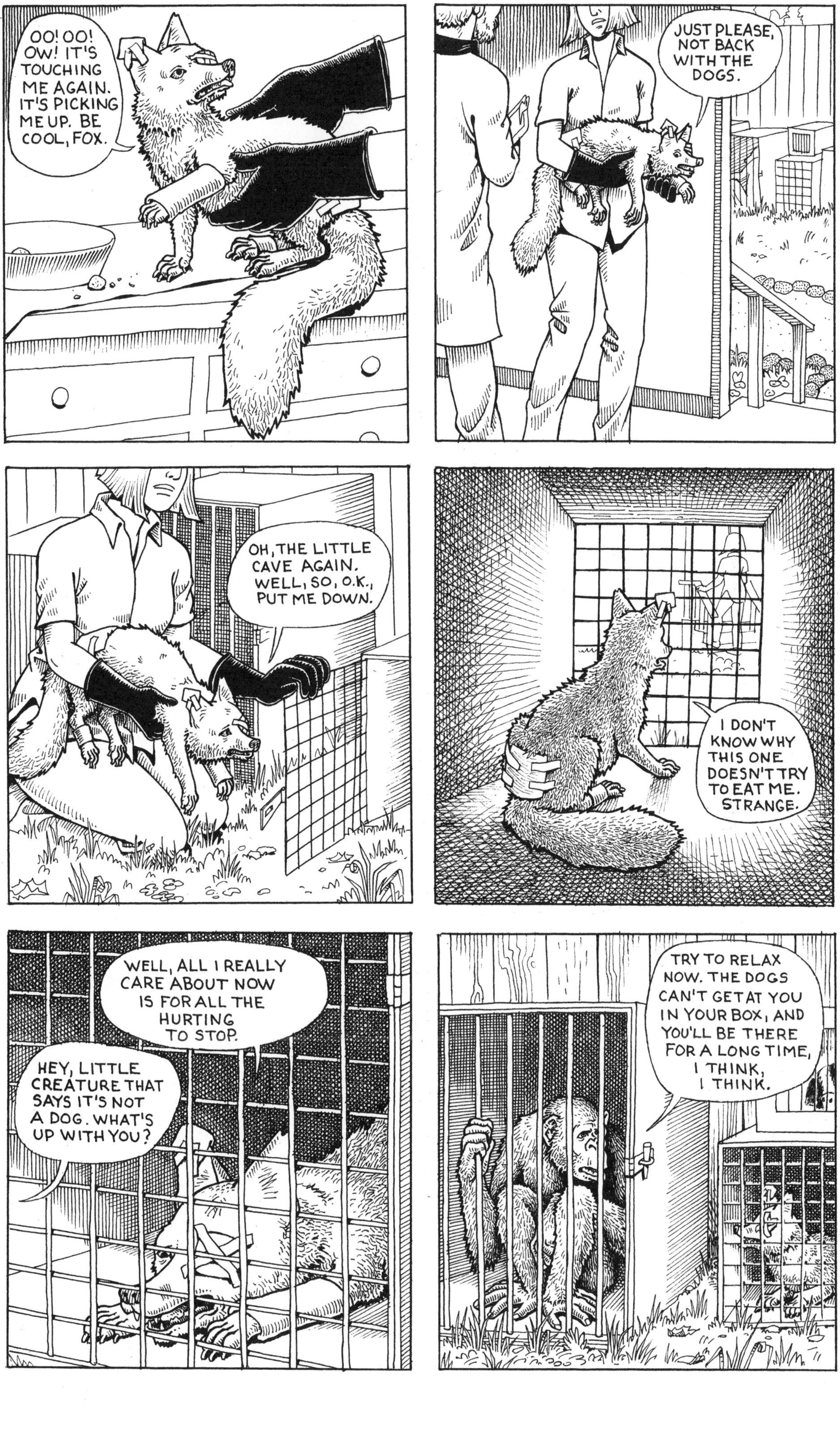
OO! OO! OW! IT'S TOUCHING ME AGAIN. IT'S PICKING ME UP. BE COOL, FOX.
JUST PLEASE, NOT BACK WITH THE DOGS.
OH, THE LITTLE CAVE AGAIN. WELL, SO, O.K., PUT ME DOWN.
I DON'T KNOW WHY THIS ONE DOESN'T TRY TO EAT ME. STRANGE.
HEY, LITTLE CREATURE THAT SAYS IT'S NOT A DOG. WHAT'S UP WITH YOU?
WELL, ALL I REALLY CARE ABOUT NOW IS FOR ALL THE HURTING TO STOP.
TRY TO RELAX NOW. THE DOGS CAN'T GET AT YOU IN YOUR BOX, AND YOU'LL BE THERE FOR A LONG TIME, I THINK, I THINK.

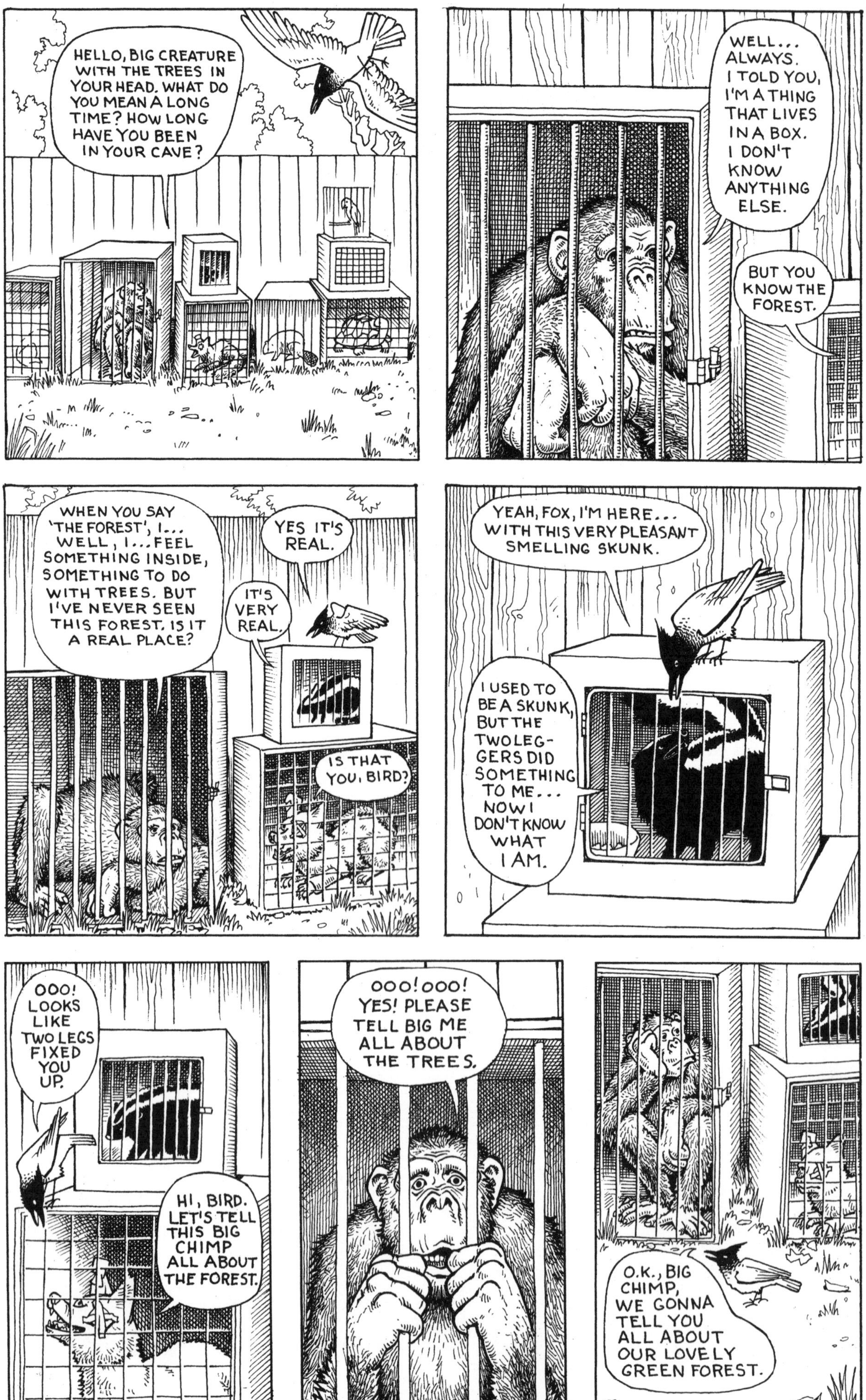
HELLO, BIG CREATURE WITH THE TREES IN YOUR HEAD. WHAT DO YOU MEAN A LONG TIME? HOW LONG HAVE YOU BEEN IN YOUR CAVE?
WELL... ALWAYS. I TOLD YOU, I'M A THING THAT LIVES IN A BOX. I DON'T KNOW ANYTHING ELSE.
BUT YOU KNOW THE FOREST.
WHEN YOU SAY 'THE FOREST', I... WELL, I...FEEL SOMETHING INSIDE, SOMETHING TO DO WITH TREES. BUT I'VE NEVER SEEN THIS FOREST. IS IT A REAL PLACE?
YES IT'S REAL.
IT'S VERY REAL.
IS THAT YOU, BIRD?
YEAH, FOX, I'M HERE... WITH THIS VERY PLEASANT SMELLING SKUNK.
I USED TO BE A SKUNK, BUT THE TWOLEGGERS DID SOMETHING TO ME... NOW I DON'T KNOW WHAT I AM.
OOO! LOOKS LIKE TWO LEGS FIXED YOU UP.
HI, BIRD. LET'S TELL THIS BIG CHIMP ALL ABOUT THE FOREST.
OOO! OOO! YES! PLEASE TELL BIG ME ALL ABOUT THE TREES.
O.K., BIG CHIMP, WE GONNA TELL YOU ALL ABOUT OUR LOVELY GREEN FOREST.

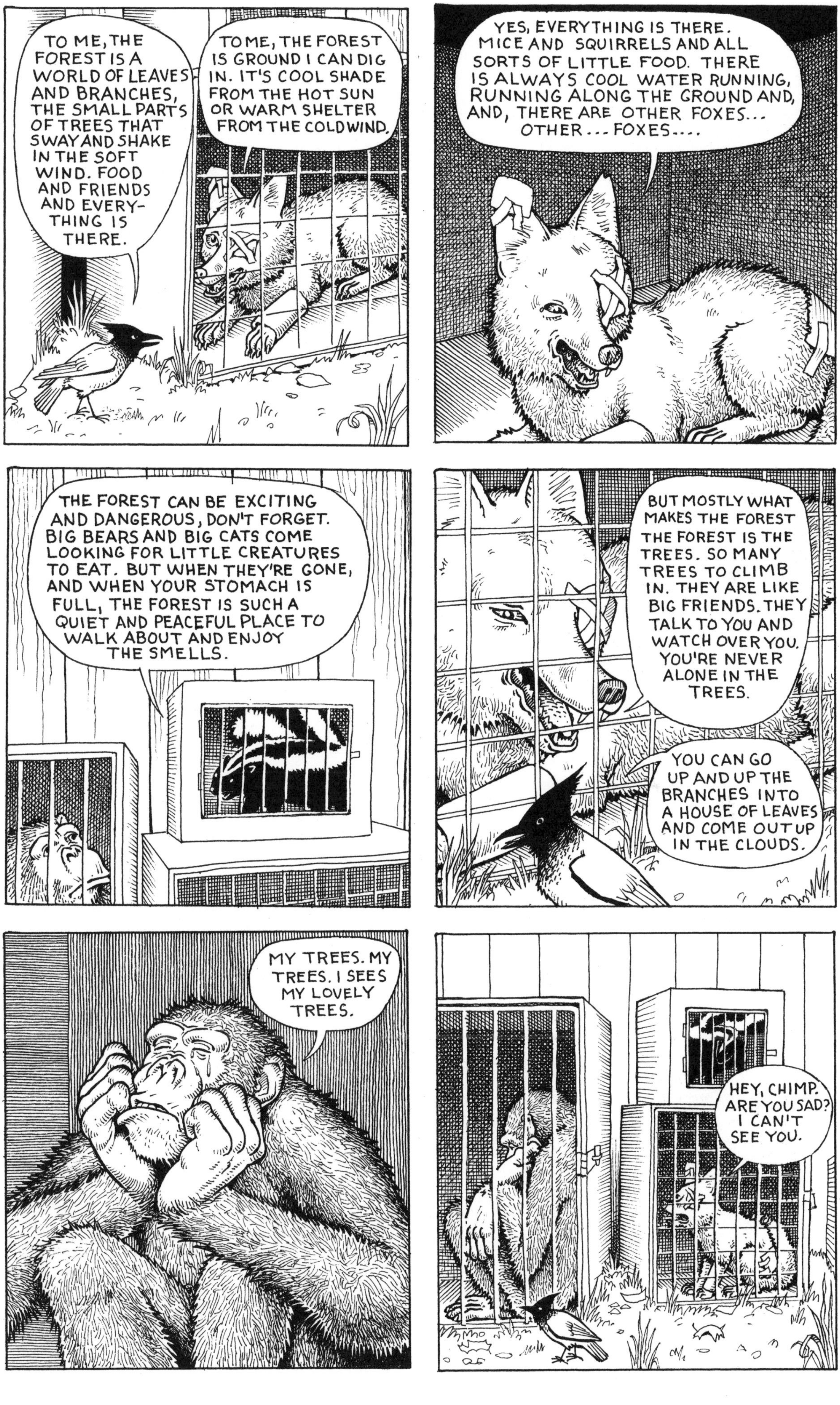
TO ME, THE FOREST IS A WORLD OF LEAVES AND BRANCHES, THE SMALL PARTS OF TREES THAT SWAY AND SHAKE IN THE SOFT WIND. FOOD AND FRIENDS AND EVERYTHING IS THERE.
TO ME, THE FOREST IS GROUND I CAN DIG IN. IT'S COOL SHADE FROM THE HOT SUN OR WARM SHELTER FROM THE COLD WIND.
YES, EVERYTHING IS THERE. MICE AND SQUIRRELS AND ALL SORTS OF LITTLE FOOD. THERE IS ALWAYS COOL WATER RUNNING, RUNNING ALONG THE GROUND AND, AND, THERE ARE OTHER FOXES... OTHER... FOXES....
THE FOREST CAN BE EXCITING AND DANGEROUS, DON'T FORGET. BIG BEARS AND BIG CATS COME LOOKING FOR LITTLE CREATURES TO EAT. BUT WHEN THEY'RE GONE, AND WHEN YOUR STOMACH IS FULL, THE FOREST IS SUCH A QUIET AND PEACEFUL PLACE TO WALK ABOUT AND ENJOY THE SMELLS.
BUT MOSTLY WHAT MAKES THE FOREST THE FOREST IS THE TREES. SO MANY TREES TO CLIMB IN. THEY ARE LIKE BIG FRIENDS. THEY TALK TO YOU AND WATCH OVER YOU. YOU'RE NEVER ALONE IN THE TREES.
YOU CAN GO UP AND UP THE BRANCHES INTO A HOUSE OF LEAVES AND COME OUT UP IN THE CLOUDS.
MY TREES. MY TREES. I SEES MY LOVELY TREES.
HEY, CHIMP. ARE YOU SAD? I CAN'T SEE YOU.

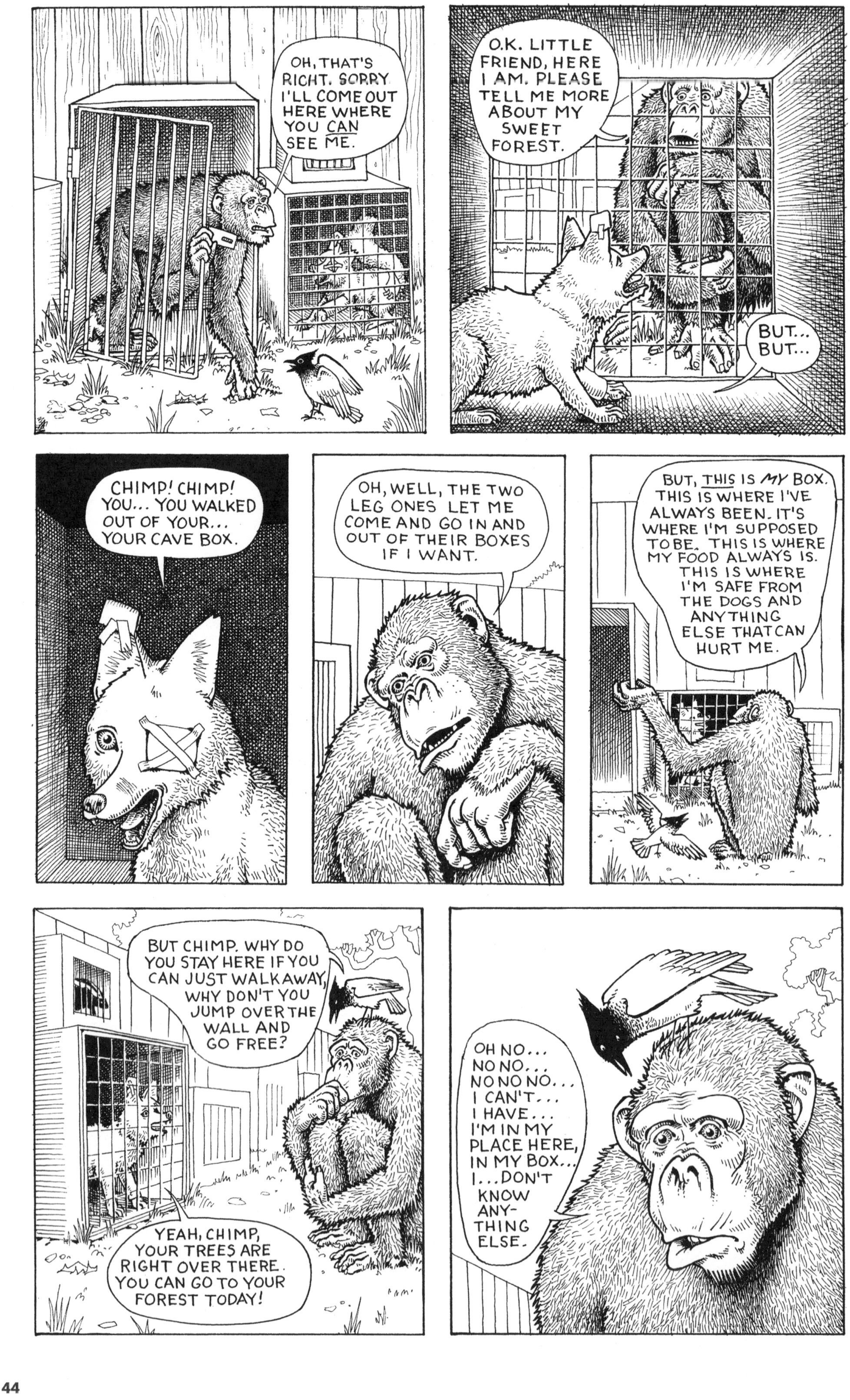
OH, THAT'S RIGHT. SORRY I'LL COME OUT HERE WHERE YOU CAN SEE ME.
O.K. LITTLE FRIEND, HERE I AM. PLEASE TELL ME MORE ABOUT MY SWEET FOREST.
BUT... BUT...
CHIMP! CHIMP! YOU... YOU WALKED OUT OF YOUR... YOUR CAVE BOX.
OH, WELL, THE TWO LEG ONES LET ME COME AND GO IN AND OUT OF THEIR BOXES IF I WANT.
BUT, THIS IS MY BOX. THIS IS WHERE I'VE ALWAYS BEEN. IT'S WHERE I'M SUPPOSED TO BE. THIS IS WHERE MY FOOD ALWAYS IS. THIS IS WHERE I'M SAFE FROM THE DOGS AND ANYTHING ELSE THAT CAN HURT ME.
BUT CHIMP. WHY DO YOU STAY HERE IF YOU CAN JUST WALK AWAY, WHY DON'T YOU JUMP OVER THE WALL AND GO FREE?
YEAH, CHIMP, YOUR TREES ARE RIGHT OVER THERE. YOU CAN GO TO YOUR FOREST TODAY!
OH NO... NO NO... NO NO NO... I CAN'T... I HAVE... I'M IN MY PLACE HERE, IN MY BOX... I... DON'T KNOW ANYTHING ELSE.

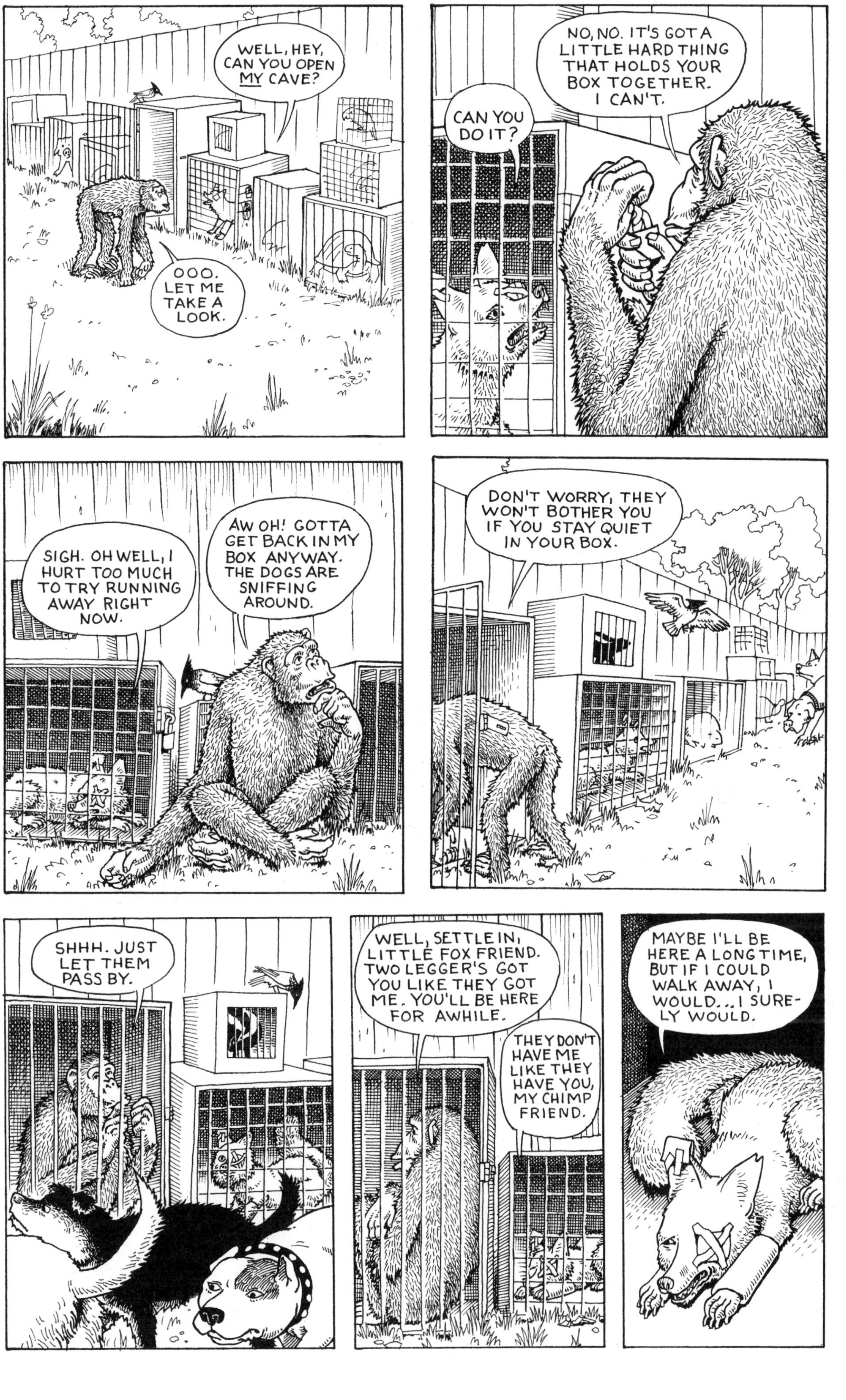
WELL, HEY, CAN YOU OPEN MY CAVE?
OOO. LET ME TAKE A LOOK.
NO, NO. IT'S GOT A LITTLE HARD THING THAT HOLDS YOUR BOX TOGETHER. I CAN'T.
CAN YOU DO IT?
SIGH. OH WELL, I HURT TOO MUCH TO TRY RUNNING AWAY RIGHT NOW.
AW OH! GOTTA GET BACK IN MY BOX ANYWAY. THE DOGS ARE SNIFFING AROUND.
DON'T WORRY, THEY WON'T BOTHER YOU IF YOU STAY QUIET IN YOUR BOX.
SHHH. JUST LET THEM PASS BY.
WELL, SETTLE IN, LITTLE FOX FRIEND. TWO LEGGER'S GOT YOU LIKE THEY GOT ME. YOU'LL BE HERE FOR AWHILE.
THEY DON'T HAVE ME LIKE THEY HAVE YOU, MY CHIMP FRIEND.
MAYBE I'LL BE HERE A LONG TIME, BUT IF I COULD WALK AWAY, I WOULD... I SURELY WOULD.

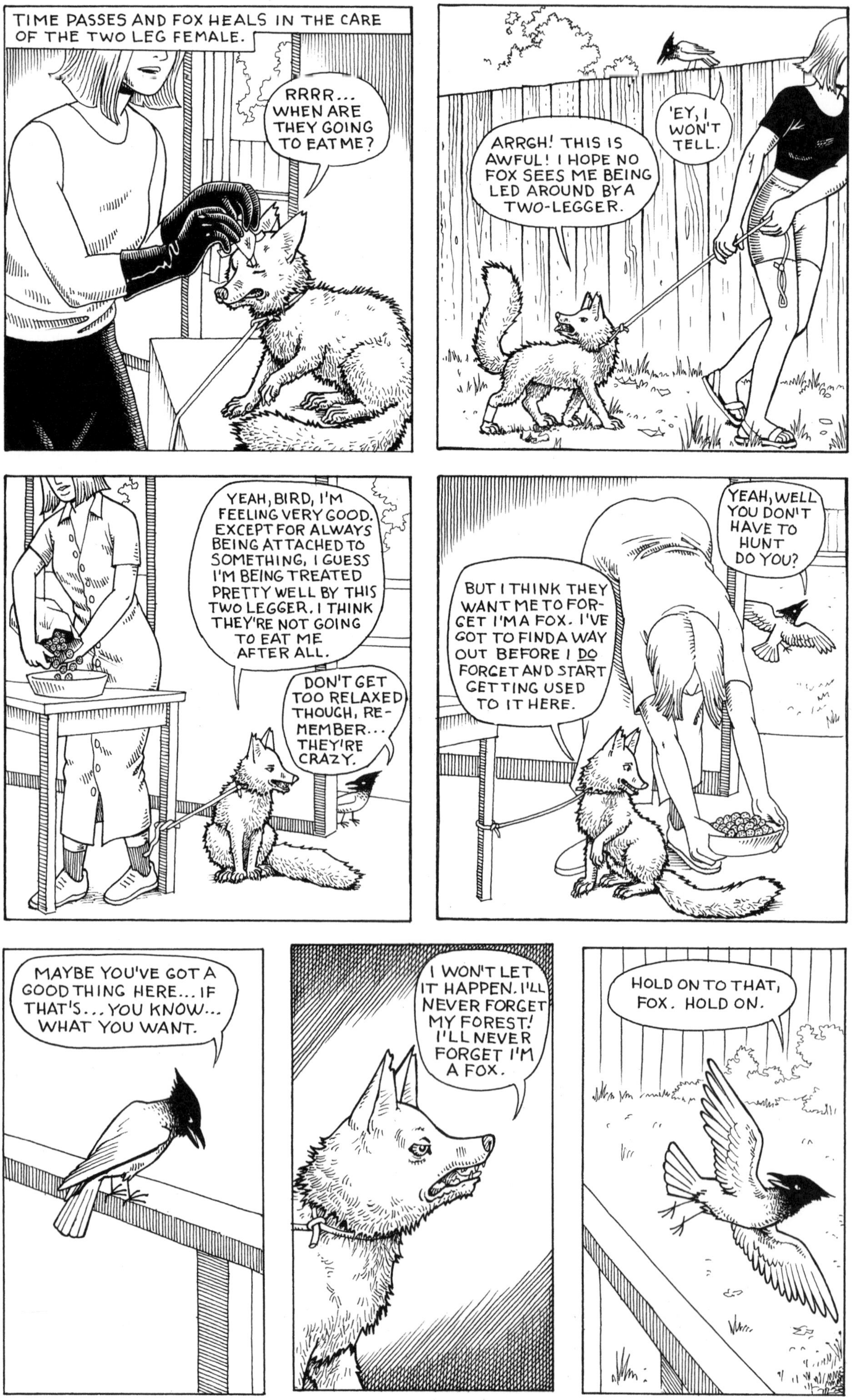
TIME PASSES AND FOX HEALS IN THE CARE OF THE TWO LEG FEMALE.
RRRR... WHEN ARE THEY GOING TO EAT ME?
ARRGH! THIS IS AWFUL! I HOPE NO FOX SEES ME BEING LED AROUND BY A TWO-LEGGER.
'EY, I WON'T TELL.
YEAH, BIRD, I'M FEELING VERY GOOD. EXCEPT FOR ALWAYS BEING ATTACHED TO SOMETHING, I GUESS I'M BEING TREATED PRETTY WELL BY THIS TWO LEGGER. I THINK THEY'RE NOT GOING TO EAT ME AFTER ALL.
DON'T GET TOO RELAXED THOUGH, RE-MEMBER... THEY'RE CRAZY.
BUT I THINK THEY WANT ME TO FOR-GET I'M A FOX. I'VE GOT TO FIND A WAY OUT BEFORE I DO FORGET AND START GETTING USED TO IT HERE.
YEAH, WELL YOU DON'T HAVE TO HUNT DO YOU?
MAYBE YOU'VE GOT A GOOD THING HERE... IF THAT'S... YOU KNOW... WHAT YOU WANT.
I WON'T LET IT HAPPEN. I'LL NEVER FORGET MY FOREST! I'LL NEVER FORGET I'M A FOX.
HOLD ON TO THAT, FOX. HOLD ON.

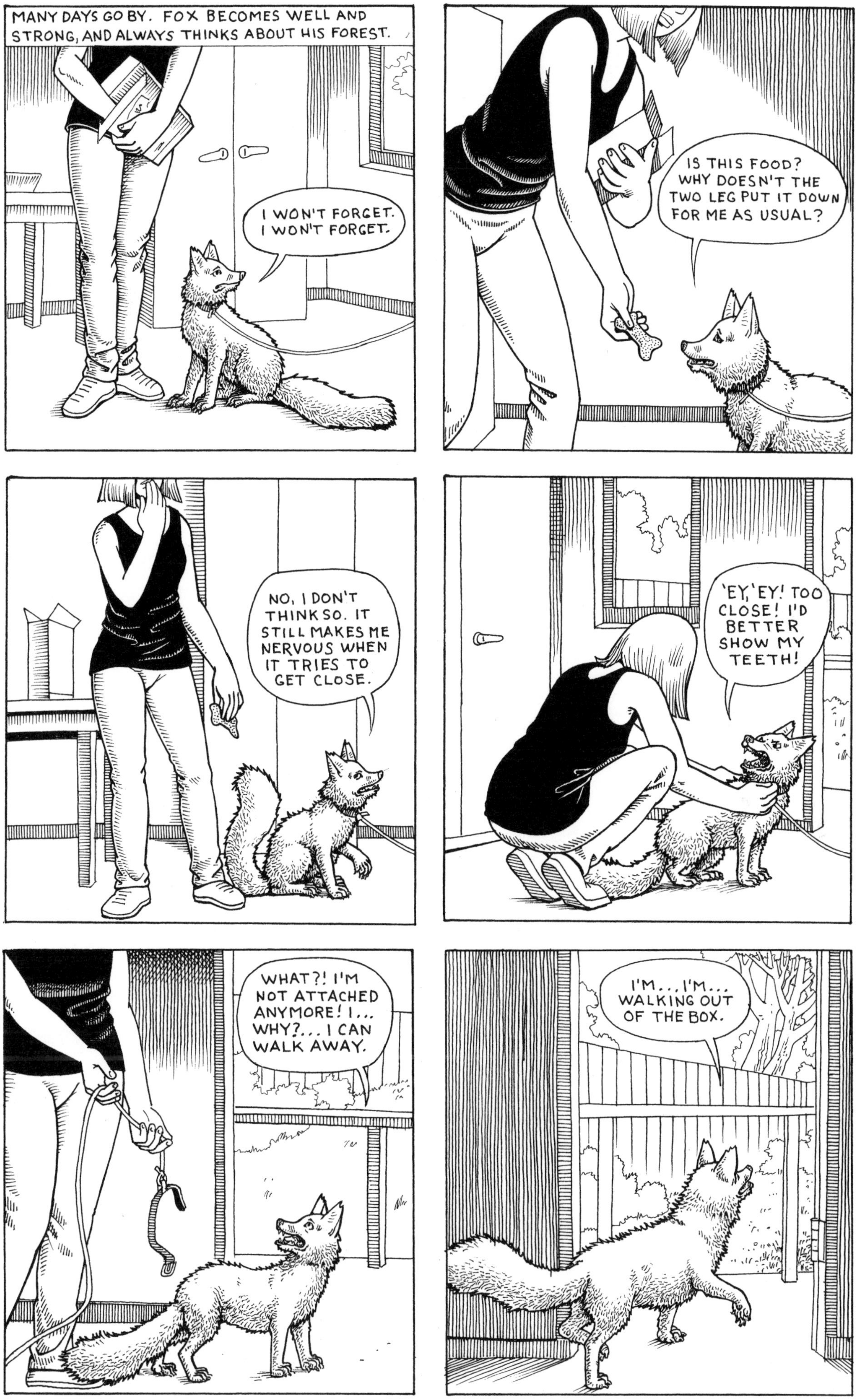
MANY DAYS GO BY. FOX BECOMES WELL AND STRONG, AND ALWAYS THINKS ABOUT HIS FOREST.
I WON'T FORGET. I WON'T FORGET.
IS THIS FOOD? WHY DOESN'T THE TWO LEG PUT IT DOWN FOR ME AS USUAL?
NO, I DON'T THINK SO. IT STILL MAKES ME NERVOUS WHEN IT TRIES TO GET CLOSE.
'EY, 'EY! TOO CLOSE! I'D BETTER SHOW MY TEETH!
WHAT?! I'M NOT ATTACHED ANYMORE! I... WHY?... I CAN WALK AWAY.
I'M...I'M... WALKING OUT OF THE BOX.

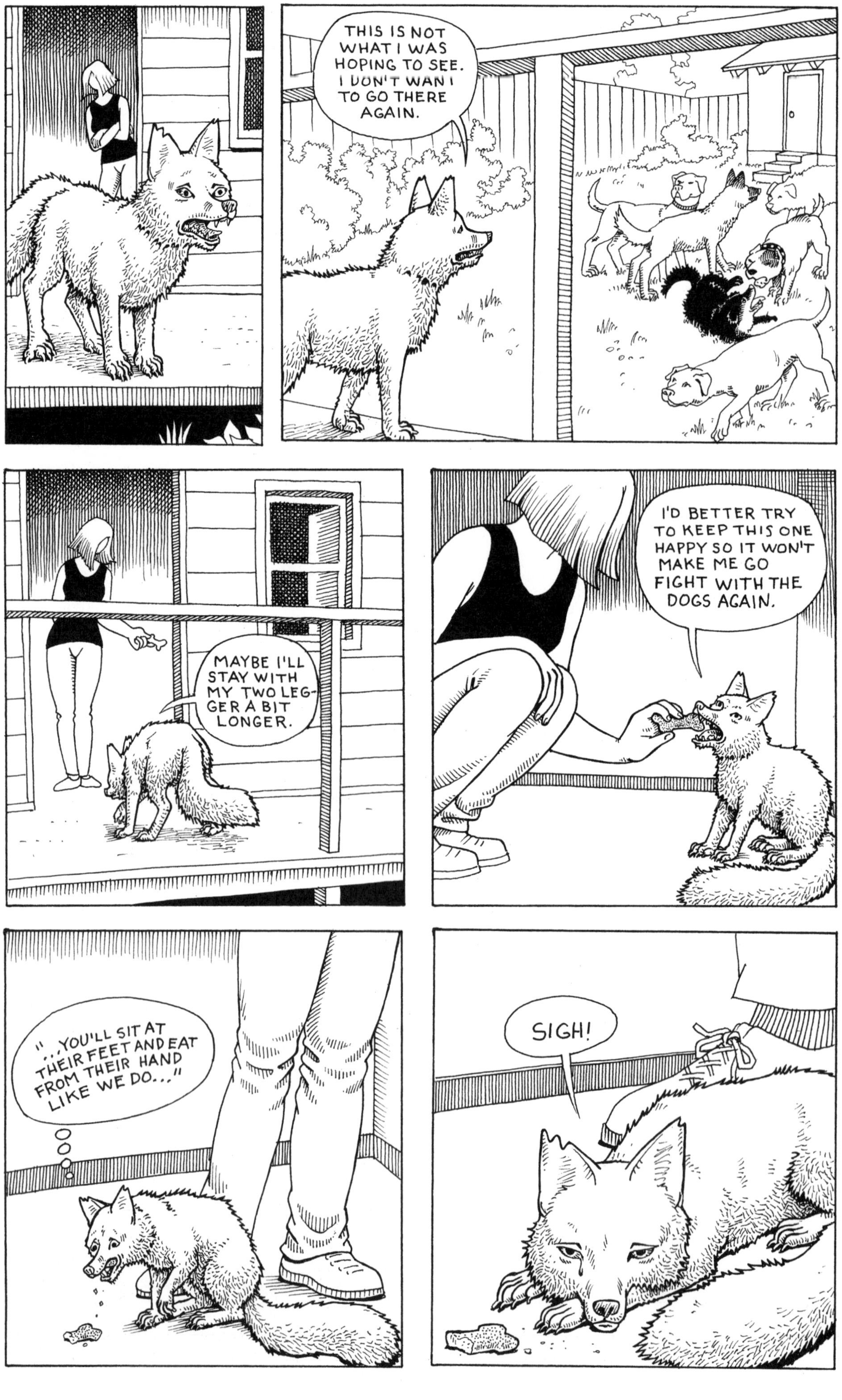
THIS IS NOT WHAT I WAS HOPING TO SEE. I DON'T WANT TO GO THERE AGAIN.
MAYBE I'LL STAY WITH MY TWO LEGGER A BIT LONGER.
I'D BETTER TRY TO KEEP THIS ONE HAPPY SO IT WON'T MAKE ME GO FIGHT WITH THE DOGS AGAIN.
"...YOU'LL SIT AT THEIR FEET AND EAT FROM THEIR HAND LIKE WE DO..."
SIGH!

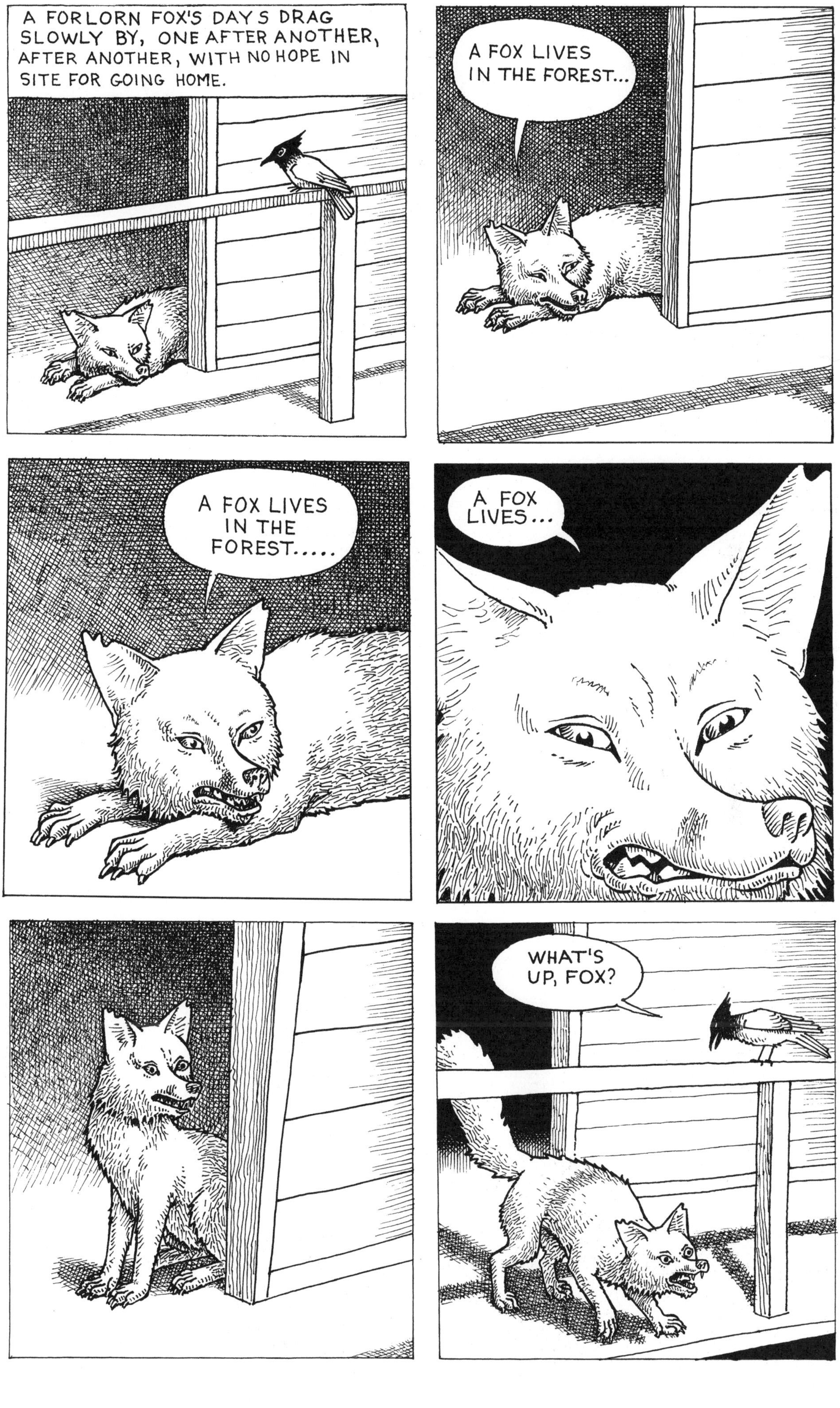

A FORLORN FOX'S DAYS DRAG SLOWLY BY, ONE AFTER ANOTHER, AFTER ANOTHER, WITH NO HOPE IN SITE FOR GOING HOME.
A FOX LIVES IN THE FOREST...
A FOX LIVES IN THE FOREST.....
A FOX LIVES...
WHAT'S UP, FOX?

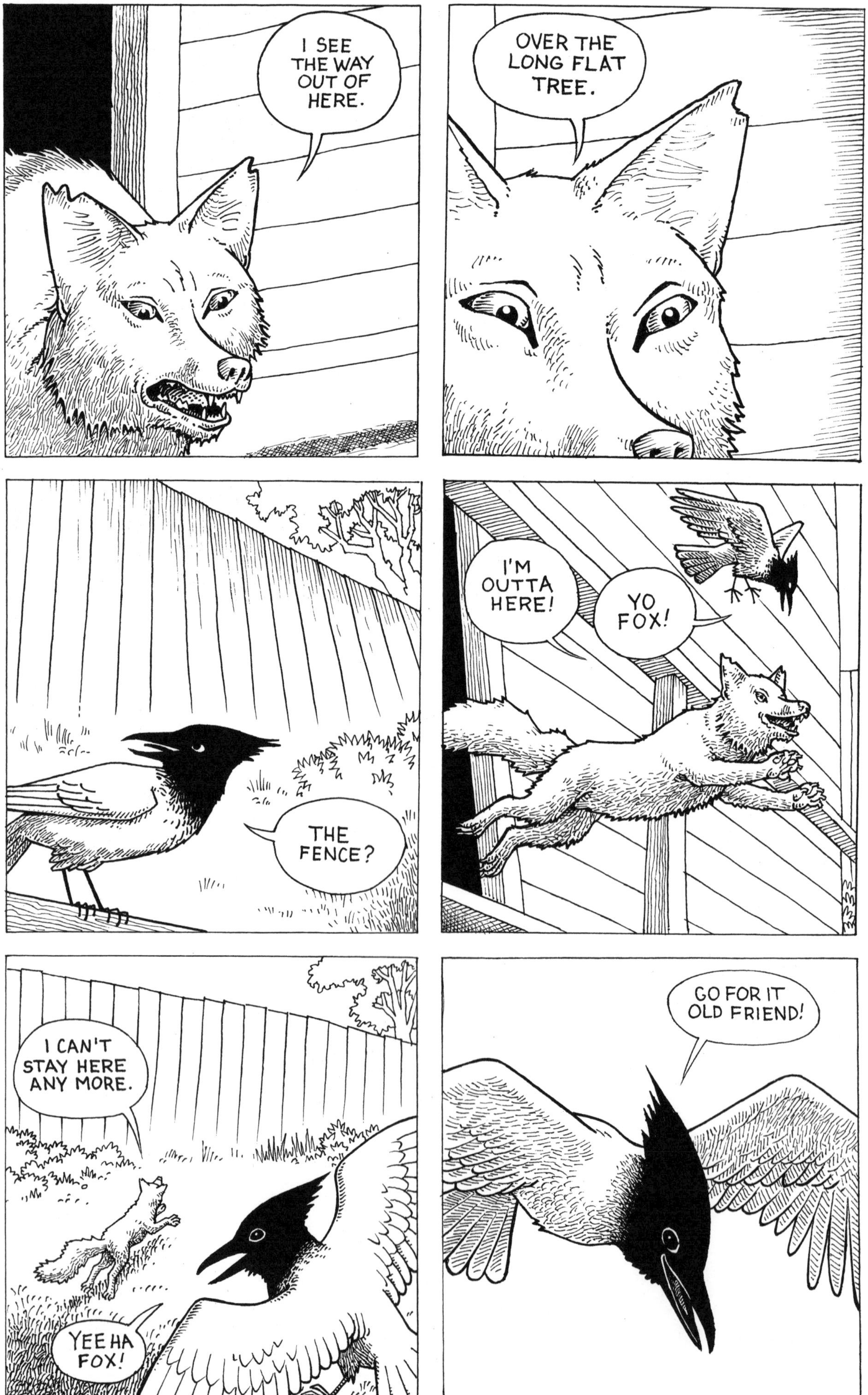
I SEE THE WAY OUT OF HERE.
OVER THE LONG FLAT TREE.
THE FENCE?
I'M OUTTA HERE!
YO FOX!
I CAN'T STAY HERE ANY MORE.
YEE HA FOX!
GO FOR IT OLD FRIEND!

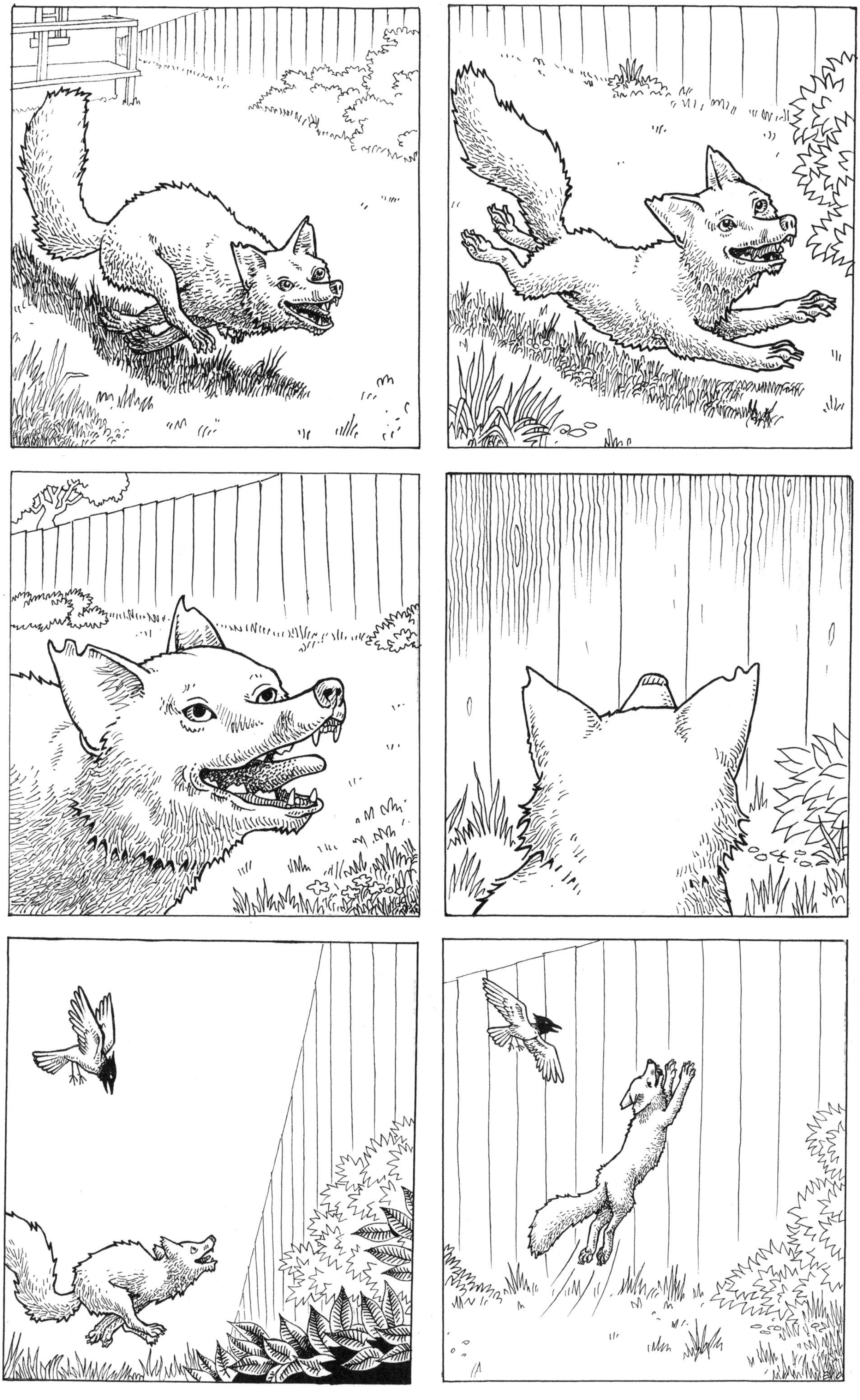

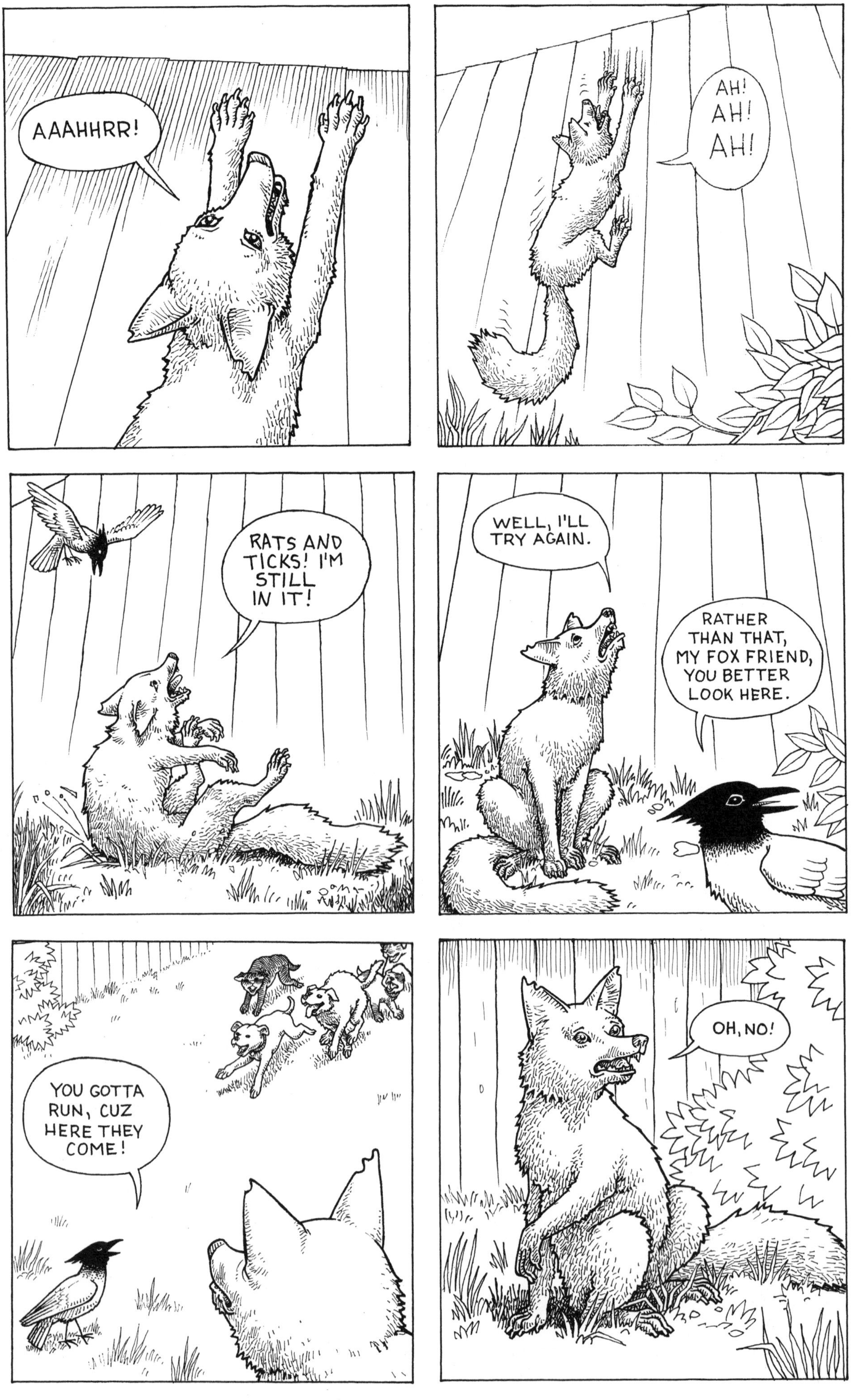
AAAHHRR!
AH! AH! AH!
RATS AND TICKS! I'M STILL IN IT!
WELL, I'LL TRY AGAIN.
RATHER THAN THAT, MY FOX FRIEND, YOU BETTER LOOK HERE.
YOU GOTTA RUN, CUZ HERE THEY COME!
OH, NO!

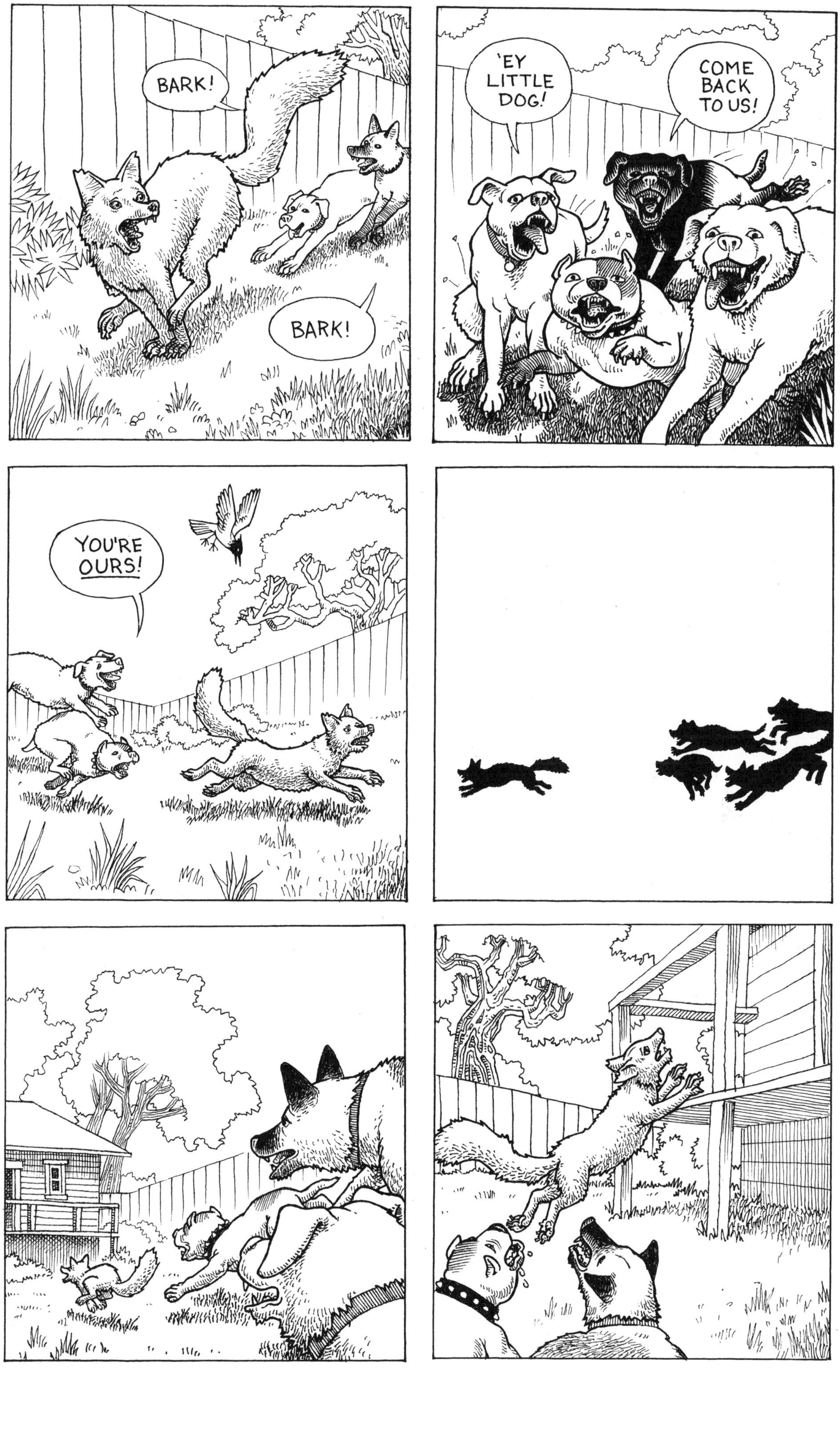
BARK!
BARK!
'EY LITTLE DOG!
COME BACK TO US!
YOU'RE OURS!

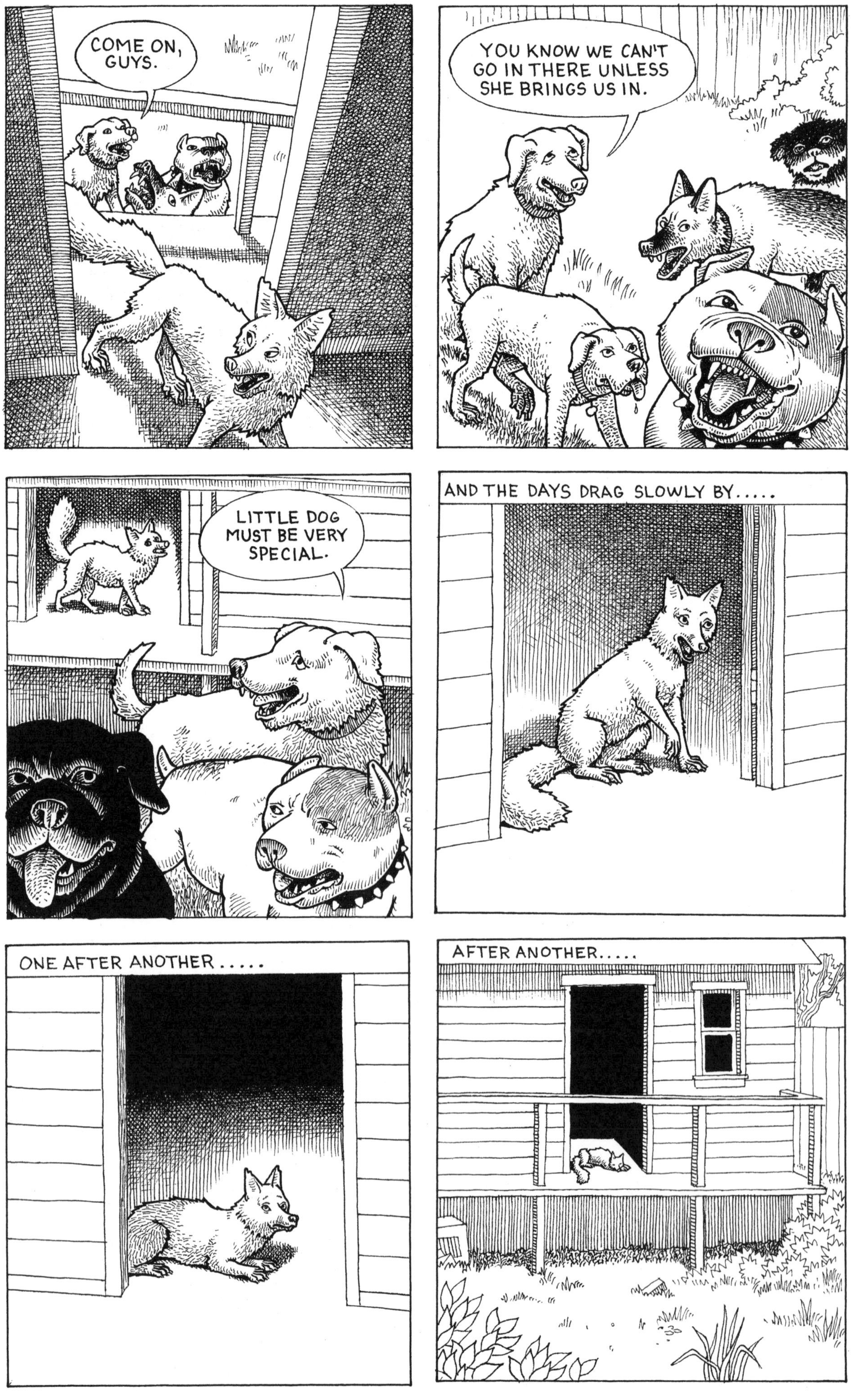
COME ON, GUYS.
YOU KNOW WE CAN'T GO IN THERE UNLESS SHE BRINGS US IN.
LITTLE DOG MUST BE VERY SPECIAL.
AND THE DAYS DRAG SLOWLY BY.....
ONE AFTER ANOTHER.....
AFTER ANOTHER.....

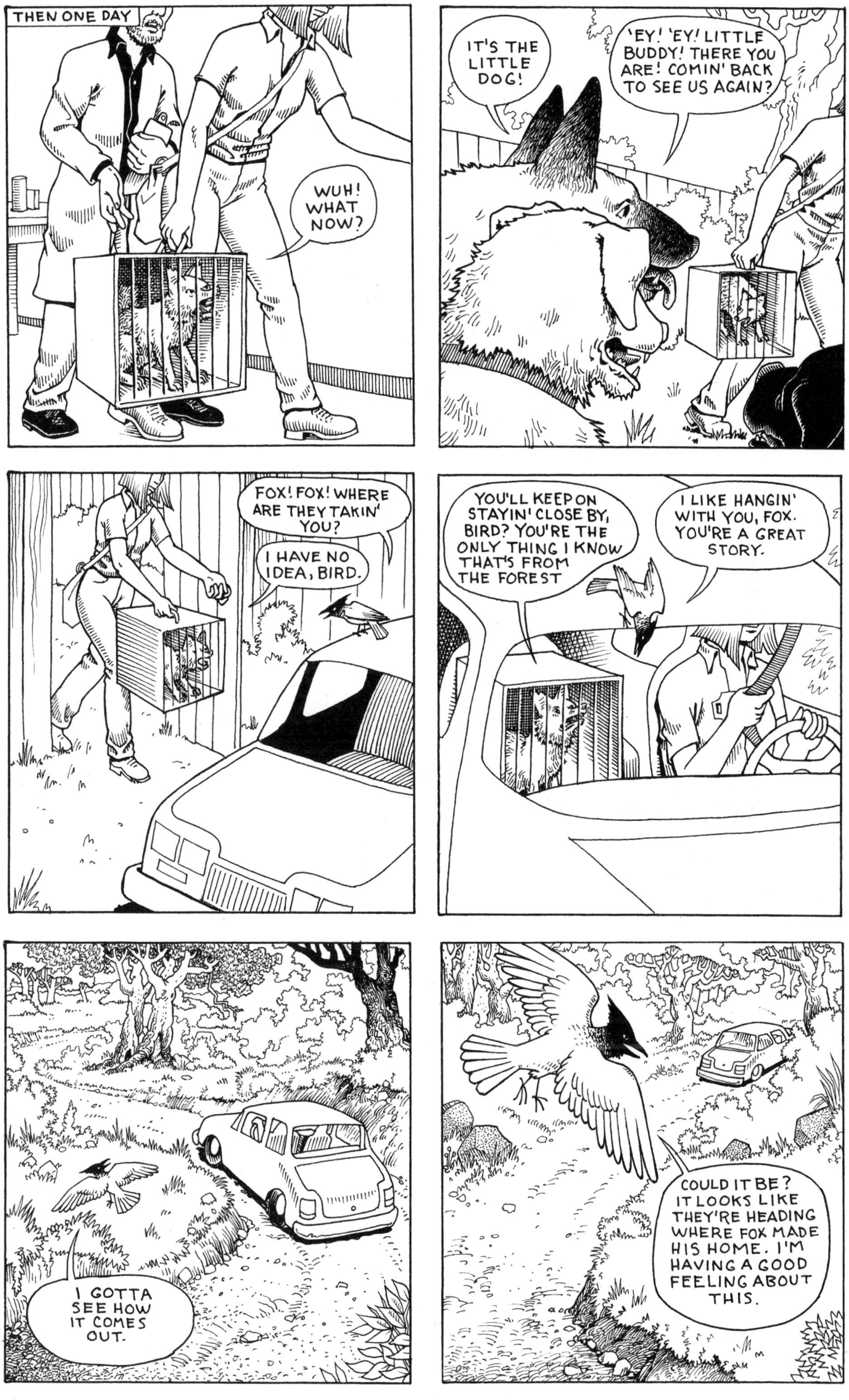
THEN ONE DAY
WUH! WHAT NOW?
IT'S THE LITTLE DOG!
'EY! 'EY! LITTLE BUDDY! THERE YOU ARE! COMIN' BACK TO SEE US AGAIN?
FOX! FOX! WHERE ARE THEY TAKIN' YOU?
I HAVE NO IDEA, BIRD.
YOU'LL KEEP ON STAYIN' CLOSE BY, BIRD? YOU'RE THE ONLY THING I KNOW THAT'S FROM THE FOREST
I LIKE HANGIN' WITH YOU, FOX. YOU'RE A GREAT STORY.
I GOTTA SEE HOW IT COMES OUT.
COULD IT BE? IT LOOKS LIKE THEY'RE HEADING WHERE FOX MADE HIS HOME. I'M HAVING A GOOD FEELING ABOUT THIS.

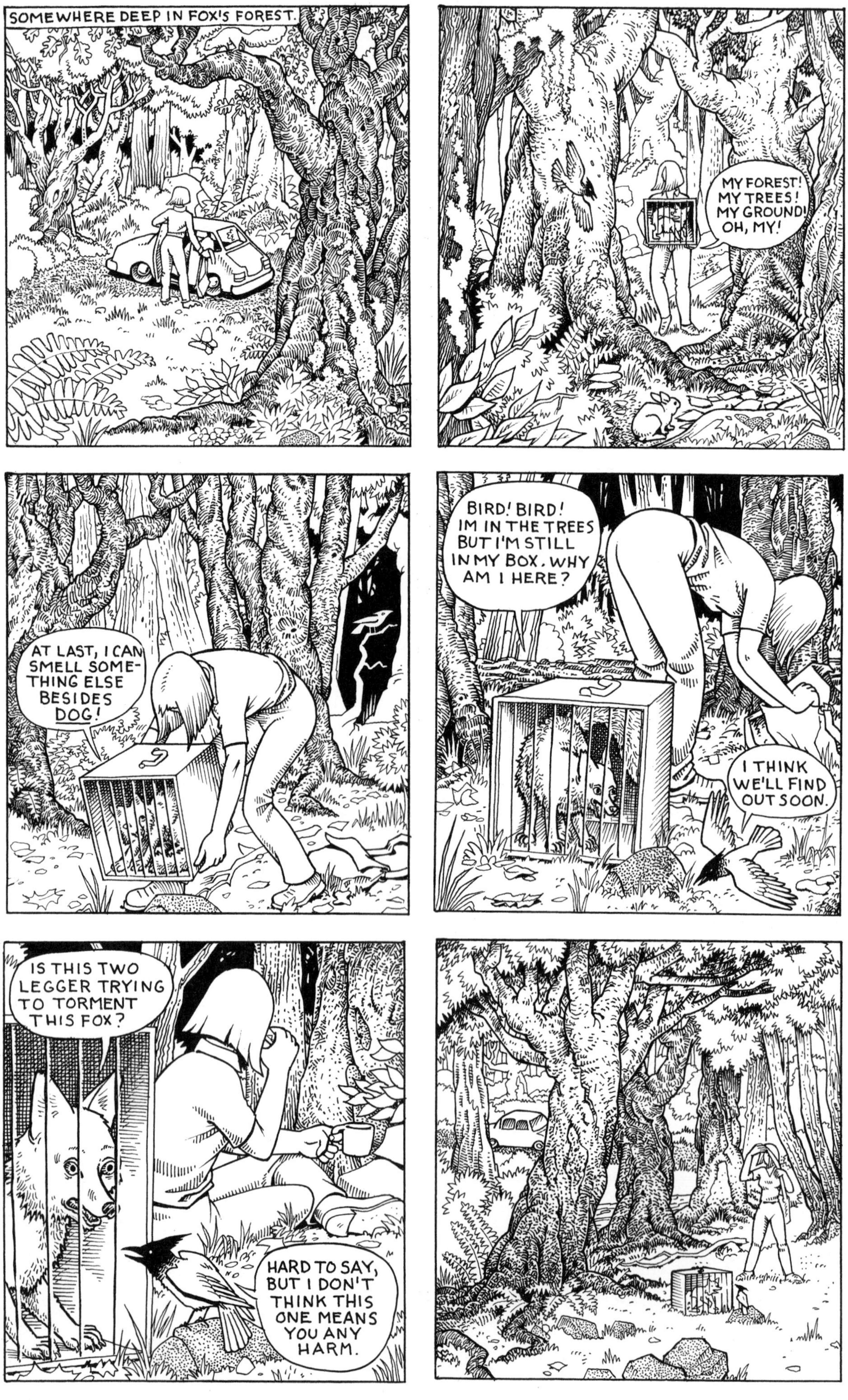
SOMEWHERE DEEP IN FOX'S FOREST.
MY FOREST! MY TREES! MY GROUND! OH, MY!
AT LAST, I CAN SMELL SOME-THING ELSE BESIDES DOG!
BIRD! BIRD! IM IN THE TREES BUT I'M STILL IN MY BOX. WHY AM I HERE?
I THINK WE'LL FIND OUT SOON.
IS THIS TWO LEGGER TRYING TO TORMENT THIS FOX?
HARD TO SAY, BUT I DON'T THINK THIS ONE MEANS YOU ANY HARM.

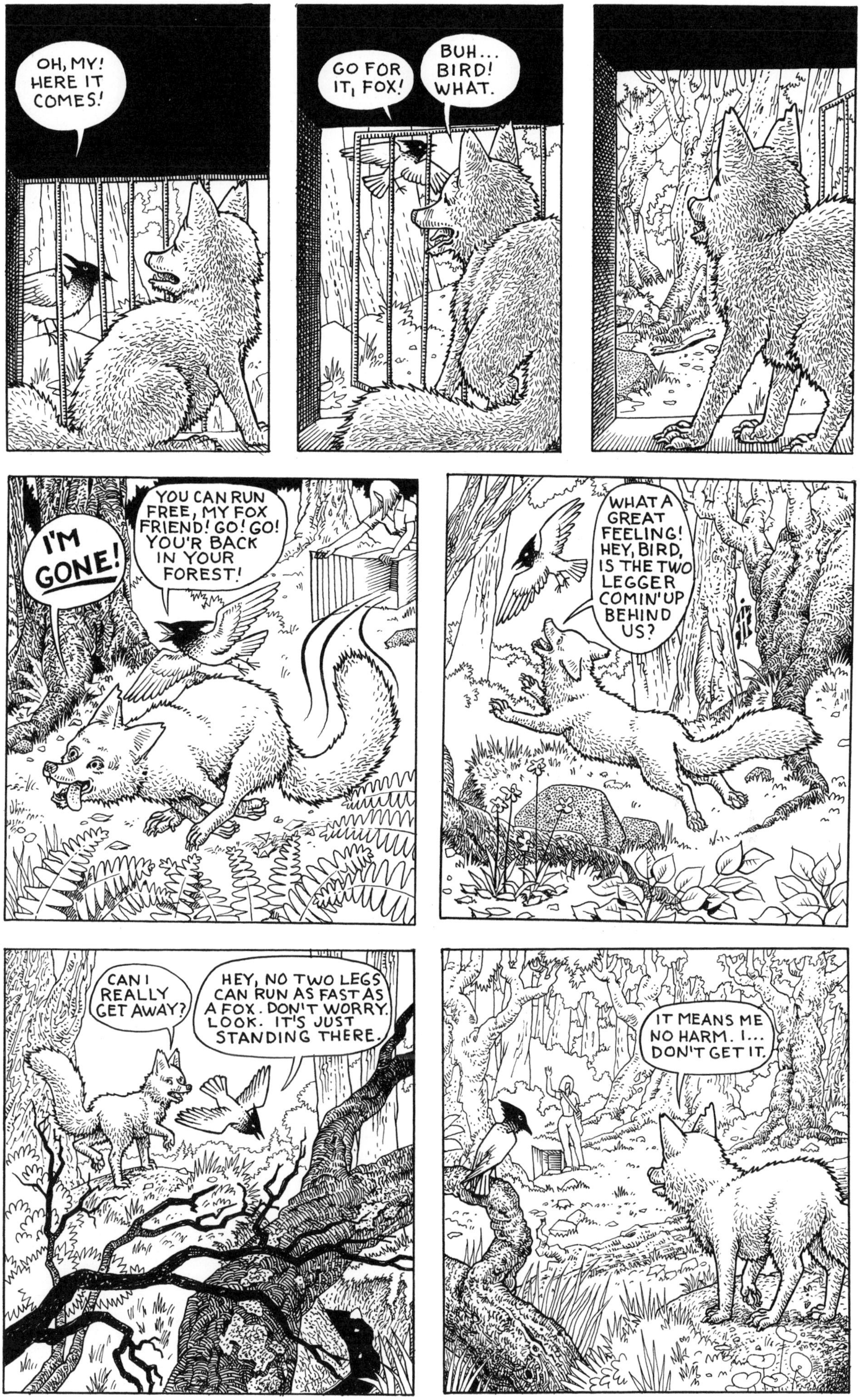
OH, MY! HERE IT COMES!
GO FOR IT, FOX!
BUH... BIRD! WHAT.
I'M GONE!
YOU CAN RUN FREE, MY FOX FRIEND! GO! GO! YOU'R BACK IN YOUR FOREST!
WHAT A GREAT FEELING! HEY, BIRD, IS THE TWO LEGGER COMIN' UP BEHIND US?
CAN I REALLY GET AWAY?
HEY, NO TWO LEGS CAN RUN AS FAST AS A FOX. DON'T WORRY. LOOK. IT'S JUST STANDING THERE.
IT MEANS ME NO HARM. I... DON'T GET IT.

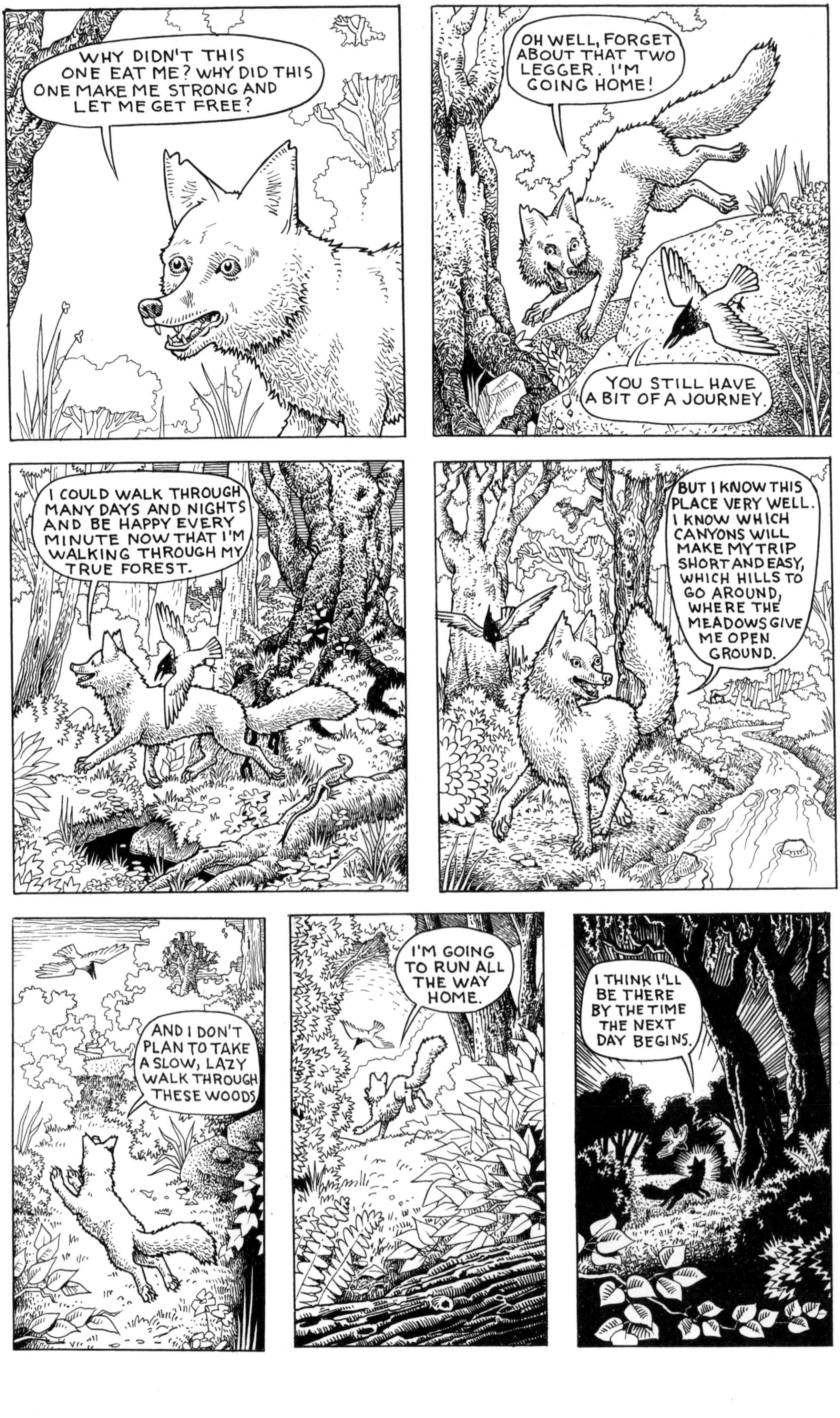
WHY DIDN'T THIS ONE EAT ME? WHY DID THIS ONE MAKE ME STRONG AND LET ME GET FREE?
OH WELL, FORGET ABOUT THAT TWO LEGGER. I'M GOING HOME!
YOU STILL HAVE A BIT OF A JOURNEY.
I COULD WALK THROUGH MANY DAYS AND NIGHTS AND BE HAPPY EVERY MINUTE NOW THAT I'M WALKING THROUGH MY TRUE FOREST.
BUT I KNOW THIS PLACE VERY WELL. I KNOW WHICH CANYONS WILL MAKE MY TRIP SHORT AND EASY, WHICH HILLS TO GO AROUND, WHERE THE MEADOWS GIVE ME OPEN GROUND.
AND I DON'T PLAN TO TAKE A SLOW, LAZY WALK THROUGH THESE WOODS
I'M GOING TO RUN ALL THE WAY HOME.
I THINK I'LL BE THERE BY THE TIME THE NEXT DAY BEGINS.

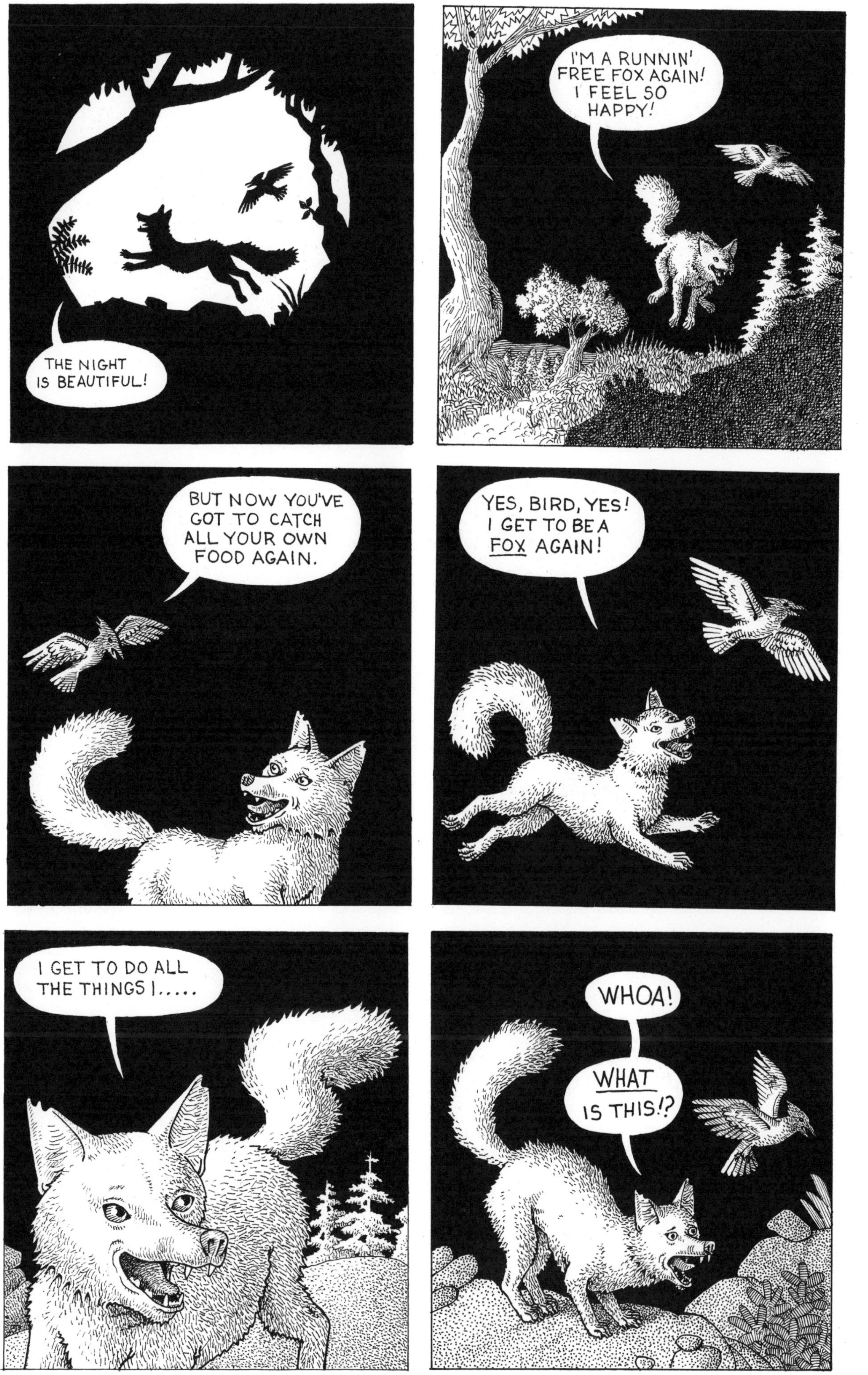
THE NIGHT IS BEAUTIFUL!
I'M A RUNNIN' FREE FOX AGAIN! I FEEL SO HAPPY!
BUT NOW YOU'VE GOT TO CATCH ALL YOUR OWN FOOD AGAIN.
YES, BIRD, YES! I GET TO BE A FOX AGAIN!
I GET TO DO ALL THE THINGS I.....
WHOA!
WHAT IS THIS!?

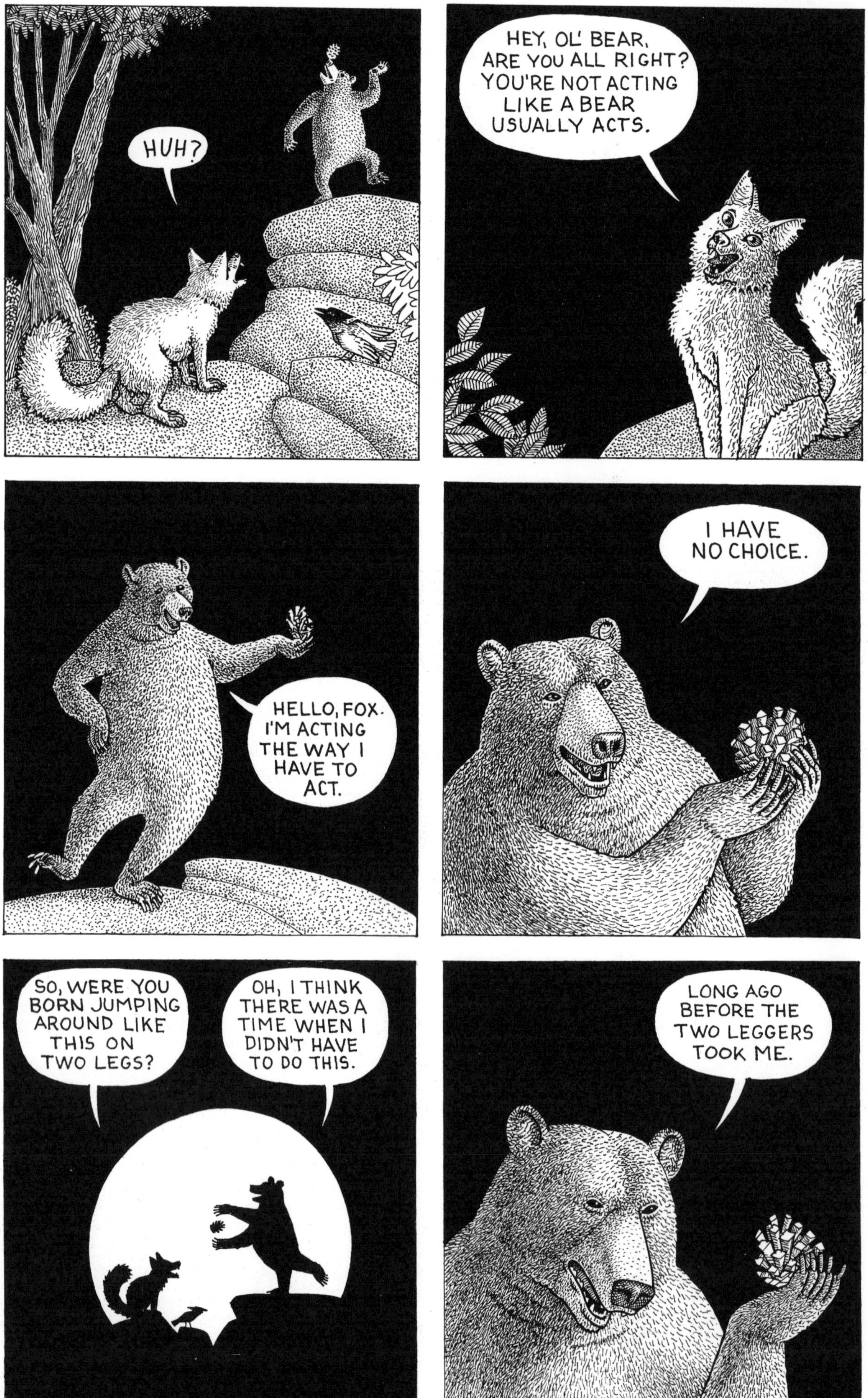
HUH?
HEY, OL' BEAR, ARE YOU ALL RIGHT? YOU'RE NOT ACTING LIKE A BEAR USUALLY ACTS.
HELLO, FOX. I'M ACTING THE WAY I HAVE TO ACT.
I HAVE NO CHOICE.
SO, WERE YOU BORN JUMPING AROUND LIKE THIS ON TWO LEGS?
OH, I THINK THERE WAS A TIME WHEN I DIDN'T HAVE TO DO THIS.
LONG AGO BEFORE THE TWO LEGGERS TOOK ME.

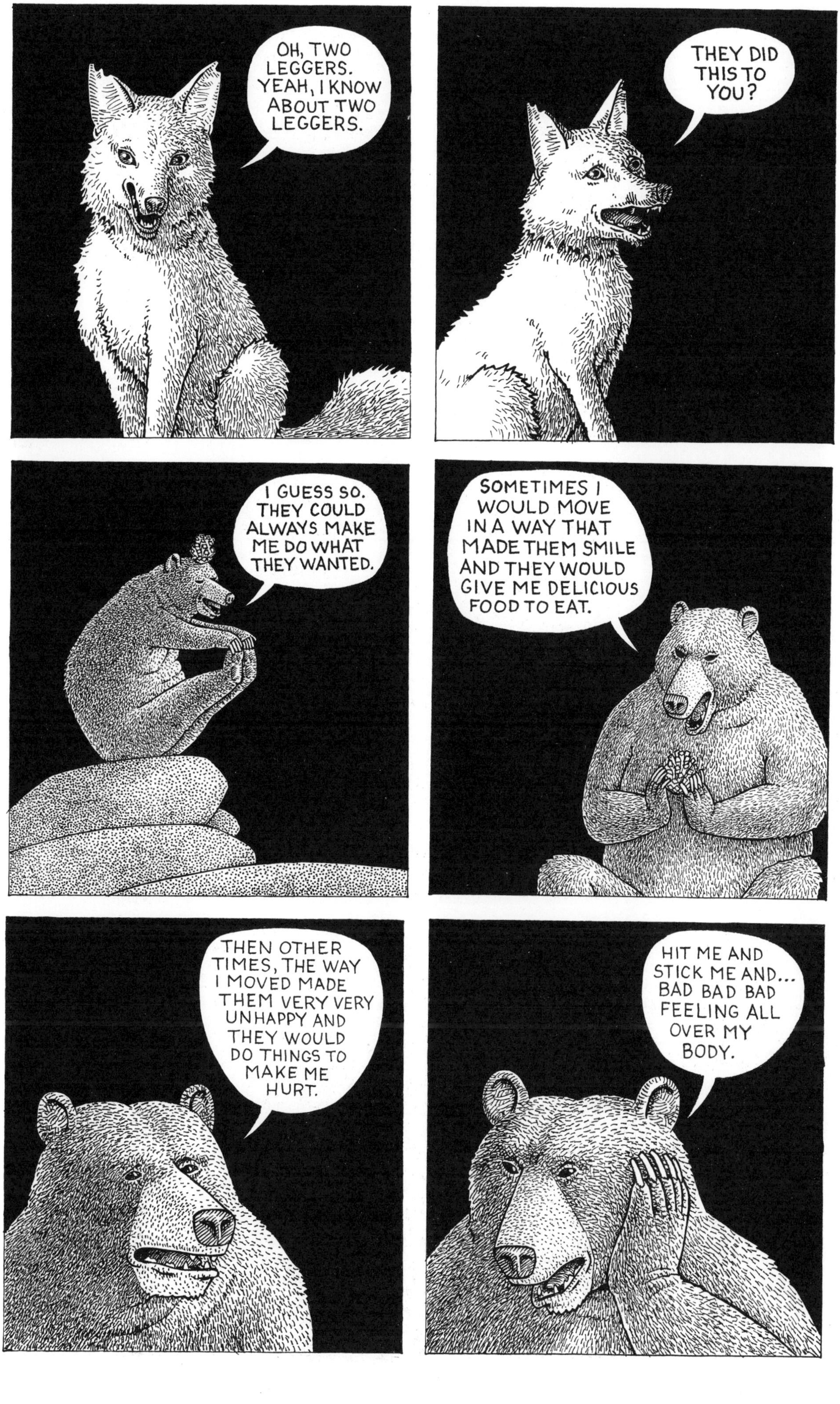
OH, TWO LEGGERS. YEAH, I KNOW ABOUT TWO LEGGERS.
THEY DID THIS TO YOU?
I GUESS SO. THEY COULD ALWAYS MAKE ME DO WHAT THEY WANTED.
SOMETIMES I WOULD MOVE IN A WAY THAT MADE THEM SMILE AND THEY WOULD GIVE ME DELICIOUS FOOD TO EAT.
THEN OTHER TIMES, THE WAY I MOVED MADE THEM VERY VERY UNHAPPY AND THEY WOULD DO THINGS TO MAKE ME HURT.
HIT ME AND STICK ME AND... BAD BAD BAD FEELING ALL OVER MY BODY.

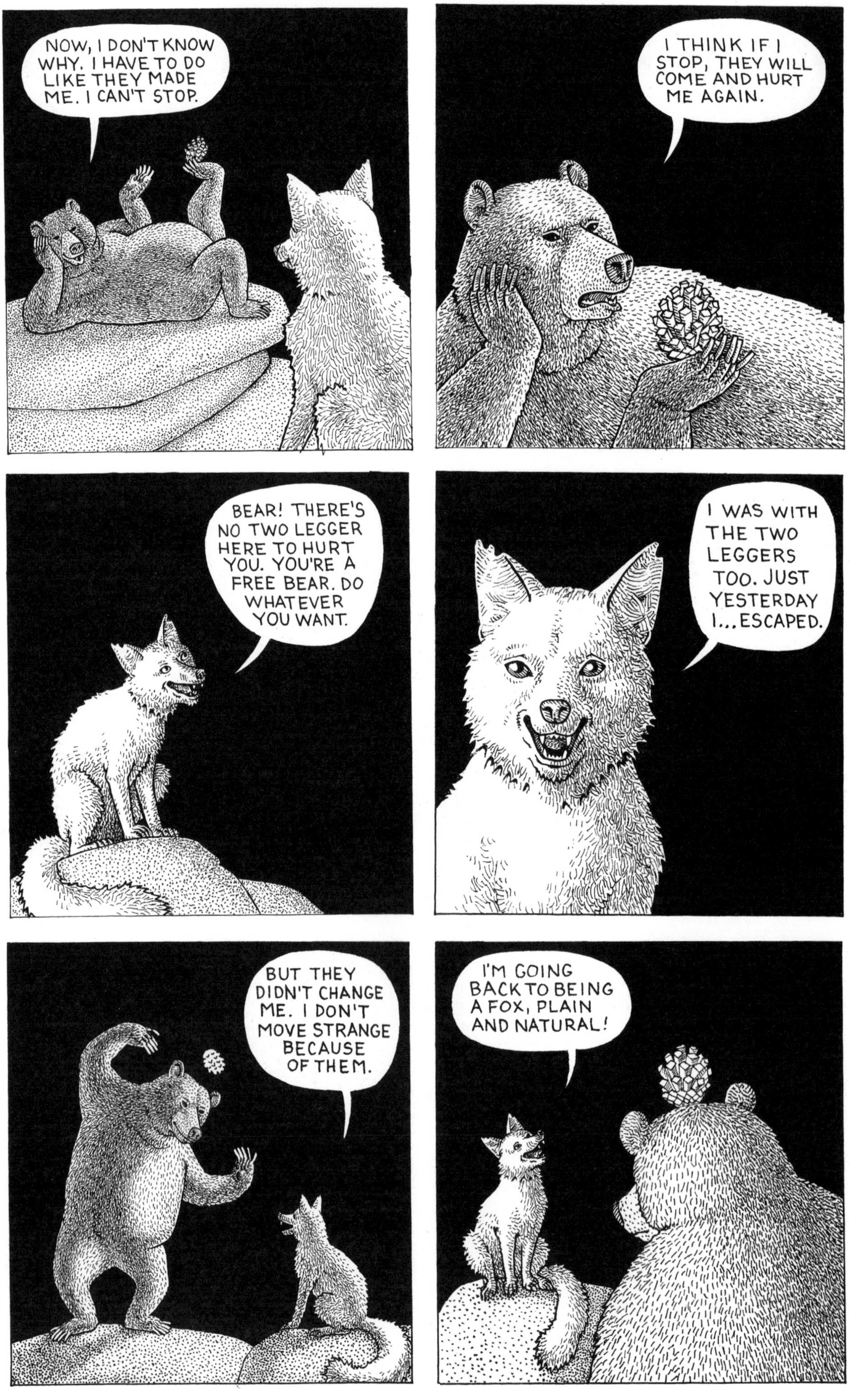
NOW, I DON'T KNOW WHY. I HAVE TO DO LIKE THEY MADE ME. I CAN'T STOP.
I THINK IF I STOP, THEY WILL COME AND HURT ME AGAIN.
BEAR! THERE'S NO TWO LEGGER HERE TO HURT YOU. YOU'RE A FREE BEAR. DO WHATEVER YOU WANT.
I WAS WITH THE TWO LEGGERS TOO. JUST YESTERDAY I... ESCAPED.
BUT THEY DIDN'T CHANGE ME. I DON'T MOVE STRANGE BECAUSE OF THEM.
I'M GOING BACK TO BEING A FOX, PLAIN AND NATURAL!

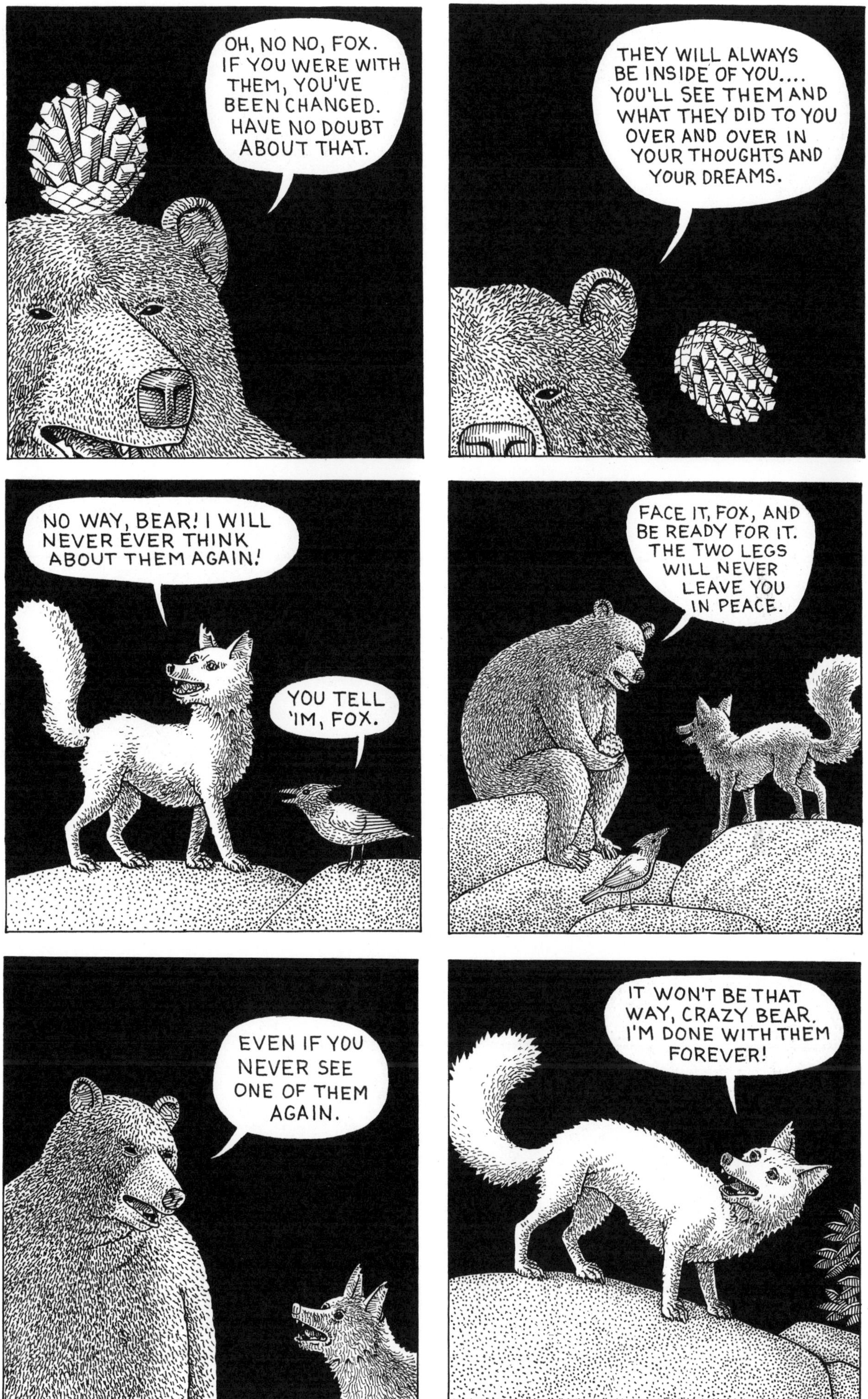
OH, NO NO, FOX. IF YOU WERE WITH THEM, YOU'VE BEEN CHANGED. HAVE NO DOUBT ABOUT THAT.
THEY WILL ALWAYS BE INSIDE OF YOU.... YOU'LL SEE THEM AND WHAT THEY DID TO YOU OVER AND OVER IN YOUR THOUGHTS AND YOUR DREAMS.
NO WAY, BEAR! I WILL NEVER EVER THINK ABOUT THEM AGAIN!
YOU TELL 'IM, FOX.
FACE IT, FOX, AND BE READY FOR IT. THE TWO LEGS WILL NEVER LEAVE YOU IN PEACE.
EVEN IF YOU NEVER SEE ONE OF THEM AGAIN.
IT WON'T BE THAT WAY, CRAZY BEAR. I'M DONE WITH THEM FOREVER!

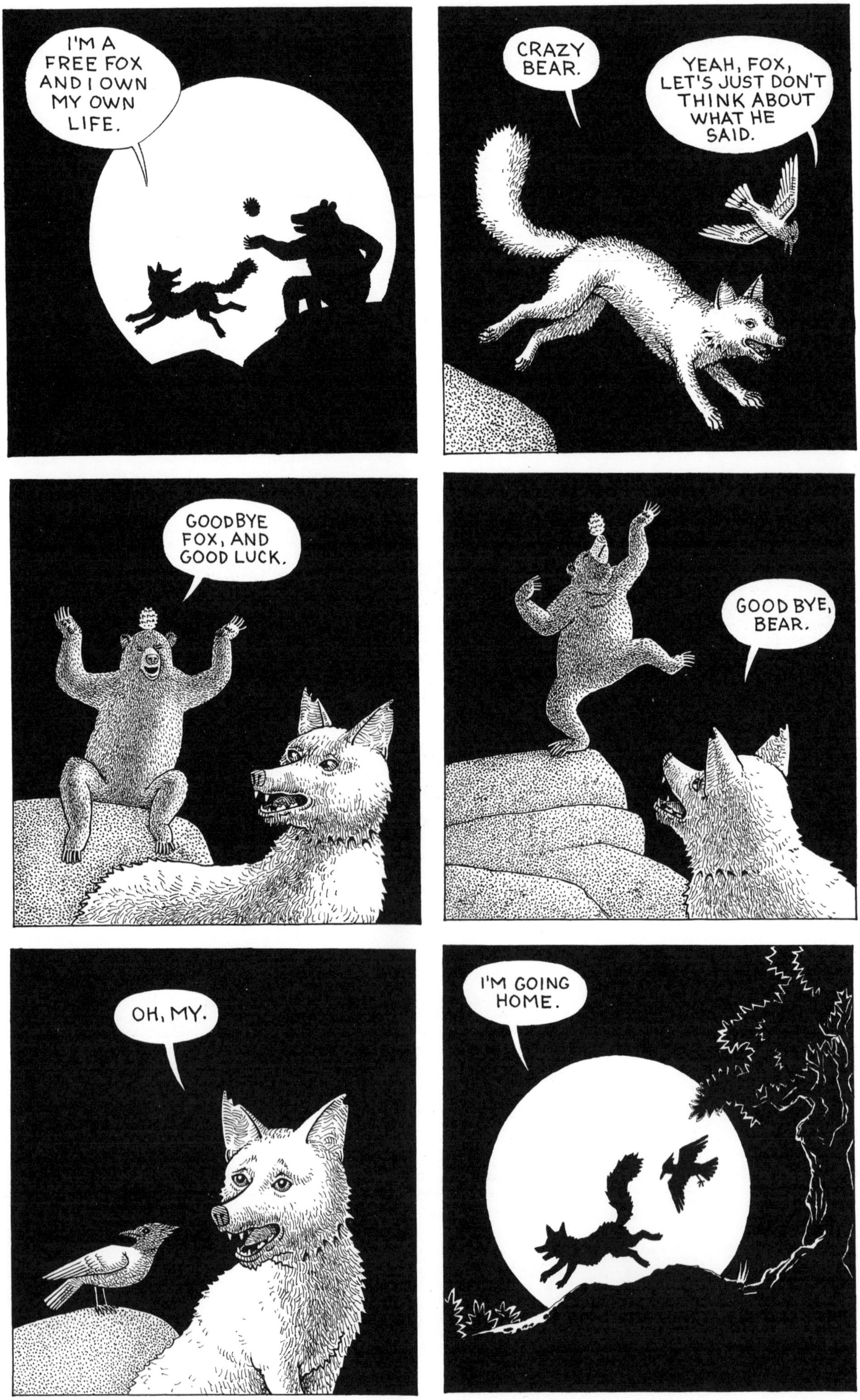
I'M A FREE FOX AND I OWN MY OWN LIFE.
CRAZY BEAR.
YEAH, FOX, LET'S JUST DON'T THINK ABOUT WHAT HE SAID.
GOODBYE FOX, AND GOOD LUCK.
GOOD BYE, BEAR.
OH, MY.
I'M GOING HOME.

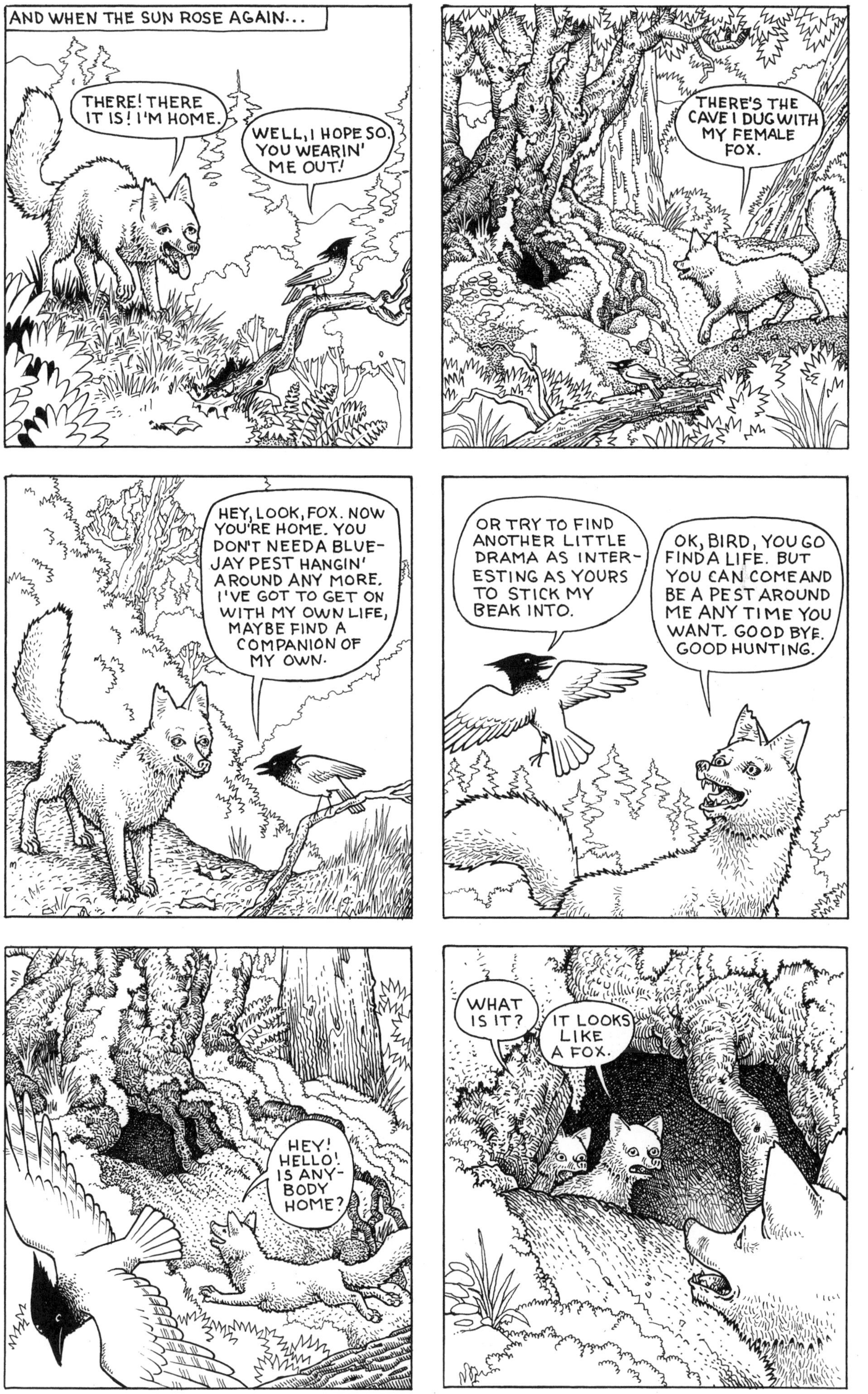
AND WHEN THE SUN ROSE AGAIN...
THERE! THERE IT IS! I'M HOME.
WELL, I HOPE SO. YOU WEARIN' ME OUT!
THERE'S THE CAVE I DUG WITH MY FEMALE FOX.
HEY, LOOK, FOX. NOW YOU'RE HOME. YOU DON'T NEED A BLUE-JAY PEST HANGIN' AROUND ANY MORE. I'VE GOT TO GET ON WITH MY OWN LIFE, MAYBE FIND A COMPANION OF MY OWN.
OR TRY TO FIND ANOTHER LITTLE DRAMA AS INTER-ESTING AS YOURS TO STICK MY BEAK INTO.
OK, BIRD, YOU GO FIND A LIFE. BUT YOU CAN COME AND BE A PEST AROUND ME ANY TIME YOU WANT. GOOD BYE. GOOD HUNTING.
HEY! HELLO! IS ANY-BODY HOME?
WHAT IS IT?
IT LOOKS LIKE A FOX.

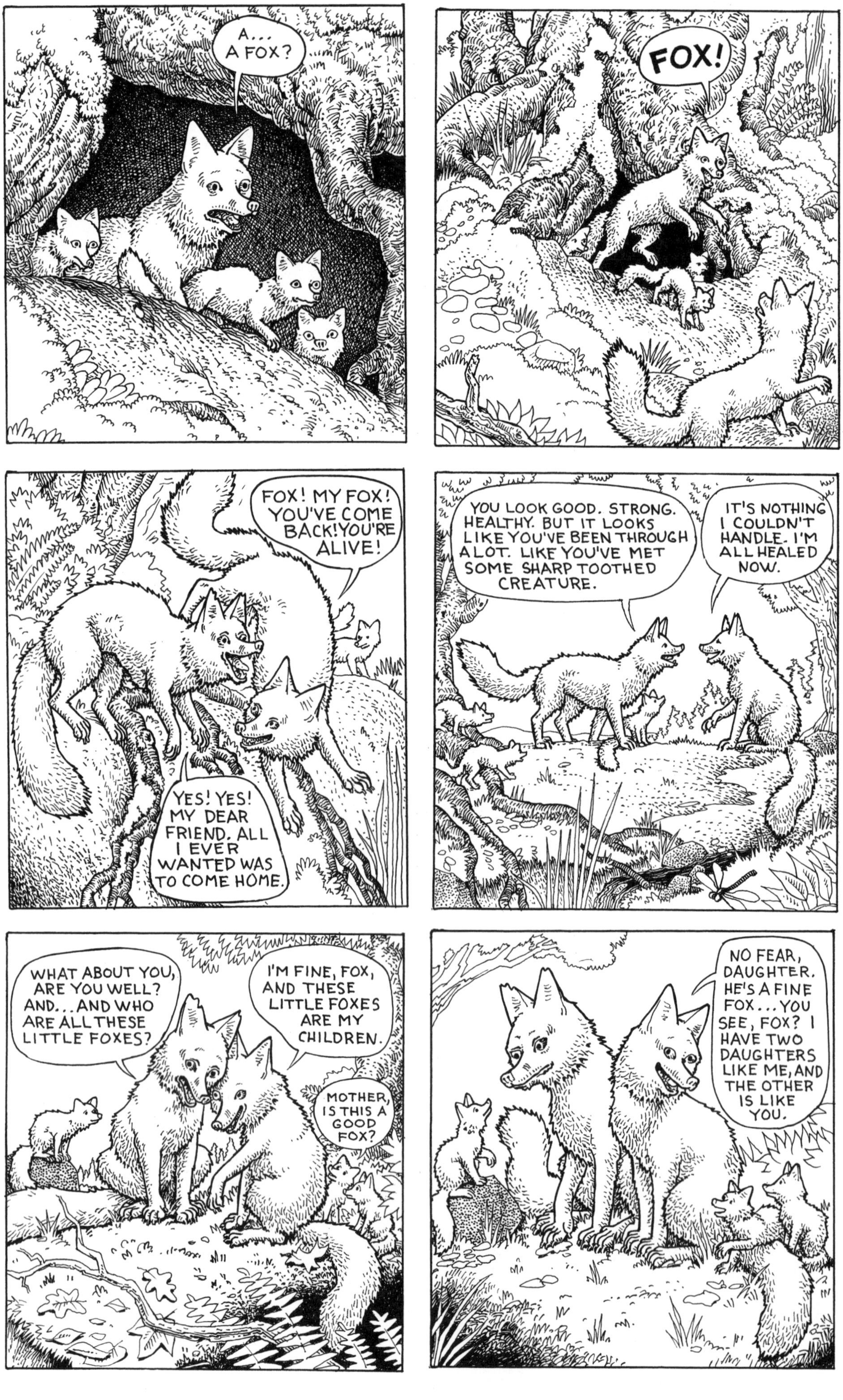
A... A FOX?
FOX!
FOX! MY FOX! YOU'VE COME BACK! YOU'RE ALIVE!
YES! YES! MY DEAR FRIEND. ALL I EVER WANTED WAS TO COME HOME.
YOU LOOK GOOD. STRONG. HEALTHY. BUT IT LOOKS LIKE YOU'VE BEEN THROUGH A LOT. LIKE YOU'VE MET SOME SHARP TOOTHED CREATURE.
IT'S NOTHING I COULDN'T HANDLE. I'M ALL HEALED NOW.
WHAT ABOUT YOU, ARE YOU WELL? AND... AND WHO ARE ALL THESE LITTLE FOXES?
I'M FINE, FOX, AND THESE LITTLE FOXES ARE MY CHILDREN.
MOTHER, IS THIS A GOOD FOX?
NO FEAR, DAUGHTER. HE'S A FINE FOX... YOU SEE, FOX? I HAVE TWO DAUGHTERS LIKE ME, AND THE OTHER IS LIKE YOU.

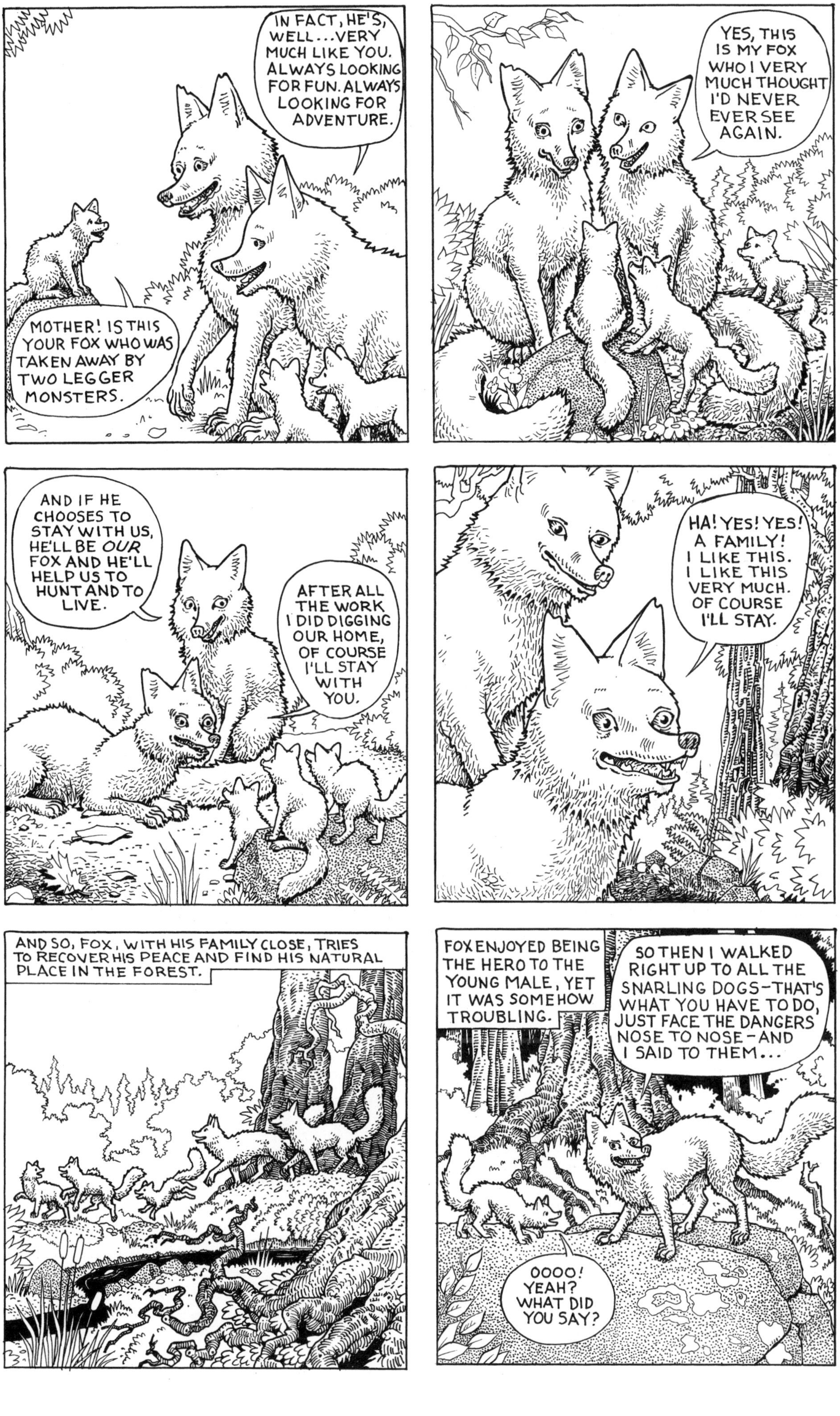
IN FACT, HE'S, WELL... VERY MUCH LIKE YOU. ALWAYS LOOKING FOR FUN. ALWAYS LOOKING FOR ADVENTURE.
MOTHER! IS THIS YOUR FOX WHO WAS TAKEN AWAY BY TWO LEGGER MONSTERS.
YES, THIS IS MY FOX WHO I VERY MUCH THOUGHT I'D NEVER EVER SEE AGAIN.
AND IF HE CHOOSES TO STAY WITH US, HE'LL BE OUR FOX AND HE'LL HELP US TO HUNT AND TO LIVE.
AFTER ALL THE WORK I DID DIGGING OUR HOME, OF COURSE I'LL STAY WITH YOU.
HA! YES! YES! A FAMILY! I LIKE THIS. I LIKE THIS VERY MUCH. OF COURSE I'LL STAY.
AND SO, FOX, WITH HIS FAMILY CLOSE, TRIES TO RECOVER HIS PEACE AND FIND HIS NATURAL PLACE IN THE FOREST.
FOX ENJOYED BEING THE HERO TO THE YOUNG MALE, YET IT WAS SOMEHOW TROUBLING.
SO THEN I WALKED RIGHT UP TO ALL THE SNARLING DOGS—THAT'S WHAT YOU HAVE TO DO, JUST FACE THE DANGERS NOSE TO NOSE—AND I SAID TO THEM...
OOOO! YEAH? WHAT DID YOU SAY?

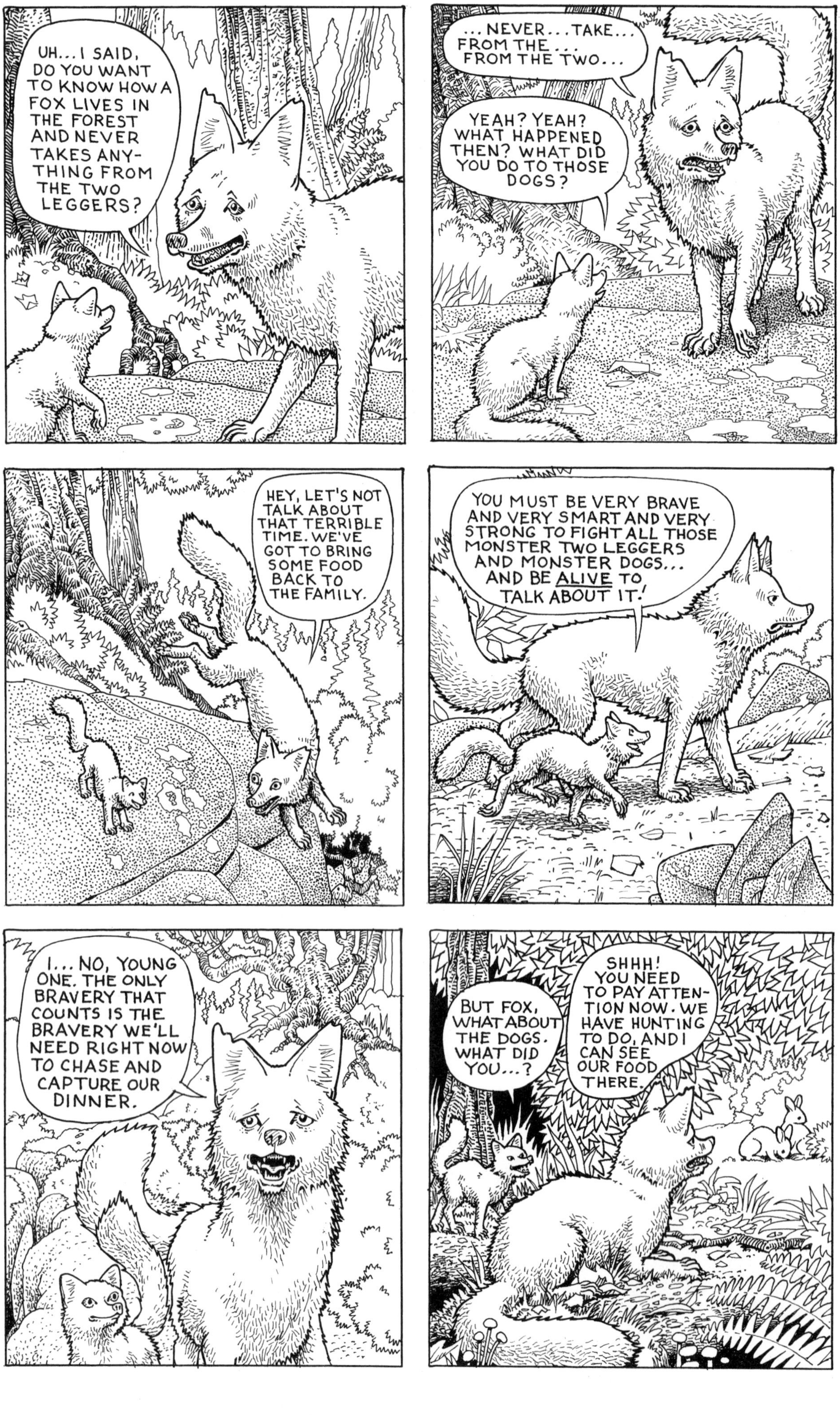
UH... I SAID, DO YOU WANT TO KNOW HOW A FOX LIVES IN THE FOREST AND NEVER TAKES ANY-THING FROM THE TWO LEGGERS?
...NEVER...TAKE... FROM THE... FROM THE TWO...
YEAH? YEAH? WHAT HAPPENED THEN? WHAT DID YOU DO TO THOSE DOGS?
HEY, LET'S NOT TALK ABOUT THAT TERRIBLE TIME. WE'VE GOT TO BRING SOME FOOD BACK TO THE FAMILY.
YOU MUST BE VERY BRAVE AND VERY SMART AND VERY STRONG TO FIGHT ALL THOSE MONSTER TWO LEGGERS AND MONSTER DOGS... AND BE ALIVE TO TALK ABOUT IT!
I... NO, YOUNG ONE. THE ONLY BRAVERY THAT COUNTS IS THE BRAVERY WE'LL NEED RIGHT NOW TO CHASE AND CAPTURE OUR DINNER.
BUT FOX, WHAT ABOUT THE DOGS. WHAT DID YOU...?
SHHH! YOU NEED TO PAY ATTEN-TION NOW. WE HAVE HUNTING TO DO, AND I CAN SEE OUR FOOD THERE.

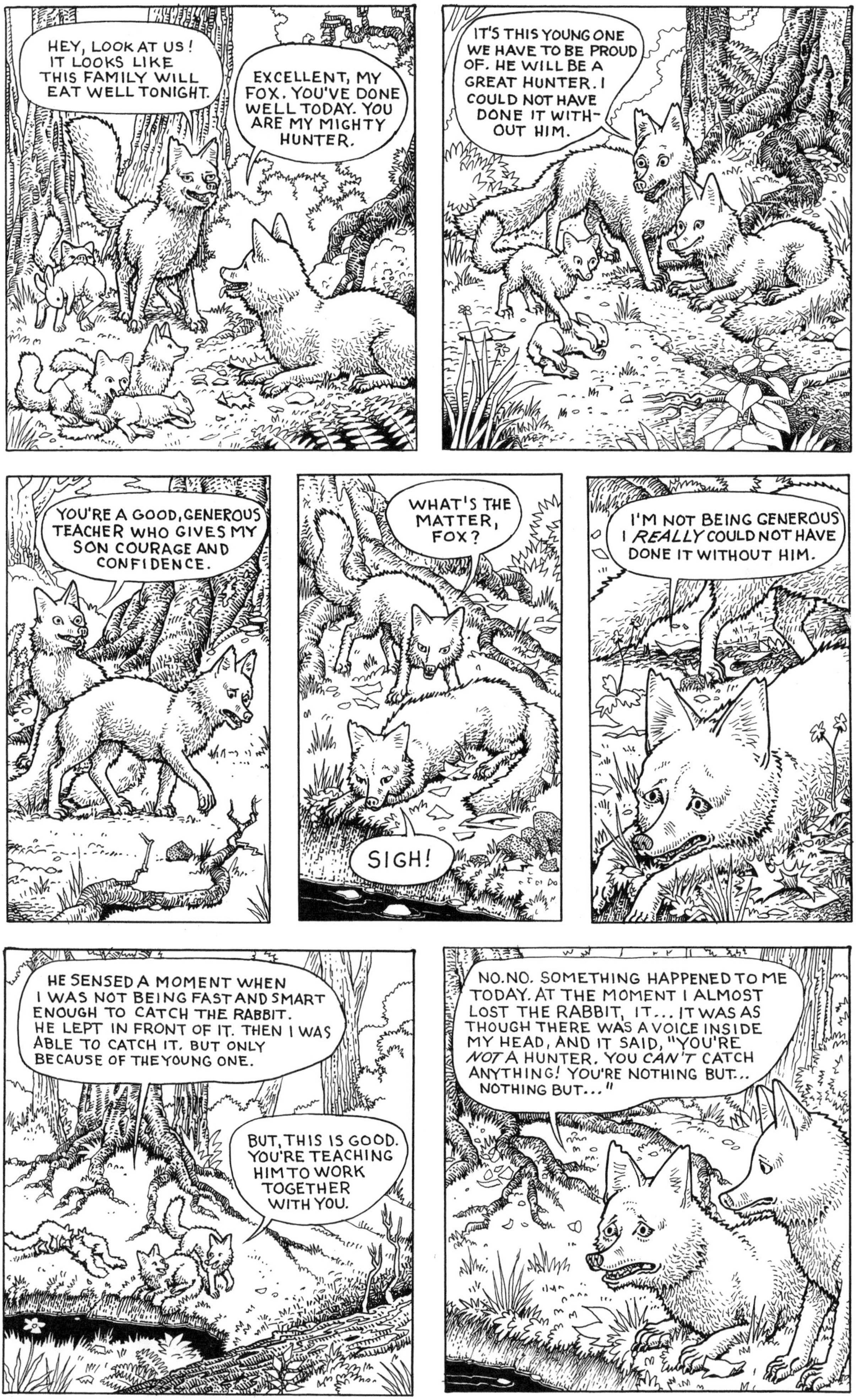
HEY, LOOK AT US! IT LOOKS LIKE THIS FAMILY WILL EAT WELL TONIGHT.
EXCELLENT, MY FOX. YOU'VE DONE WELL TODAY. YOU ARE MY MIGHTY HUNTER.
IT'S THIS YOUNG ONE WE HAVE TO BE PROUD OF. HE WILL BE A GREAT HUNTER. I COULD NOT HAVE DONE IT WITH-OUT HIM.
YOU'RE A GOOD, GENEROUS TEACHER WHO GIVES MY SON COURAGE AND CONFIDENCE.
WHAT'S THE MATTER, FOX?
SIGH!
I'M NOT BEING GENEROUS I *REALLY* COULD NOT HAVE DONE IT WITHOUT HIM.
HE SENSED A MOMENT WHEN I WAS NOT BEING FAST AND SMART ENOUGH TO CATCH THE RABBIT. HE LEPT IN FRONT OF IT. THEN I WAS ABLE TO CATCH IT. BUT ONLY BECAUSE OF THE YOUNG ONE.
BUT, THIS IS GOOD. YOU'RE TEACHING HIM TO WORK TOGETHER WITH YOU.
NO. NO. SOMETHING HAPPENED TO ME TODAY. AT THE MOMENT I ALMOST LOST THE RABBIT, IT... IT WAS AS THOUGH THERE WAS A VOICE INSIDE MY HEAD, AND IT SAID, "YOU'RE *NOT* A HUNTER. YOU *CAN'T* CATCH ANYTHING! YOU'RE NOTHING BUT... NOTHING BUT..."

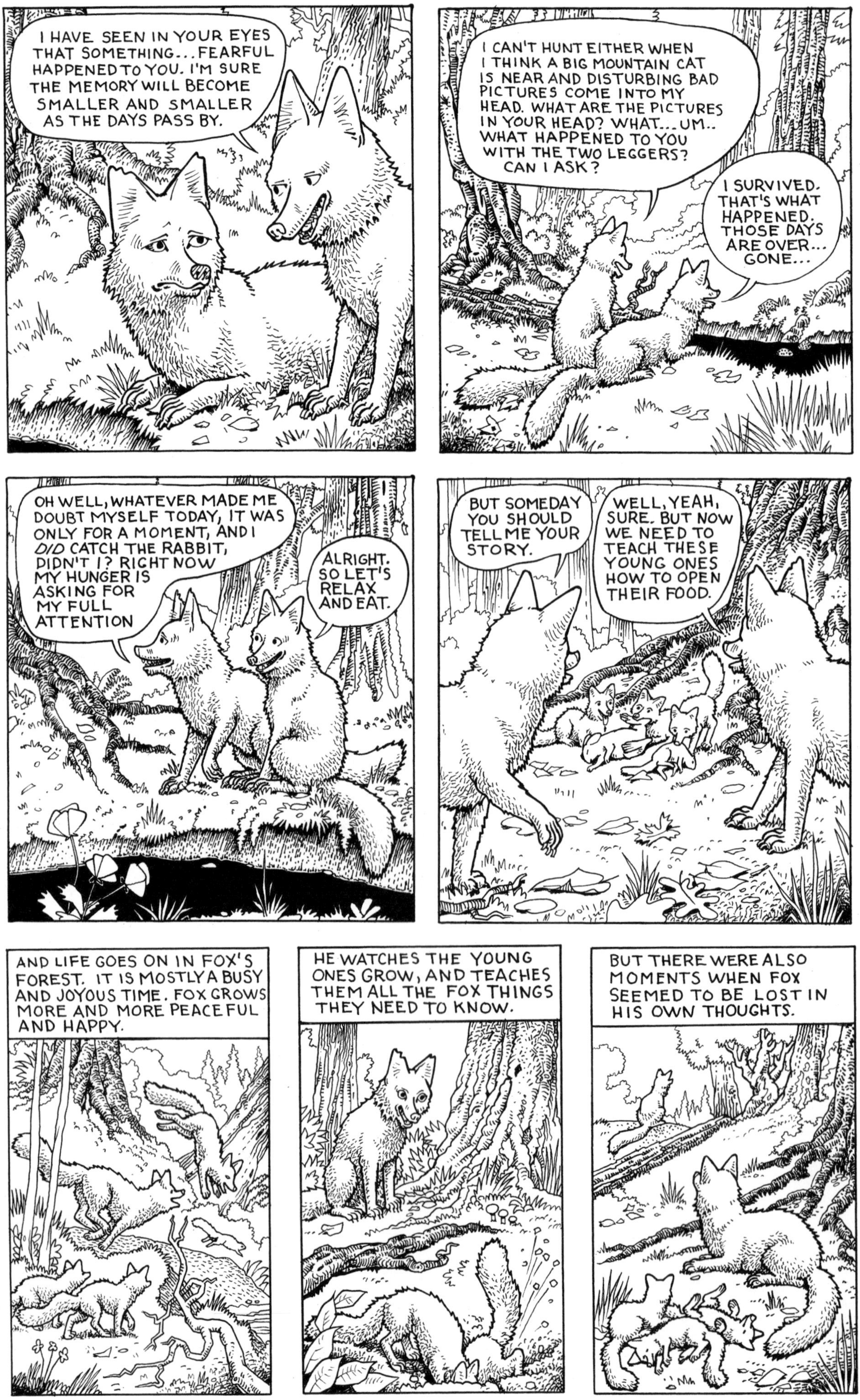
I HAVE SEEN IN YOUR EYES THAT SOMETHING... FEARFUL HAPPENED TO YOU. I'M SURE THE MEMORY WILL BECOME SMALLER AND SMALLER AS THE DAYS PASS BY.
I CAN'T HUNT EITHER WHEN I THINK A BIG MOUNTAIN CAT IS NEAR AND DISTURBING BAD PICTURES COME INTO MY HEAD. WHAT ARE THE PICTURES IN YOUR HEAD? WHAT... UM.. WHAT HAPPENED TO YOU WITH THE TWO LEGGERS? CAN I ASK?
I SURVIVED. THAT'S WHAT HAPPENED. THOSE DAYS ARE OVER... GONE...
OH WELL, WHATEVER MADE ME DOUBT MYSELF TODAY, IT WAS ONLY FOR A MOMENT, AND I *DID* CATCH THE RABBIT, DIDN'T I? RIGHT NOW MY HUNGER IS ASKING FOR MY FULL ATTENTION
ALRIGHT. SO LET'S RELAX AND EAT.
BUT SOMEDAY YOU SHOULD TELL ME YOUR STORY.
WELL, YEAH, SURE. BUT NOW WE NEED TO TEACH THESE YOUNG ONES HOW TO OPEN THEIR FOOD.
AND LIFE GOES ON IN FOX'S FOREST. IT IS MOSTLY A BUSY AND JOYOUS TIME. FOX GROWS MORE AND MORE PEACEFUL AND HAPPY.
HE WATCHES THE YOUNG ONES GROW, AND TEACHES THEM ALL THE FOX THINGS THEY NEED TO KNOW.
BUT THERE WERE ALSO MOMENTS WHEN FOX SEEMED TO BE LOST IN HIS OWN THOUGHTS.

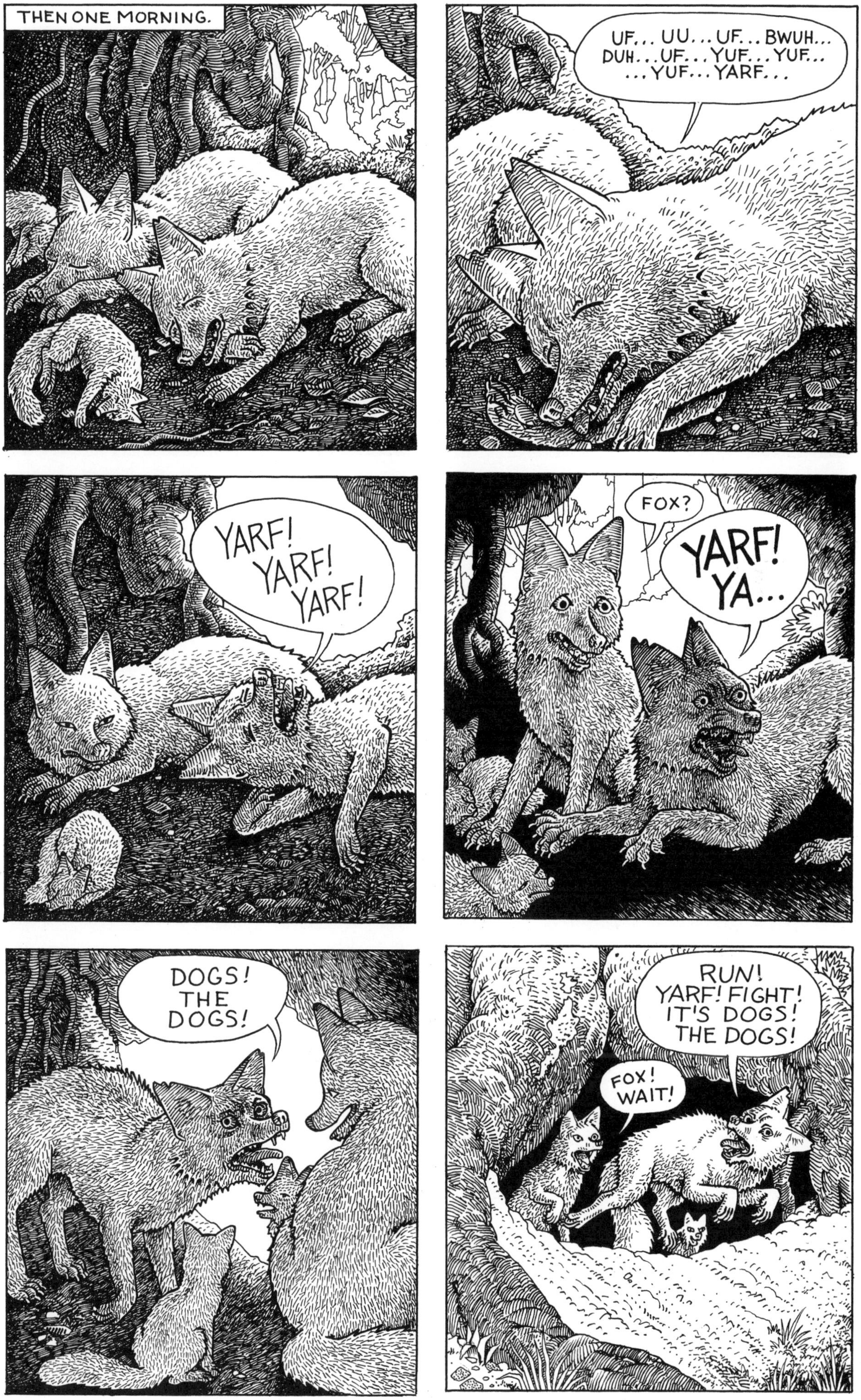
THEN ONE MORNING.
UF... UU... UF... BWUH... DUH... UF... YUF... YUF... ...YUF... YARF...
YARF! YARF! YARF!
FOX?
YARF! YA...
DOGS! THE DOGS!
RUN! YARF! FIGHT! IT'S DOGS! THE DOGS!
FOX! WAIT!

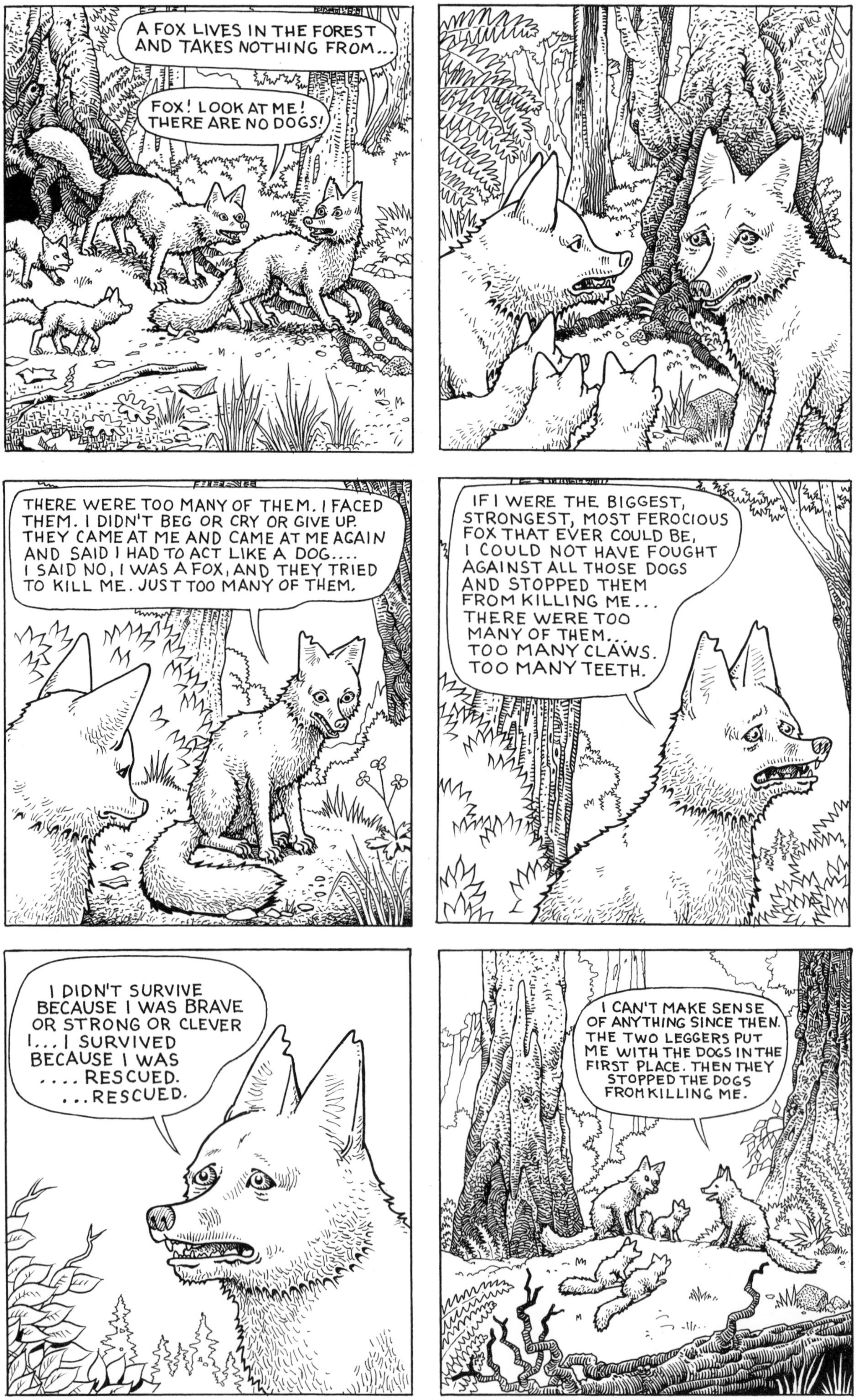
A FOX LIVES IN THE FOREST AND TAKES NOTHING FROM...
FOX! LOOK AT ME! THERE ARE NO DOGS!
THERE WERE TOO MANY OF THEM. I FACED THEM. I DIDN'T BEG OR CRY OR GIVE UP. THEY CAME AT ME AND CAME AT ME AGAIN AND SAID I HAD TO ACT LIKE A DOG.... I SAID NO, I WAS A FOX, AND THEY TRIED TO KILL ME. JUST TOO MANY OF THEM.
IF I WERE THE BIGGEST, STRONGEST, MOST FEROCIOUS FOX THAT EVER COULD BE, I COULD NOT HAVE FOUGHT AGAINST ALL THOSE DOGS AND STOPPED THEM FROM KILLING ME... THERE WERE TOO MANY OF THEM... TOO MANY CLAWS. TOO MANY TEETH.
I DIDN'T SURVIVE BECAUSE I WAS BRAVE OR STRONG OR CLEVER I... I SURVIVED BECAUSE I WAS .... RESCUED. ...RESCUED.
I CAN'T MAKE SENSE OF ANYTHING SINCE THEN. THE TWO LEGGERS PUT ME WITH THE DOGS IN THE FIRST PLACE. THEN THEY STOPPED THE DOGS FROM KILLING ME.

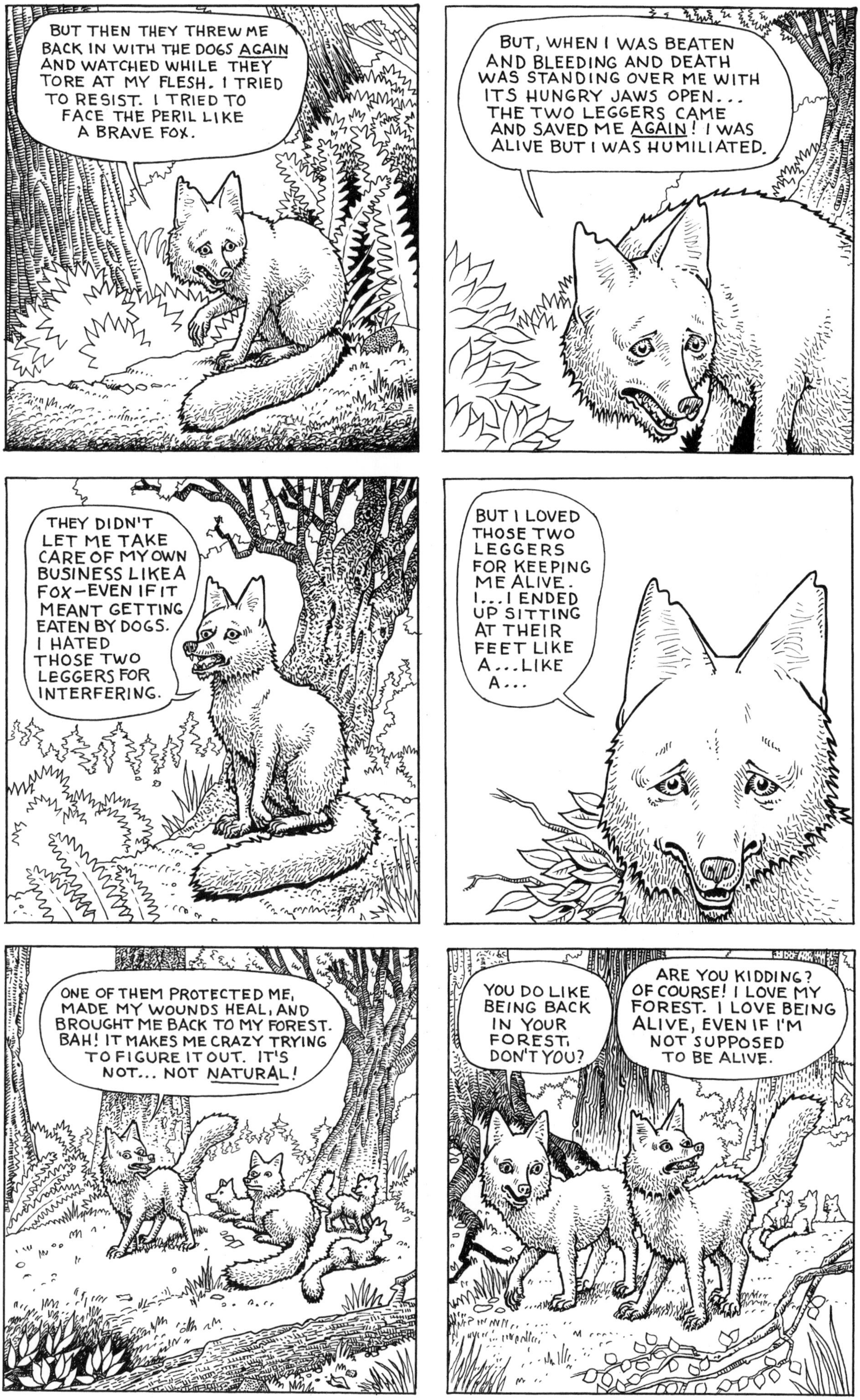
BUT THEN THEY THREW ME BACK IN WITH THE DOGS AGAIN AND WATCHED WHILE THEY TORE AT MY FLESH. I TRIED TO RESIST. I TRIED TO FACE THE PERIL LIKE A BRAVE FOX.
BUT, WHEN I WAS BEATEN AND BLEEDING AND DEATH WAS STANDING OVER ME WITH ITS HUNGRY JAWS OPEN... THE TWO LEGGERS CAME AND SAVED ME AGAIN! I WAS ALIVE BUT I WAS HUMILIATED.
THEY DIDN'T LET ME TAKE CARE OF MY OWN BUSINESS LIKE A FOX—EVEN IF IT MEANT GETTING EATEN BY DOGS. I HATED THOSE TWO LEGGERS FOR INTERFERING.
BUT I LOVED THOSE TWO LEGGERS FOR KEEPING ME ALIVE. I... I ENDED UP SITTING AT THEIR FEET LIKE A... LIKE A...
ONE OF THEM PROTECTED ME, MADE MY WOUNDS HEAL, AND BROUGHT ME BACK TO MY FOREST. BAH! IT MAKES ME CRAZY TRYING TO FIGURE IT OUT. IT'S NOT... NOT NATURAL!
YOU DO LIKE BEING BACK IN YOUR FOREST, DON'T YOU?
ARE YOU KIDDING? OF COURSE! I LOVE MY FOREST. I LOVE BEING ALIVE, EVEN IF I'M NOT SUPPOSED TO BE ALIVE.

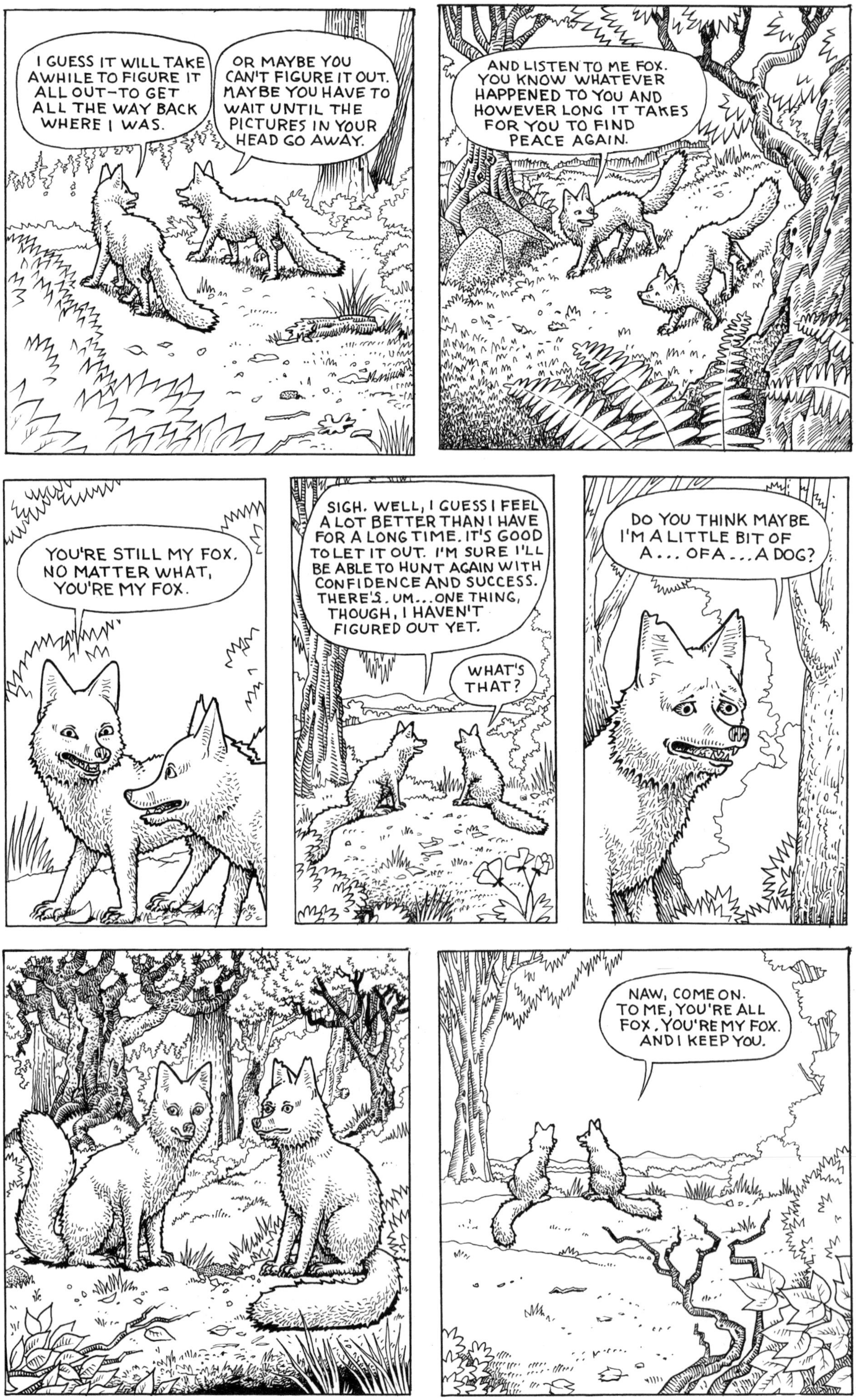
I GUESS IT WILL TAKE AWHILE TO FIGURE IT ALL OUT—TO GET ALL THE WAY BACK WHERE I WAS.
OR MAYBE YOU CAN'T FIGURE IT OUT. MAYBE YOU HAVE TO WAIT UNTIL THE PICTURES IN YOUR HEAD GO AWAY.
AND LISTEN TO ME FOX. YOU KNOW WHATEVER HAPPENED TO YOU AND HOWEVER LONG IT TAKES FOR YOU TO FIND PEACE AGAIN.
YOU'RE STILL MY FOX. NO MATTER WHAT, YOU'RE MY FOX.
SIGH. WELL, I GUESS I FEEL A LOT BETTER THAN I HAVE FOR A LONG TIME. IT'S GOOD TO LET IT OUT. I'M SURE I'LL BE ABLE TO HUNT AGAIN WITH CONFIDENCE AND SUCCESS. THERE'S...UM...ONE THING, THOUGH, I HAVEN'T FIGURED OUT YET.
WHAT'S THAT?
DO YOU THINK MAYBE I'M A LITTLE BIT OF A... OF A... A DOG?
NAW, COME ON. TO ME, YOU'RE ALL FOX, YOU'RE MY FOX. AND I KEEP YOU.

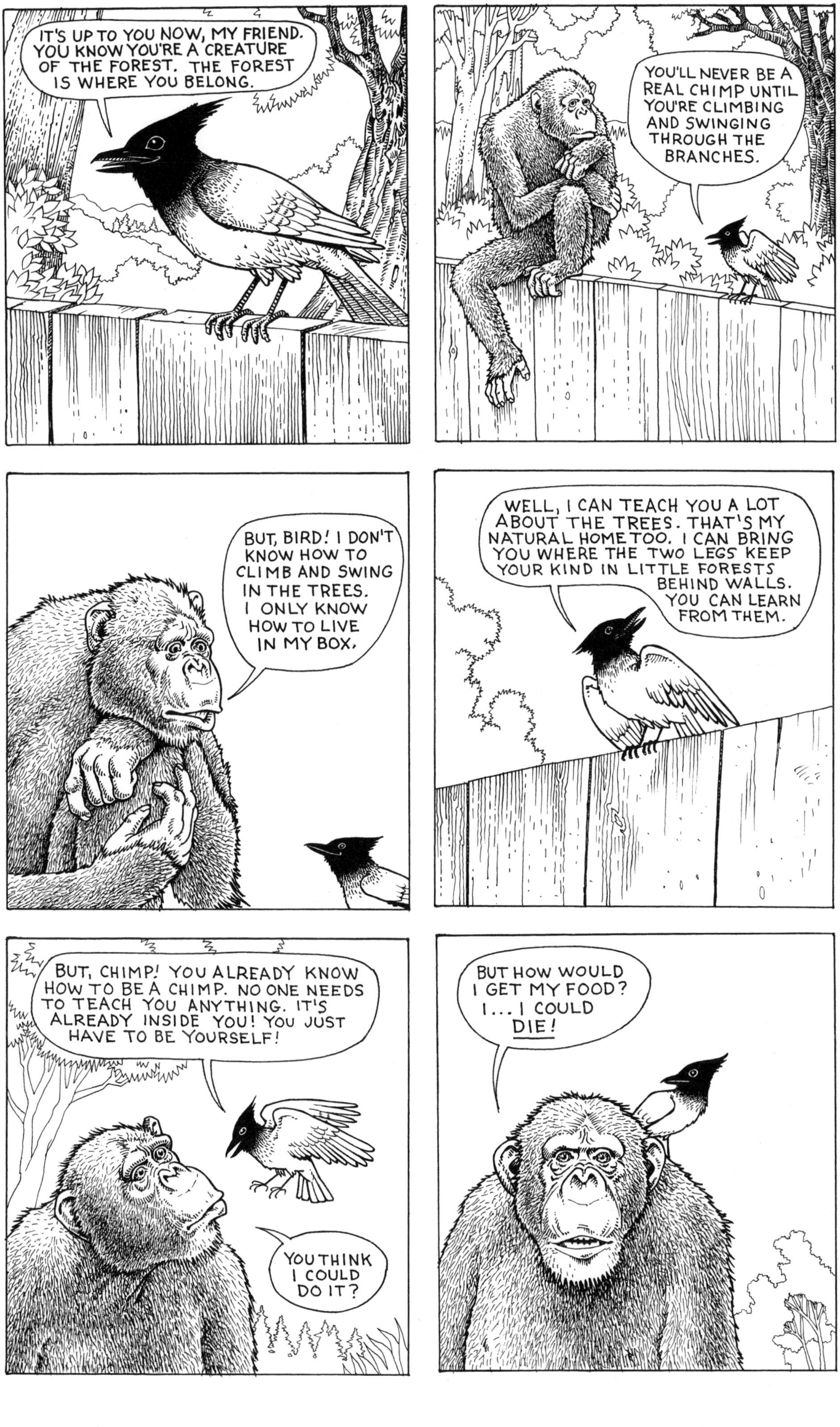
IT'S UP TO YOU NOW, MY FRIEND. YOU KNOW YOU'RE A CREATURE OF THE FOREST. THE FOREST IS WHERE YOU BELONG.
YOU'LL NEVER BE A REAL CHIMP UNTIL YOU'RE CLIMBING AND SWINGING THROUGH THE BRANCHES.
BUT, BIRD! I DON'T KNOW HOW TO CLIMB AND SWING IN THE TREES. I ONLY KNOW HOW TO LIVE IN MY BOX.
WELL, I CAN TEACH YOU A LOT ABOUT THE TREES. THAT'S MY NATURAL HOME TOO. I CAN BRING YOU WHERE THE TWO LEGS KEEP YOUR KIND IN LITTLE FORESTS BEHIND WALLS. YOU CAN LEARN FROM THEM.
BUT, CHIMP! YOU ALREADY KNOW HOW TO BE A CHIMP. NO ONE NEEDS TO TEACH YOU ANYTHING. IT'S ALREADY INSIDE YOU! YOU JUST HAVE TO BE YOURSELF!
YOU THINK I COULD DO IT?
BUT HOW WOULD I GET MY FOOD? I... I COULD DIE!

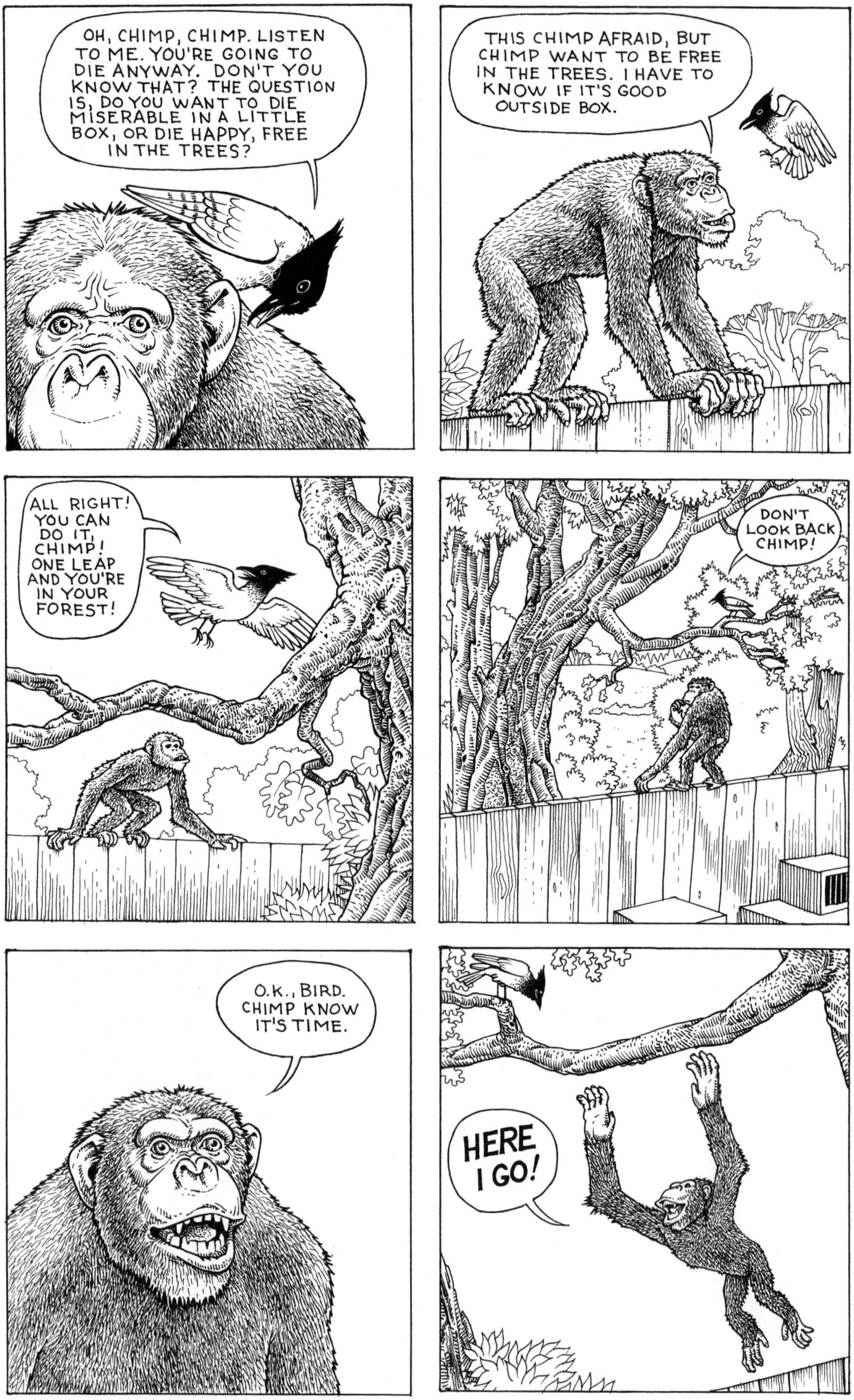
OH, CHIMP, CHIMP. LISTEN TO ME. YOU'RE GOING TO DIE ANYWAY. DON'T YOU KNOW THAT? THE QUESTION IS, DO YOU WANT TO DIE MISERABLE IN A LITTLE BOX, OR DIE HAPPY, FREE IN THE TREES?
THIS CHIMP AFRAID, BUT CHIMP WANT TO BE FREE IN THE TREES. I HAVE TO KNOW IF IT'S GOOD OUTSIDE BOX.
ALL RIGHT! YOU CAN DO IT, CHIMP! ONE LEAP AND YOU'RE IN YOUR FOREST!
DON'T LOOK BACK CHIMP!
O.K., BIRD. CHIMP KNOW IT'S TIME.
HERE I GO!